Order of the Ice

The Order Trilogy, Volume 2

Lila Mary

Published by Lila Mary, 2024.

This is a work of fiction. Similarities to real people, places, or events are entirely coincidental.

ORDER OF THE ICE

First edition. November 19, 2024.

Copyright © 2024 Lila Mary.

ISBN: 979-8227507143

Written by Lila Mary.

Also by Lila Mary

The Order Trilogy
Order of the Sun
Order of the Ice

Standalone
The Red King's Mystical Suitors
The Lover With Five Names

Table of Contents

CHAPTER ONE 1
CHAPTER TWO 20
CHAPTER THREE 33
CHAPTER FOUR 48
CHAPTER FIVE 67
CHAPTER SIX 80
CHAPTER SEVEN 94
CHAPTER EIGHT 106
CHAPTER NINE 120
CHAPTER TEN 139
CHAPTER ELEVEN 160
CHAPTER TWELVE 185
CHAPTER THIRTEEN 199
CHAPTER FOURTEEN 212

CHAPTER ONE

"Oh, my Saints!" Cerrick doesn't know how he finds the breath to speak.

"I did tell you to trust me," Edlyn shouts.

They're plummeting toward the ground at an alarming speed, the wind roaring around them. Their arms are locked tight around each other, and all Cerrick can see is the blur of the Gryting Sea.

We are going to die, he thinks. *We are going to die, our bodies lost to the sea, and Andor will have won, and Njord will never know—*

"Trust me," Edlyn yells again. All Cerrick can do is hold on tighter.

Saint Renalie, take mercy on me, he thinks as he shuts his eyes and buries his face in Edlyn's neck. Her arms squeeze tight around his shoulders.

Cerrick braces to hit the jagged rocks lining the water, braces for a brief flash of pain, braces for nothingness. Instead, they hit the water with a mighty splash.

He gasps involuntarily as freezing water fills his mouth, followed swiftly by panic. Cerrick didn't know cold could be cold like this. It bites into him, numbing, and he flails uselessly. He tries desperately to lift his head above the water high enough to breathe, spreading his arms to push the water back. Powerful white rapids push against him, sweeping him away.

Cerrick never learned how to swim. He could never fight this, not with his heavy clothes dragging him down, his head bobbing under the water as he gasps for breath. He swallows some of the water and chokes, coughs, trying to keep his head afloat.

Edlyn's arm locks around him with a determined strength. She knows how to swim, she knows what she's doing. Cerrick surrenders to her, relieved beyond words that she's alive.

She *lets* the water sweep them away, angling them toward the rocky banks as best as she can. Cerrick goes limp, trying to conserve what little energy he has left. Saints, he hates this. He hates the cold. He hates the sea.

Edlyn guides them in a slow slant toward the banks, treading through the torrent of white foam. Each breath is a struggle, each movement a fresh cold torture.

Cerrick doesn't dare close his eyes, the currents of water washing over them send a fresh wave of panic through him. If they're in this cold too long, their bodies will simply shut down. When they get out, they'll have to work quickly to get warm.

Edlyn guides them to the banks, grasping for a hold on one of the rocks jutting out over the water. She still has a tight hold of Cerrick, and her hair is plastered to her face, but her teeth are grit with steely determination. Her hand slips from the rock, likely slick with salt. It's brittle, cracking off at the base.

"Cerrick," she gasps. He convinces his frozen limbs to get back in working order and grabs for the bank with both hands. It takes several tries to get a good grip, and when he finally does, he's nearly too weak to pull himself up. But he fights through it for Edlyn's sake.

At last, Cerrick hauls himself out of the water. Kneeling on the freezing rock, shivering, Cerrick reaches a hand down to pull her out. He almost topples into the water himself with nothing to anchor him, and Edlyn is heavy, made doubly so by her sopping clothes.

Together, they heave and haul each other to safety. Cerrick lays flat on his back and heaves for breath, too exhausted to speak. He just wants to lay back and collapse, let the winds have him, but that would defeat the whole fight they've just been through. They've only gotten through the first step. The harder part lies ahead.

Edlyn slaps his shoulder in thanks, and Cerrick begins slowly dragging himself to his feet. "Come on," she says, somehow finding the strength to speak. "Need to—warm—"

"I know. Save your strength."

She laughs unexpectedly. Cerrick looks up, wondering if she's delirious, when he sees the open mouth of a dark cave behind the rocks.

With no other option, Edlyn leads the way inside. The instant relief from the wind and the roar of the sea is staggering, and Cerrick nearly collapses again. It's dark, where he belongs, but Saints, he would love a fire right now.

Don't think about it. The very idea of such blistering warmth will make him ache and burn through his numb haze. He can't afford to dream about it. Thoughts of a blistering heat capable of bringing one back from the darkness of unyielding cold brings thoughts of blazing Njord.

He peers around for anything to start a fire with, anything at all. Edlyn is busy shucking her cloak, and motions for his. Cerrick readily gives it up. A fire and warm clothes. That's what they need.

He sinks down onto the cave floor, allowing his body some respite at last. Edlyn rigorously removes her wet clothes, and Cerrick begins sluggishly doing the same. They're both shaking and shuddering, and if Cerrick had the breath, he would be swearing. He still can't feel his fingers. Most of his body is numb.

Edlyn evidently has the breath. "Fucking Saints," she gasps. "Fucking Andor. Bastard of the heavens."

The thought of Andor is daunting, far too much for Cerrick to contemplate right now. But they're alive. Both of them, somehow, miraculously alive. They won't remain that way much longer unless they get warm.

From the impenetrable blackness comes a steady and routine clicking. Edlyn whips around, drawing one of the knives from her sopping cloak. Cerrick is uncomfortably weaponless. He must've dropped his own dagger when they were falling.

"Show yourself," Edlyn snaps. "Who's there?"

Cerrick rubs his arms and his freezing bare chest as the clicks get louder, closer. He braces for Andor himself to walk through the darkness and end them, end this, but when the figure emerges it's not Andor. The man standing there with tired eyes, hair flopping into his face, hunched over with his weight braced on his cane is none other than Brandr Tofte.

"Brandr?" Edlyn exclaims. "What in Saint Irena's heaven are you doing here?"

Duke and Oligarch Brandr Tofte smiles. "I would ask you the same." He tosses them each a huge, soft blanket. "Here, before you freeze. I couldn't make a fire even if I could bend down, but here." He tosses flint and a pile of sticks onto the ground.

Edlyn scoops up her blanket and wraps it around her shoulders, Cerrick does the same. It's thick, heavy, and best of all, *warm*. He shudders pleasantly and dries his soaked hair with a corner of it as he finally starts to get feeling back in his fingers.

"Thank you," Edlyn says, taking the flint in one hand and her dagger in the other, "but please, explain."

"There's a passage that leads from the back of the palace to here, through the cave system above the sea. I've known about it for years."

"No, I meant explain why and how you're here helping us." Edlyn asks. "How did you know we needed help? Did you see us fall?"

Brandr grimaces. "Questions later. Let's get you warm first."

He hovers while Edlyn uses the flint and the blade of her knife to make a spark on the sticks. Cerrick sits slumped against the wall, clutching the blanket close. "You didn't happen to bring spare clothes, did you?"

Brandr unshoulders a pack and dumps it at his feet just as Edlyn gets a spark to catch and ignite into a sizable flame. Cerrick scoots closer to it, rubbing his hands together as close to the fire as he dares get. Brandr stays standing, his white hands clasped around the head of his cane. "I would join you, but it's not easy for me to sit on the floor of a stone cave and get back up again. This is temporary. I have somewhere I can take you, to help you. I am going to help you beyond this point, if that wasn't clear."

Edlyn peels her hair pack from her face, toweling it with a corner of her own blanket. Cerrick begins pulling on the new clothes—fit for winter in Kryos, thick with wool and fur. He could sob. He's never known such a pleasure. "Where and how and why?" Cerrick asks. His voice is thin to his own ears.

"Andor and I—" Brandr cuts himself off, shakes his head. "I knew you would end up like this. Edda and I both did. We've been waiting, preparing."

"Even back then," Cerrick says quietly, "before I went to Aeton, you knew. And you said nothing."

"You wouldn't have believed me, and I couldn't afford to lose your trust. Anyone who gets burned by Andor has to discover for themself just how odious he is. He's remarkably good at preserving an image. Until it's shattered before your very eyes, no one and nothing can convince you otherwise." Brandr's voice grows gruff. He dips his head. Cerrick wonders what lurks behind those green eyes.

Now that Cerrick knows he's not going to die of the cold or a plummet to his death, he finds the space to be angry at Andor. Not even angry, though of course that too simmers under the surface. The burning sting of betrayal hurts far worse than any temporary red rage Bertie taught him to hold onto.

"You're right," Cerrick says, a painful truth to swallow. He's never been a man of blind devotion. During his first days of employment with Andor, he picked the lock of his desk drawer to see what kind of secrets the man had—and found nothing, of course. Cerrick believed in him. He thought Andor was someone he could trust. Someone with whom he could rebuild and start anew.

Another dream lost to the sea.

They sit by the fire until warmth has returned to their bones, until Cerrick's hair has dried enough not to make him shiver. Brandr just stands quietly beside them with the fire painting his pale face orange.

Edlyn finally grunts and struggles to her feet, picking up her sopping clothes. Cerrick does the same, sighing at the heavy weight of Njord's cloak in his arms. The last remnant of Njord he has with him.

"Let's make sure we don't leave any evidence behind," Edlyn advises, bundling up everything of hers into a tight ball and stuffing it into the empty sack that Brandr used for the dry clothes. She steps out and tosses the bundle into the water.

Cerrick tosses everything but the cloak.

"We need to get out of here before Andor thinks to check," Brandr says. "Sometimes he comes down here for air like I do."

Brandr lifts a torch from the wall and dips it into the fire before Edlyn snuffs it out. Cerrick and Edlyn follow Brandr and the click of his cane up the winding cave path. Cerrick kicks himself for never having discovered this, as long as he's worked in the palace.

At the top of the path, they reach a short wooden door. Ducking his head, Brandr says, "Hold this, please." He passes the torch to Cerrick and pulls out a rusty keyring with a rusty key, almost comically huge. "Only the oligarchs and anyone they choose to tell have access to this key," Brandr says as he fits the key into the lock. It's surprisingly quiet.

The door swings open. Cerrick isn't as familiar with the lower floors of the palace, so he doesn't recognize where they are. They seem to be in a storage closet with more stairs awaiting them.

Brandr starts to step out, and Cerrick grabs his arm. "Are we going to run into Andor?"

Brandr shoots him a withering look. "Why would I be so careful down there if I was just going to lead you straight to him? I have this, kid. We'll be fine. Trust me."

"I won't," Cerrick snaps, his voice breaking. "I have had my trust betrayed too many times, most recently by your boss who had never given any indication I should be suspicious of him. That was not an hour ago. How do you expect me to believe you aren't going to lead us right into Andor's arms? Perhaps you only helped us because he wanted us alive."

Brandr nods. "I see Andor trained you well."

"Not just Andor." Cerrick has both his parents and Bertie to blame for that.

Brandr knew they were going to be betrayed. If he could know such a thing ahead of time, he must know about their history in the Ice. They have nothing left to lose. Cerrick can speak freely.

"You're right," Brandr says. "You can't trust me. Yet. If you would like me to leave you here, I will do so and tell no one of your whereabouts. I swear on the Saints, I have no loyalty to Andor."

"Start by telling us where you're taking us," Edlyn says.

"My manor in Fura."

Edlyn and Cerrick exchange startled glances.

"From here, I'm taking you to the stables. We'll be taking the fastest route in the palace that I know of," Brandr says. "I will protect you."

Cerrick shakes his head. "Don't promise that, either. Just be honest and you might gain my trust. Take us through the safest, quietest route. It doesn't have to be fast as long as Andor still believes we're lost to the sea."

Brandr smiles. "Oh, it will be a while before he even starts to guess otherwise."

"I wouldn't mind a little bit of speed, nonetheless," Edlyn cuts in. "Being under the same roof as that bastard makes my skin prickle. Brandr?"

They both look to Cerrick for objection, but when he says nothing, Brandr says, "Yeah. Follow me."

Brandr takes the torch back only to blow it out, leaving it in a sconce just outside the wooden door. "I take walks here often, and I'm far from the only one to come down here," he says. "Andor won't think anything of it if he's here before the torch cools."

Locking the door, he leads them up through the darkness with confident steps. Cerrick trips over Edlyn's heels enough for him to hiss at Brandr to slow down.

Brandr leads them in a steady uphill climb. The foggy windows they pass show the dim light of a Kryc morning. Cerrick's first morning back in his home would be beautiful if the circumstances weren't so dismal. They pass a few low doors, the steps down to the wine cellar.

The layout reminds Cerrick of his childhood home in Grenivik, with similar dim windows looking out upon the sea.

Just glimpsing the rushing white water through the frosted windows makes him shiver and pull his blanket tighter around his shoulders. He wishes to the Saints his cloak was dry. It's heavy in his arms.

Brandr leads them ever upward, a slow incline that's kinder on Cerrick's feet than stairs but tiring nevertheless, especially after his ordeal. Andor's betrayal, the fall into the sea, the fire, the whirling revelations happened no more than two hours ago. It feels like a lifetime.

Cerrick pities the version of himself that was happy in Holbeck, happy to believe in Andor, as much as he envies him.

Finally, they reach another door, which Brandr calmly pushes through. Light falls over them, and Cerrick panics, but Brandr appears unconcerned. Doubt about his loyalties crosses Cerrick's mind again.

Cerrick brushes Edlyn's hand and whispers for one of her knives, and she presses one into his hand without a sound. The cold metal against his warming palm makes him shiver again, but it's a relieving kind of discomfort. It wakes him up, sharpens his mind. He slides the knife up his sleeve.

"It's okay," Brandr says, checking both ways before stepping into the light, into a small storage room. They appear to be taking the long route through looping hallways around the perimeter of the palace. Cerrick blinks into the bright light of the overhead chandelier.

Brandr dashes across the room to the next door, opening it and waving them through. Cerrick follows, and the stress begins to melt away with every step.

A chase like this is what he's made for, even if their pursuer is not immediately on them. It's invigorating, addicting, and for the moment, Cerrick trusts Brandr. He has a knife. He's just survived falling out of a window and into the Gryting Sea. The cold water made him feel unstoppable.

Before long, they're running, or moving swiftly with a cane in Brandr's case. "We're—almost there," Brandr wheezes, laughing merrily. Edlyn sprints by them both.

They push through another set of double doors, and at last Cerrick recognizes where they are. With the palace built into the cliffside, only the top floor is visible from the south side and the city.

Most people, especially the workers, bypass the elegant front doors in favor of the private side entrance.

But here, the lower floors rest within the mountain, visible only from the north side—from the sea. Ships coming into the port of Rinnfell are the only ones with the honor of seeing the north face.

The lights and windows become familiar the farther up Cerrick walks. From the bowels of the palace to the top. Emerging back into polite society. A monster, reborn.

The offices are deserted this early in the morning. Brandr leads the way to the side entrance Cerrick has used every day he's worked here. Being out in the open like this tickles at Cerrick's instincts, no matter the discretion.

While Brandr fumbles with the door, Cerrick glances back at the hallway of oligarch offices. Andor is probably still in there, nursing his wounds and repairing his window. Cerrick shivers as Edlyn's hand on his back shepherds him out the side door.

The blast of cold is sudden and unwelcome, and Cerrick pulls his blanket tighter around himself. Brandr pays the stablehand for a fresh horse and retrieves his own, a short one with a rich black coat. The tall chestnut horse goes to Cerrick and Edlyn to share.

Edlyn claims the seat in the back of the saddle before Cerrick can argue. "What?" she asks. "You got to sleep last night on the horse. When we fell into the sea, I pulled us to safety. I made the fire. I haven't slept since the night before last. It's time I got my turn to rest, don't you think?"

Cerrick climbs up and lets her slump against his back, arms bracketing his waist. She sighs and goes quiet, tightening her protective grip. They move out.

Brandr leads the way down the western trail Cerrick has glimpsed many times but never traversed. From what he's heard, it's the route one takes when one wants to leave Rinnfell discreetly. Cerrick remembers the very public ride from Rinnfell to Holbeck, in the carriage with the driver and the route that Andor handpicked. The thought of ever obeying that bastard's whim makes him burn now, but without him Cerrick would've never met Njord.

That thought stirs the pit in the depths of his stomach.

That thought is going to ruin him.

He will trust Brandr as long as he shows he can be trusted. The moment he proves he isn't, Cerrick will use his knife, or simply take Edlyn with him and slip away.

Where would they go? Where *can* they flee that Andor won't hunt them down?

Andor will learn they're alive eventually, but for now, they're free. They have a valuable head start they can't afford to squander. For now, in this precious slot of time, they can go anywhere. They're free.

Would Bertie chase them to the Oslands, to Tailing, to Ressegal, to the far sides of the Gryting Sea? He won't be willing to let them go free, not without a fight. Bertie needs the money they owe him. More than that, he needs his reputation intact. If rumor spreads that he let a pair of debtors slip through the cracks, it would do irreparable damage.

Cerrick wonders if he and Edlyn still have a reputation in the Ice. If they're still known as the villainous bastards who betrayed the cause and killed seven Ice members in the process. He wonders if enough time has passed that the only ones who remember them are the people who were there when they were. Evan. Kara.

Names Cerrick hasn't thought of in almost two years. Cerrick hasn't seen Bertie's face since the night he and Edlyn fought their way free from the inside out, cutting through anyone who entered their path. Bertie's final words to him were a brutal curse, remorseless and furious. That night, Cerrick resigned himself at long last to the reality that Bertie had never truly cared for them. They were just playing pieces for him to nudge and discard as he pleased.

"Hey, kid," Brandr calls, cutting through Cerrick's thoughts. "You still with me?"

Cerrick swallows the lump in his throat. "Yes." The westward path is narrow, lined on both sides by leafless white trees with narrow trunks. No red leaves here, no green grass, no bright flowers. Kryos is blank and colorless in a way Cerrick never truly noticed until he went to Holbeck and discovered just what sunshine and color could do.

There's no life here. The bleakness sucks the life out of its occupants.

Shaking those thoughts away, Cerrick asks, "How's your leg? Can't be that comfortable for you, on a horse."

Brandr laughs, a gentle, warming sound. "We have a long way to go, it's too early to be asking me that yet. Me and my leg are old enemies. I'll be fine. How are you? Warm enough?"

"Yeah." Cerrick keeps his voice quiet so as not to disturb Edlyn. He allows himself to drift off to the horse's motion, leaning back into Edlyn for support. She grumbles and shifts as he dares close his eyes—not for long, he doesn't want them to topple over, but his nap on her back last night wasn't enough. He's nurturing a desire for a warm, safe place to rest. A desire not to get back up and check over his shoulder during another endless day. Has he not earned a period of rest?

Holbeck was his period of bliss. The dream has been shattered. It ended before his eyes when he crashed through Andor's window with the wind whistling in his ears. It ended last night, when Edlyn told him she would go on without him yet he chose her anyway. It ended when Erline Asger confessed to having her own book robbed. When Njord threatened divorce. When Cerrick chose to leave.

The red leaves of Vegertha Valley, kissing Njord in the cabin and their palace rooms, the easy companionship of the Hagens and the endless sunshine—they were Cerrick's version of Saint Irena's heaven. One does not get there without great sacrifice in their life, and one does not get to remain forever in a great cloud of peace. Not on earth, not in heaven. Nothing can last. Everything must be broken eventually, especially peace, especially bliss.

He landed himself here. Now he must live with it.

The trees block the wind better here than in the city, so Cerrick's shivering is kept to a minimum. The only sound is Edlyn snoring at his back and hooves clopping in the snow.

Snowflakes are falling softly. Cerrick sticks his tongue out to catch one, watching the back of Brandr's cloak shift with movement as he struggles not to fall asleep.

Like last night, the time fades and blends with the weather until finally, Brandr's voice drifts through Cerrick's foggy head. "We're here."

Edlyn startles against his back, jerking awake as violently as she always has. She and Cerrick both swear. Brandr laughs warmly.

Cerrick turns his bleary eyes to *here*. There was no movement and no noise, no sign of other people. Not the reception he was expecting to find upon arriving at an oligarch's house.

Brandr's manor isn't in the center of a bustling city, on the top of an icy hill, or buried in a beautiful forest like most oligarch homes. Brandr's home is modest in comparison, a plain building three stories tall. A wraparound balcony lines the second floor, gleaming with fresh snow and ice. It's large and handsome and spacious enough for dozens of people. Brandr proudly told him that he had it built from the ground up.

Yet it rests in the middle of nowhere in a field that's not exceptionally beautiful. The only thing of note in the front yard is the large ice lake. Cerrick remembers the day of ice skating in Holbeck. Njord's gentle hands guided him, and his smile warmed Cerrick through.

He tears his eyes from Brandr's frozen lake.

The manor is flanked by dead forest to the west and north. At one time, the forest was probably beautiful and lush—if northern Kryos was ever lush—but now it's bleak and dreary.

"It's nothing special, I know," Brandr says. "Probably not what you were expecting. You're not alone in thinking that, but it's my home, and I wouldn't have anything else."

Cerrick slides off the horse, disentangling himself from Edlyn and realizing too late how numb his legs are. He almost falls into the snow, but Edlyn is right there to catch him. Again, he's reminded of Njord's ever present strength and willingness to help.

Saints, being away from him is going to be hard. If it hasn't even been a full day and Cerrick's already been reminded of him twice, what does that spell for the future?

The three of them hitch their horses to the trees and skirt around the lake to the front of the house. The entrance is nestled in the back, blanketed by the trees.

Brandr leads them inside through the sliding glass door. It's fogged up from the cold, but Cerrick spots a flickering lamp inside. Would Brandr leave a light burning like that? Cerrick doesn't know how long he was in Rinnfell before rescuing them, but the more than likely conclusion is that someone else is here keeping the lights on.

Brandr doesn't live totally alone. He's an oligarch. At the very least, he probably has servants, although that would go against his reclusive tendencies. Cerrick hasn't seen any other signs of life. The manor doesn't have a garden since the climate wouldn't support it, but the lake is clear of debris, the trees are trimmed, and the thorny hedges have been pruned into perfect rectangles. Most houses in northern Kryos don't look so utterly desolate. That light inside is the first sign of warmth and life here.

Despite the light, the house is cold. Cerrick is used to entering buildings and shuddering through the temperature adjustment, but this house is hardly any warmer than the outdoors. The light they spotted outside is from a lonely lantern on the kitchen counter, burning low. "It'll be warmer once I get the fire going," Brandr promises.

The house is also dark, but Cerrick searches the dark corners while Brandr is taking off his cloak. The house is richly furnished, the kitchen well stocked, and the wooden floors polished to a shine. A dark wood staircase sits at the back of the large sitting room, the railing similarly polished.

The sight of feet making their way down the steps almost makes Cerrick jump out of his skin. A pale hand hugs the railing. A voice floats towards them. "Brandr? Is that you?"

Cerrick's mouth falls open as the figure comes into view, holding a bright lantern in her left hand.

"Yes, Edda," Brandr says, his voice melting into gentle peace.

"Edda Holman?" Edlyn says, slightly strangled. Edda is a moderately common name in Kryos, but there's no mistaking who's wearing the blue gown with an elegance only Duchess Holman could emanate. The gown shows her arms and back, the bodice beaded in white and silver.

Her nails are painted a dazzling red, and her eyes shine in the yellow lamplight. She's dressed like she's going to a wedding instead of waiting in Brandr Tofte's house. She steps like she's walking on air. Saintly.

Edda's smile only widens when she sees Cerrick and Edlyn. "My dears. How lovely it is to see you and find you safe," she says, wrapping her arms around them both. She's far taller than them both, making for an awkward hug, but her warmth in both a literal and figurative sense makes Cerrick feel at home. He's thought long and hard about what exactly home means to him, but for now Edda provides safety—a novel commodity.

Cerrick is too shocked to hug her back. After giving a starstruck Edlyn a hug, Edda hugs Brandr, closing her eyes and breathing him in. He looks just as surprised to find her dressed so finely during this time. She was ousted from the council of oligarchs just two nights ago. She seems to be adjusting well.

When she lets him go, he holds onto her arm for a moment. He looks into her eyes. "What's the occasion for this?" he asks, gesturing to her dress.

"We are in a dark time. You keep your house dark, my dear. What better time to wear something that reminds us of a beautiful light?" She smiles. *You are the beautiful light,* Cerrick thinks. The brightest and best of the oligarchs. The first one sacrificed to Andor's treachery.

"You're right." Brandr holds her wrist a little too long to be passed off as an innocent greeting. Cerrick and Edlyn exchange glances.

"You're hiding Edda Holman out here?" Edlyn asks, interrupting their moment. Cerrick glares at her, more conscious than he once was of giving lovers their privacy.

Edda and Brandr jump apart, Edda smoothing down her dress as if there's any wrinkles in it. Brandr runs a hand through his hair. "Yes," he says, clearing his throat. "We arranged it long before she was ousted. If anything ever befell either of us, we made a promise that we would house the other and care for them as best we could."

"So you've known for a while," Cerrick says, "that Andor's treachery was inevitable."

Edda gives him a pitying look. "Child, you're one of the last to know."

"We'll go over all of that in a bit," Brandr says, rubbing his hands together. Cerrick has never seen him without his forest green cloak, but it turns out he wears plain black underneath. No jewels, no gold. Plain, but deceptive. "You're right, Edda, the house is freezing. You could've made a fire." Idle remarks, like they've lived together for years instead of two days.

"I didn't know where your firewood was. I searched everywhere."

"Ah. I should've told you where it was." Brandr strides to the door, swearing as he bumps into things in the dim light. The humanity of this oligarch, so simple yet so striking, makes Cerrick laugh.

"Do you truly have no servants, Brandr?" Edlyn asks, following him. Not knowing where else to go, Cerrick wanders after them. Brandr lifts a hatch in the corner of the large, dark room, kneeling down with a groan to pull the handle. He rises to his feet with difficulty, accepting the hand Edlyn offers him with a murmur of thanks.

"No," he says, stepping down into the cellar. Cerrick and Edlyn follow carefully, mindful of their steps in the darkness. Luckily, Brandr lights a lantern on the table at the bottom of the staircase, illuminating a small room stacked with chopped firewood.

"I have always lived alone, and I like it that way. I prefer to see to my own chores. The grandeur of the palace exhausts me." He lifts a few large logs of wood and passes them to Edlyn. "Do you mind carrying this?"

She takes the bunch and marches back up the steps. Brandr takes a bundle of wood with a pre-tied handle wrapped around the logs. The more Cerrick looks, the more of those he spots in the great stack. Brandr gently pushes him out of the way as he trudges back up the steps and blows out the light, carrying the bundle by the rope.

Edda is sitting with her feet up on Brandr's sofa. Brandr kneels at the fireplace in front of her and throws the logs into it, stacking Edlyn's to the side and starting the fire with the kindling and matches sitting on the mantle.

Edlyn sits beside Edda on the couch, but Cerrick is too uncomfortable with Edda's unexpected presence and the remaining respect he has for oligarchs who deserve it that he sits on the floor beside Brandr. It's just as cold as he feared.

Cerrick warms his hands in front of the flames as they start to roar. The silence isn't comfortable, nor is it awkward. The air is still. Holding its breath in anticipation as Brandr stretches his leg out on the floor.

"I'll go cook us a meal," Edda says with the tone of someone who means to give privacy where it's needed, rising.

"No, I'll do it," Brandr says, struggling to his feet instead.

Edda gives him a look. "You've done enough for both me and them. You do more than enough all the time. Let me do something for you for once."

"No, I insist you stay here," Brandr says as he gets the support of his cane back under him. "You cooked everything yesterday. Really, Edda, you're wonderful, but I'm not the one who just lost my job and is now facing the shame of the public and the papers."

"Being ousted gives me more time to do things like cook for you," Edda argues, more cheerfully than the average person would. Then again, this is Edda Holman, the woman who has a smile for every situation. Despite her protests, she remains settled on the couch as Brandr clicks his way to the kitchen. Edlyn rises to help him.

Cerrick can feel the restlessness vibrating off her, the need to occupy herself and her thoughts, help do that which needs to be done so she can get the information she wants faster. Even if she weren't waiting for answers from Brandr, she's always hated people who don't help where help is needed.

Which leaves Cerrick sharing space with Edda, silent while he considers the warning she gave him at Queen Brenda's party.

"I'm happy this happened to you," Edda says quietly at last, drawing his eye. Cerrick raises an incredulous eyebrow. "I'm not happy you have to go through this turmoil," she clarifies, "the sting of betrayal, but I'm glad you're finally aware of Andor's every egregious crime. That you won't ever be taken in by his pretty words again."

Cerrick looks into her brown eyes, finding a stoic, calm fury there that he's not used to seeing on her sweet face. "Yeah," he finds himself saying. "I am, too."

Better this void in his chest than a day more believing Andor's lies.

CHAPTER TWO

It is midmorning, so Brandr cooks breakfast in classic Kryc style; crisp, buttery pastries with eggs or berry jam baked within. Upon their collective surprise at how quickly he was able to make the pastries, he says he keeps a supply of ready made dough for occasions just like this. He shrugs bashfully. Cerrick and Edlyn exchange glances.

While Cerrick is eating the pastries along with the sausages Edlyn helped fry up, he asks where Brandr learned to cook like this. They're all sitting around Brandr's square kitchen table, which is little more than a marble countertop with wooden legs bolted to the floor.

Brandr shrugs and smiles. "I wasn't always a rich duke who worked in a palace. There were times I had to cook for myself. When I was young, my father taught me what he knew. The rest I picked up myself."

"I thought you were letting me cook yesterday because you were terrible," Edda accuses, devouring another of the egg pastries. "How did you let me in there to make mediocre stew when you had this up your sleeve?"

"Well, I saved us all from stew for breakfast today," Brandr shoots back, smiling at her easily.

As they eat, the air in the room warms from the fire roaring in the hearth behind them. Something is stirring, like the inner workings of a storm brewing. Cerrick sets down his napkin and resolves to take control.

"Brandr," Cerrick asks, "what really happened to your leg?" Brandr always explained his limp as a seafaring accident in his younger days, but Cerrick thinks better of that now. Now, when nothing is certain.

"I was going to tell you about that. Might as well get it over with." Brandr braces his leg on the table with a grimace and pulls his trouser leg up to show them the scar. It's long and jagged, faded with time. "Andor got one over on me."

"How?"

Brandr smiles and shakes his head. "I was a fool, that's how. He invited me on a seafaring trip about thirteen, fourteen years ago. That part of the story is true. I was only a few years older than you. This was shortly after I was elected to my first term as oligarch, and I was eager to curry favor and keep myself on the path for reelection. Everyone in Kryos admired him. Many of the same still do. I took his offer without any hesitation. Look where that got me.

"The story doesn't start there. Andor breaking my leg is the middle of the tale of my tumultuous life." He frowns. "Did I mention Andor broke my leg?"

Cerrick remembers to close his mouth. Edlyn's is still open.

Brandr sighs. "What I'm about to tell you mustn't go past the confines of this room, but I suppose you knew that already. Nothing here is for common ears. If you want to trust me but you find yourselves still hesitating, I will dispel those doubts now. I worked for the Order of the Ice, under Bertie's father, when I was seventeen until I was twenty two."

"You fucking *what?*" Edlyn demands, lurching from her seat.

Brandr smiles grimly. "You heard me right. You wondered why you couldn't find anything incriminating on me in Aeton. Why Alfred skipped over me in his quest for knowledge. Here. This is it."

He draws a breath. Edda's hand drifts in circles over his back, and he leans into it. "I've never had a chance to say so on my own terms except to Edda."

"You should've told us when you found out we were in the Ice," Edlyn says. "When did you find out? When Carr joined the Sun, perhaps? That's when Andor was told."

Cerrick himself is a bit confused about the timeline.

"I discerned it on my own long before he did," Brandr says. "The way you carry yourselves, your paranoia—some claim it's a trait of the Sun, but I know the difference. Maybe because I've never worked in the Sun, but I know what Bertie's family ingrains into you."

Cerrick buries his head in his hands at the thought of *Brandr*, of all people, working for Bertie's father. Cerrick doesn't know as much about him and the old regime, but if Bertie's father was anything like him, it can't have been good.

Bertie never talked about family or loved ones. In the Ice, family was simply something to exploit. A weakness. Edlyn only told Cerrick about her family in private, fractured chunks.

Brandr says, "I left the Ice and tried to bury all my connection to it, all those old habits, but Andor found out somehow. Perhaps one of my former colleagues spilled the secret. Perhaps one of Andor's spies ran a check into my history. One of you.

"No doubt he wanted to keep close eyes and ears on all his oligarchs. Anyway, he took me, young and dumb and eager to prove myself despite my experience in the Ice, on that sea trip. We sailed across the eastern Gryting, on the tamer side. We went to the largest island in the channel to catch a glimpse of the wild geese there. At least, that's what I was told.

"We spent three glorious days at sea," Brandr says. "I had been on the water before, but it was a novelty that had yet to wear off. I didn't mind the cloudy skies because the sea was so beautiful." His hand drifts through the air, painting a scene with his gestures. His eyes are low as he imagines those three glorious days, a small smile on his face.

"The sea foam was spectacular, and the water this gorgeous pale blue-green. Of course, you two have experienced it, so you know what I mean. Up there on the deck of a ship, safe from the waves and the power of the ocean, observing the sea—especially to twenty eight year old me—was incredible.

"And then came the fourth day. Andor sat me down after a meal that made me sleepy and loose tongued and pliable. He'd drugged me." Brandr sighs. "He told me, quite gently as he often does, that he knew about my old job. Knew everything I'd hidden. Knew the extent of my crimes. He threw me down and—and broke my leg. The butt of that Pointstaff can do some real damage."

Brandr ducks his head. Only Edda is close enough to see his face. "He told me the break was a reprimand for daring to enter his oligarchy with such a secret lurking in my past. He told me he admired my audacity, but that I needed to be reminded of my place. He told me what would happen if I ever thought of revealing how my leg was truly broken. We had each other bound. I could never tell on him, and he wouldn't tell on me. He held that chip over my head."

He raises his head. "We were supposed to dock at the island, but we were blown off course to the coast of Aeton. It was another day to the healers, and he made sure my leg didn't set right. He may as well have sat on it, for all the damage he did. He didn't leave my side. When we finally reached Aeton, I had to stay for months before the healer deemed me fit to travel again. Hence my closest companion; the cane.

"We are going to get our revenge," Brandr vows. "Not just for this leg and my shattered dreams, but for you and Edlyn getting thrown out of the window, Edda being ousted over an outdated rule that's been abused for Andor's convenience. We are going to fix it all."

Edda lays a hand over Brandr's, a chastisement.

"More than just revenge," Brandr corrects. "We are going to create change. Corruption in Kryos has become normalized, but we cannot continue to let it be. Not this generational tradition of dirty family business, threatening and bullying and stealing, ousting those whose only crime is their bloodline. And me—I know I will be next on Andor's list. I know it."

Edda squeezes his hand again. Brandr gives her a reassuring smile.

"Andor wants to abuse Kryos' outdated and twisted system of voting oligarchs out and in because he thinks he knows what's best for our future. But that's not what Kryos was meant to be. He should not float under the surface of the law by using his loyalists to bully people into silence. Kryos does not belong to him, it's not his to do with as he pleases, and it's time we reminded him of that."

"What exactly do you mean to do, Brandr?" Edlyn asks quietly, with a quiet sort of power in her voice. The air is deathly still. "It could turn into the seventh rebellion if you want it to be."

Brandr sets his teacup down. It's loud as thunder in the quiet of his kitchen. "I want it to be."

Cerrick swears under his breath.

Brandr smiles, and it's so different from his other smiles so far. This one isn't friendly and warm, nor is it a soul deep weariness. This one twists his mouth into a sharp smirk, turning his eyes to the glimmering green of storm clouds.

"I've been thinking about this since that day at sea. I've thought about what I would do, how I would do it. The only thing that's stopped me is a lack of allies and lack of evidence against Andor. To prove his corruption in a high court, I would need much more than what I had, something more concrete than rumors and snippets and hunches. My leg was my word against his. My involvement in the Ice is my word against his, but he's Head Oligarch, and he has perfect weapons against all the others.

"I won't get anywhere trying to deny it, and I'm tired of hiding. When he denounces me, I'm not going to deny it. I'm going to bring about his downfall with the three of you."

Chills run down Cerrick's spine.

Brandr continues, "So, as sorry as I am that you and Edlyn were betrayed so terribly, that you had to go through the betrayal I went through thirteen years ago, I'm eternally grateful for your efforts."

"All the credit goes to him," Edlyn says, slapping Cerrick on the back. "I was confined to Kryos. We only met a few times a month to discuss his findings and for me to bring him news."

"Edlyn...we're partners in everything," Cerrick tells Brandr. "We were both betrayed. We share the credit, the pain, and the responsibility."

Brandr nods. "My apologies. I've already come up with a name for our rebellion. A mocking of Andor's prize organization, a mocking of the order that raised all three of us. The Order of the Phantom."

Cerrick grins. Brandr looks from face to face, at the delight in all of their expressions, the kindling flaring to life in their hearts.

"We will follow you," Edlyn vows. "You will help us take down Andor? We will follow you, whatever you need."

Cerrick doesn't agree with such blind trust, though he suspects such a feeling is just an old instinct biting at him. Fresh wounds still festering. It's only been a few hours since Andor betrayed him, but Cerrick's not sure that wound will ever heal with time. All things must, but Cerrick has been taught to hold grudges well and hold them long.

"I do not want that to be my legacy," Brandr says. "I will not be your leader. The public would not accept another oligarch at the head of the rebellion."

"What does that matter?" Edlyn interjects. "If we're rebuilding Kryos, all the common laws will be uprooted and new ones planted in their place. We will be the ones to choose them."

Cerrick buries his head in his arms at the thought of rebuilding Kryos. Talking about rebellion is all good and well, but uprooting the entire country as Edlyn is suggesting, changing everything they've ever known into what they want it to be…

This is always how it starts. A grievance needs airing out, a grievance shared by a handful of tired people. An angry yet productive conversation over a meal. Smoldering plans.

Is this how the rebels felt the first six times? Certain of a problem, even more certain that no one but them could fix it? Unsure if they're strong enough, passionate enough about the cause to go through with such a monumental task?

Edlyn looks at him, nudging his leg with her foot. "You could still go back, you know," she says quietly. "Tell him that something went amiss and that the weather delayed your horse. When the public catches wind of what we're doing and he puts the pieces together, you could admit your sympathy to our cause but nothing more.

"Your family is noble, involved in politics. You publicly live in Rinnfell. He'd never be the wiser that you were anything more than a silent supporter of our cause. He'd follow you anywhere."

Cerrick is not so sure he would if he knew the truth. Precisely why he'll never find out.

Going back to Njord after last night…the thought is alien and daunting. Cerrick came with Edlyn fully expecting to never return. The option of going back to Holbeck after he's sorted his business here never came to mind. Eating breakfast in Brandr Tofte's kitchen while discussing a seventh rebellion never came to mind either.

Could he do it? Go back to Njord and the Hagens and his blissful heaven, pretending nothing is amiss? Could he look Njord in the eyes and assure him nothing ever was?

Would Njord still trust and love him blindly, or would Cerrick grow afraid of slipping up and run away? Would he crumble under the weight of loving Njord with only half of himself? Any and all options are likely. Holbeck feels a world away instead of a few hours' ride.

"No," Cerrick says. "I can't. It would tear me apart." He came with Edlyn because he couldn't bear the thought of loving Njord halfway, yes, but he also couldn't bear to sit in a crafted heaven while knowing she was here wreaking the havoc that they always have together. She couldn't do this alone, though she'll never admit it, and he won't admit that he doesn't want her to do it without him.

Edlyn nods sharply. "It would destroy anyone." She pats his hand. "So, you're in?"

"I was never not in." He scratches his head and smiles, trying to cover up his inner turmoil. He's with her, always.

"Where do we start?" Edda asks, gently guiding them back to the heart of the matter. "Sigrid and Erika Thorpe had a daunting task indeed when they began their rebellion. I'm at a bit of a loss on where we begin."

Brandr smiles and stirs the storm. "I've had an idea of where to start for years, but I told you that I lacked allies. Allies and a hope I have rarely possessed. I thought the situation was hopeless, that the corruption of Kryos was truly carved into its branches. That nothing could ever change. You've surely been in the taverns. You know what they say when you complain and wish for change."

"Start the rebellion yourself," Cerrick supplies, recalling words he uttered on that night so long ago, the argument that drove him out of the tavern he visited with his college acquaintances and into the southwest streets. Into the arms of the Ice, into Bertie's captivating clutches. He's never fully escaped them.

Every awful second of that year in the Ice flashes before his eyes in a moment. Every moment of despair, every moment spent wishing he wasn't sleeping in that black townhouse with a back breaking mattress and a light that never seemed to burn at full brightness. Edlyn beside him, Edlyn behind him, Edlyn holding him up, Edlyn supporting him, helping him survive.

He wanted out. He wanted out so badly. Away from Bertie's grin, out of his arms, of Cerrick's head.

At night, left alone with his thoughts and Edlyn sleeping quietly at his side, he yearned for freedom. One of those nights when he laid awake pondering his life before the Ice, wondering if he'd ever had a life before the Ice, he woke Edlyn and proposed the maddest plan he'd ever come up with: escape.

They fought hard for their freedom, and the price was seven souls sent to Saint Renalie—he very much doubts they joined Saint Irena. And for what? Is this really freedom? He's in deep debt to the Ice, and now that he's about to declare war on his former employer, he won't be able to pay off that debt for a long time. He avoids that thought for now, though he suspects it'll be the least of his problems soon.

He still lives on the edge of the southwest region, though he hasn't set foot in the apartment in months. He still has to see Evan's face every month and contend with old memories—memories of when Cerrick was the greatest force in the Ice.

The flower, Bertie called him, while he called Edlyn the fury. A notable difference in reputation, certainly something Cerrick was mocked for when he and Edlyn went to intimidate other gangs. Bertie meant it in jesting at first, mocking the skinny, slippery boy whose life he spared at Edlyn's request. After a while, the nickname grew into a form of respect and perhaps even reverence. Not from Bertie, but from new recruits, lesser members of other gangs.

Perhaps they refer to a poisonous flower, he heard whispered a few times. *He must have a fearsome reputation behind that name. Perhaps he's a frightening warrior, and the nickname is an irony.*

If anyone is a frightening warrior, it'd be Njord. But Njord is a storm, not a measly flower, nor a violent fury. Njord is slow building, contained, yet eventually destructive if he desires to be. Cerrick is glad he never truly got on Njord's bad side.

Would it have just been better to give up hope and stay in the Ice, doing what Cerrick is unfortunately and surprisingly good at? Threatening, stealing, intimidating, expanding the flock at Bertie's orders? Or does that make him no better than Skad and Gustav doing Andor's bidding?

Of course he's glad he left. Every time he contemplates the what ifs, Njord's face pops up behind his eyelids. For that alone, it was worth it to change the entire course of his future in a single night.

"We are going to use the Order of the Ice," Brandr says, cutting through the turmoil in Cerrick's mind, "the way they used us. We will start with our revenge there."

"You must be out of your mind," Edlyn says. Cerrick is inclined to agree with her, but not in the way her tone of voice suggests. "Ask *Bertie* for help? Willfully go back there to treat with him? That would be his dream, and our nightmare."

"I worked for his father, who is dead now," Brandr says calmly. "I have no loyalty to Bertie. I never met him. His father didn't want his son embroiled in that world, believe it or not, but Bertie was forced into the position of leader too young when his father was killed without naming an heir."

Cerrick hasn't learned much about Bertie's rise to power, certainly not anything he'd believe from Bertie's own lips. It works in Bertie's favor for everyone to assume that he's always been in power, that he's immortal and invincible. Time is short in the gangs, just surviving one day to the next, and Bertie's father was old news by the time Cerrick joined.

"We need allies," Brandr says. "We're going to have a hard time finding them. Unless you can summon a sizable army of Tailings who'd be willing to rebel against the Kryc government, or you have a secret contact in Ressegal, we'll need to find them here. No one is more outspoken against the government and the oligarchy than the Ice. Think about that."

"You're an oligarch, though," Cerrick says, leaning back and crossing his arms. "Have you thought about that?"

"I have. At length. Agonized over it, actually." Brandr's tone of voice is cheery, his fake smile bright. "But more importantly, I used to be one of them. That's what I'll get Bertie to focus on. I'll put away my heavy cloaks and shined boots and rings if that's what he wants, if that's what it takes to make him *see*. I will—I will embrace that part of myself. I'll do what Bertie's father was always telling me to do. I keep trying to bury that part of myself, but it keeps worming its way back out at every transgression."

"Embrace the monster," Cerrick says before he can think better of it. Words Bertie said to him so many times as they looked in the mirror together, Bertie's hands on his shoulders with a manic grin very different from Cerrick's stoic frown. Bertie begged him over and over to make full use of his potential, but Cerrick always rolled his eyes and waved him off. *I am not like you. I am only here because the other option was death. I am here biding my time.*

"Embrace the monster," Brandr repeats. Bertie must've adopted that phrase from his father, probably from rumors or stories or a secret set of instructions his father left him despite Brandr's claim he didn't want Bertie involved with the Ice. Perhaps Bertie even picked it up from the other Ice members as he found his footing. Cerrick would pay to see how Bertie struggled in those initial days.

Brandr continues, "Saints help me, if that's what it takes, I will do it. Can you?"

"If that's what it takes," Edlyn says before Cerrick can answer. He nods, distracted and intimidated. She's always been quicker to embrace the monster. She's always been surer of herself and her actions and her knives in those streets. He never doubted her dedication to her craft. Sometimes like now, it's eerie how easily she slips back into that role. *The fury.*

"Anything it takes," Cerrick says. Pretending to fit back in with the Ice and with Bertie is a small consequence for the long term goal of dethroning Andor. Brandr smiles, proud and pleased. Cerrick would do anything to earn that kind of approval again.

Behind his eyes Cerrick sees the dimly lit, wet, and dirty streets of southwest Rinnfell again, but he breathes through the cloying fear in his chest. He can do this. Moment by moment.

Edda's red nails on the table, shining in the lamplight, draw him out of his head again. She looks Brandr in the face, shaking her hair out of her eyes.

"You know you could always come to me in times of need," she says. "That my door will always be open to you if you need wounds tended, or mediocre stew cooked, or the comfort of warm arms around you. I am your friend, Brandr, and to you two as well." She smiles at them. "Those same offers extend to you. However, in order for me to join this cause and support you fully, in times of war as well as peace, there are some rules I must set. They cannot be broken."

Brandr bows his head and waits.

"This can't be purely about revenge. We cannot do this purely for us. We can tear down Andor and his dreams, but we have to build something in its place. We cannot be destructive and leave it that way. You say you don't want to have a legacy of leading a movement to pit one oligarch against another. You want something bigger. Well, so do I. I want to leave a legacy of creation. Of justice.

Something new. Something big and beautiful and right, that gives people hope."

"The seventh era of Kryos," Edlyn says. "That's what we'll build. The Order of the Phantom, you say, Brandr? Operating in the shadows, leaving little trace to incriminate them?"

She grins. As monstrous as it is, as sharp, as harsh, Cerrick likes it. *Whatever it takes.* Seeing her like this again, looking in a mirror and learning to stomach the man he sees looking back at him, isn't going to be hard as he hoped. As he thought.

"I like it."

CHAPTER THREE

This is the second time Cerrick has ridden back into Rinnfell in the last two days, and each time has been different. He still rides double with Edlyn, conserving heat and sharing silent worry. At least they're both well rested now.

Last night, Cerrick slept beside Edlyn in one of Brandr's guest beds, just like they used to in the Ice. The upper floor was warmer than the bottom, with a fire burning in every room to keep them cozy in bed. They spent the day finalizing plans and taking some much needed rest.

Brandr prepared more otherworldly food—sandwiches made with a cured and beautifully seasoned ham stored in his cold cellar, and a strong eastern Kryc cheese. He pressed them flat on a hot griddle over the fire in his kitchen. Cerrick sat at the counter and watched, eagerly inhaling the smell.

Cerrick entrusted Brandr with every detail of the scandal he unearthed in Holbeck, filling in the gaps of his knowledge. Relinquishing such a secret was hard, and he's still learning to trust Brandr in entirety. However, it was gratifying to watch the shock play out on Brandr's face at every egregious detail.

Cerrick was starting to believe Brandr couldn't be caught off guard, but it turns out Edda is the harder one to startle. She met every detail with the same sad smile—not surprise, not chagrin, but grim acceptance.

Brandr brought them meal after meal, grinning at the reactions he garnered. Cerrick suspects that cooking for the people he treasures is his way of winding down, his calming practice. Edda harped upon the point, "Really, Brandr, this is better than most food I've had in the palace kitchens."

"I see we've discovered my proper place in the palace hierarchy," Brandr jokes, sitting down to eat with them. Cerrick marveled at the ease with which he carried himself, smiled, spoke.

At the palace, Brandr always seemed weary and out of his element, as if he'd rather be anywhere else. Therefore, it makes sense that he's most comfortable in his own home, but Cerrick didn't think it was possible for him to be this easygoing.

Cerrick wouldn't choose to ride into Rinnfell with anyone else. Edda put on riding clothes today so she could ride with Brandr, wearing a plain brown cloak instead of an oligarch's finery. Edda removed all signs of her own glamor except the red paint from her nails, referring again to the necessary glimmer of light in a dark time.

It's barely sunrise. They wanted to slip into Rinnfell under the cover of nightfall, and the earliest parts of the morning are the time where the city is quietest.

Their horses' hooves clop along the otherwise silent cobblestone streets. Cerrick catches the stench of smoke from the fires burning in the top of metal barrels, heating the frozen lower city streets. Further off, the smoke from the factories in the central city wafts close. Rinnfell was built around them and their great, shining pipes that reach into the sky like the arms of a tree.

They're confronted by an unobstructed view of the palace on the incline in the distance, but it doesn't serve as a symbol of Kryc grandeur the way it used to. Now, it's a symbol of fear, the same as the Ice townhouse. It's quite sad, if Cerrick's honest, how quickly its image has deteriorated.

If Cerrick peers far enough, he sees the edge of his and Edlyn's apartment building, the yellow lantern hanging on the street corner. It's on the west side of the street, only a few blocks down from the street that leads to the Ice townhouse.

He can't see their unit from here, but mere sight of the peeling beige paint is enough to make Cerrick yearn for home.

Edlyn glances back at him, her eyes shining in the light of a streetlamp. Her mouth is drawn in a thin, grim line, and it's not hard to read her thoughts, as they mirror his own.

Cerrick wonders when he'll set foot inside their apartment again, collapse onto the old couch, sleep in his tiny bed, freeze his feet on the wooden floor. At least the view from their balcony is lovely, if one likes looking down on a snowy street of riders and leafless trees. At least it has light.

Brandr and Edda's horse turns sharply right, and Cerrick is forced to draw a harsh breath. This corner won't ever leave his mind. It lies from across an alley cloaked in darkness where water probably still pools in the street, guarded by twin townhouses like gargoyles. Twin sets of dying flowers line the balconies with their chipping paint. The flowers are too colorful, too full of life to survive here.

All the townhouses on this street are painted a black that soaks up all light, except for little patches of orange light from low burning lamps. It's by the light of said lamps that Cerrick glimpses the street. He's hit by a wall of memories.

Walking to work in the palace, unable to afford a horse or carriage, Cerrick avoided every hint of this place. He was never exactly sure what he feared.

Did he fear getting sucked back in, believing Bertie and his lies and the glory painted in Cerrick's own mind? Did he fear what Bertie might do to him if he dared come back? A knife in his chest would've been better, a sweeter relief than the mountain of debt.

Cerrick will never let Bertie kill him or Edlyn. They tread into Bertie's territory again now, but if he lays so much as a finger on Edlyn—

They pass the corner where Evan meets him to collect payment. Slowly, they approach the looming black townhouse. Far too close, far too formidable in Cerrick's vision as Brandr's horse pulls to a halt before it. Edda slides off and helps Brandr down, handing him his cane. Cerrick tries his best to swallow his nerves, landing hard on solid ground after Edlyn.

They hitch the horses to a dead lamppost outside, and Brandr gets his cane under him. Without anything further to stall them, they look to one another and then at the ominous black door lit by a single, dim overhead light.

"Cerrick," Brandr says, "would you like to…?"

"No, I really wouldn't."

"What were you going to do when we got here," Edlyn snaps, "cower in the shadows? You have to face him eventually if we're going to do this."

Cerrick swallows. "Bertie lives off fear. If he sees me afraid, he'll be more likely to join our cause. Let's let him think he can get something out of me."

"He doesn't live off uncertainty, and that's what you're exuding right now. Not fear." Edlyn fixes the collar of the simple brown cloak Brandr lent him. This one defends against the merciless Kryc winters with a fur trim at the top, just enough to get away with in this district. "You're not afraid, and your logic is sound, even if it's false. You are not afraid. I will cut off my own arm before I see you afraid of Bertie."

"Only you can scare me," he assures, patting her arm with his uncomfortably bare and frozen hand.

"So go before I put the fear of the Saints into you," she says, slapping his shoulder and shoving him toward the door.

Cerrick takes a breath, almost asks *why me and not Brandr*, but stows those foolish words. He stands on the stoop for a long while, unable to raise his fist. The others give him time and silence.

The idea of someone walking out while he's still unprepared is what finally sets him in motion. Cerrick raises his fist and bangs on the door with the token impatience and defiance of the gangs. He's surprised how easily that knock comes back to him.

Cerrick didn't see any lights on in the upper levels of the townhouse, but it takes a while for any sign of life to stir within the building. Most of them will likely be sleeping, and the others out wreaking havoc on the town.

From within, he hears a muffled curse, several bangs, more loud curses from others trying to sleep. Cerrick bites back a delirious smile. Footsteps, grumblings, more swearing. And then, with his heart in his mouth, the door opens.

Evan. Behind him, Bertie.

Evan's mouth immediately drops open, but Bertie's widens into a grin. Cerrick stands frozen as Bertie sidles to the front, wrapped in a brilliant silver cloak. "Well, well. Here's a face I never thought I'd be lucky enough to see again."

Cerrick swallows. He didn't hear Edlyn approach, but suddenly she's there at his left side, brushing his hand and shaking her hair out of her face. Defiant as ever. "Two," Bertie says, never losing his grin. One of many unnerving things about him—he never stopped smiling. When Bertie's smile disappeared, it meant bad things.

"I thought you two didn't want anything more to do with me, so I want nothing more to do with you," Bertie says brightly, then slams the door in their faces.

For a moment, Cerrick is too shocked to act, then Edlyn nudges him again. Cerrick yanks open the door again, the wood like ice under his fingertips. Fitting. He can't believe he's doing this. "Don't be so dramatic. We're here for help."

Bertie's smirk makes him burn.

"Don't give me that look," Cerrick snaps, pushing inside. "We're the best you ever had, don't deny it. You should be on your knees thanking us for gracing you with our presence."

Bertie says nothing until he gets a look at Brandr. Cerrick takes pleasure in the way his smugness deflates.

"Out of my way, kid," Brandr says, nudging Cerrick out of the way, evidently fed up with Bertie's pettiness. He doesn't need a rich cloak or rattling wooden cloak ornaments to be intimidating. The hunch of his back when he leans on his cane gives him a towering power. Bertie is short, but even someone tall would bend back before Brandr's form. He stands in the way of the light.

"Listen, kid," he says with a scowl, "I worked with your father. I had a modicum of respect for him, which is why I killed him myself. I gave him a grand, fitting end, what he would've wanted, instead of giving that prize to someone less adequate. I loved him, I bedded him, but I hated him. You know how it goes in these circles."

Bertie nods slightly. Cerrick never in his year here saw Bertie respond to anyone like that—with submission instead of simple acknowledgement. Bertie leaning his head back, eyes wide with fear, is also something new. Something precious. Cerrick drinks it all in.

"He killed Bertie's father?" Edlyn mutters beside him, quiet enough only for the two of them to hear. Cerrick barely dares to breathe or think lest he miss Brandr's words.

"Because of him, I am going to give you a chance," Brandr barrels on. "I need your organization, but don't think for a second that I need *you*. You're half my age if a day, and I could take over the Ice in a few minutes if I wanted to. I don't want to, I don't have the damn time, but you'd do well to remember the possibility. So, you're going to let us in, and we're going to talk, and you're going to agree no matter what I say. Does that get through your smoke addled skull?"

A thin sliver of light from the overhead lamp paints Bertie's terror for all to see. Evan lingers in the background, wire rimmed spectacles and flaming hair, with a lantern in hand. To his credit, he hasn't dropped it yet despite his comical shock.

"Yes," Bertie squeaks, actually *squeaks*. He steps out of the way, stumbling right into Evan and startling them both. What a sight, these hardened gang members startling like scared children. "Uh—come in."

Brandr shoots him a smile and motions the other three inside. Evan catches a glimpse of Edda for the first time, and his mouth, which just closed, opens again. Cerrick can't help but smile as Brandr's warm hand on his back guides him inside, murmuring, "Here we go."

The door closes, trapping them in with the darkness and the heat and the memories.

It smells the same as the day Cerrick left, like smoke and blood and the heady scent of pine. The air is hot, just as thick and hard to breathe as Cerrick remembers. He exhales his way through it now.

It's pitch dark, and Evan's lantern is the only thing keeping them from tripping over the furniture. Such a problem was probably what made Bertie and Evan curse when they came to answer the door.

Cerrick could navigate here easily in the dark or in the light, and he catches himself falling back into old habits and nearly following Bertie to the stairs. Edlyn's hand on his arm is a silent, strong support, a support he attempts to return.

Brandr strides confidently through the room. Cerrick wants to ask him how much has changed since he was last here, but he doesn't dare speak so openly in front of Bertie.

"Sit," Bertie says, sending Evan around the room to light the candles in the wall sconces. The curtains are always drawn in this big sitting room, and Cerrick remembers now how tight this space has always been. Not an ounce of joy or hope could exist here.

He takes a seat on a couch facing the door, wondering how many bloodstains lie beneath him that he can't see.

Edlyn sits beside him, unwilling to part from him for even a moment. Is she making up for all the time they spent apart while he was in Holbeck, or is she hovering protectively because of where they are? Either way, he's happy. He likes having her close.

Brandr and Edda seat themselves in individual chairs beside each other. Brandr leans forward with his forearms braced on his knees. He looks eager, his face drawn, his cane clutched in his left hand.

Bertie takes a while to settle down, fluttering around the room and giving meaningless instructions to Evan. Cerrick suspects he's holding onto his authority as long as he can. Cerrick keeps looking at Evan, but he refuses to meet Cerrick's eyes.

"You said you'd be seeing us again," Cerrick says to Bertie before he can help himself. He knows he should let Brandr say his piece before he ruins it with the mess brewing in his own mind, but he needs to say this. Over a year since he and Edlyn left, all the words he longed to say to Bertie have been bottled up with nowhere to go. Out they come now. "Why did you just shut the door on us?"

Bertie looks at him, still wide eyed. He's not smiling. "You killed seven of us," he says, his voice low with a twinge of sadness and disapproval. It doesn't cut like it used to. Cerrick sits up straighter.

He waits for more, but Bertie stays silent. Cerrick and Edlyn exchange glances. Bertie busies himself rearranging cushions on the couch across from Cerrick. Another oddity. He's never liked to fumble around, he likes to save time and get to the point.

"Right," Brandr says, sick of waiting, "so, Bertie. Meet the Order of the Phantom." He sweeps his hand across his companions.

Bertie pauses, then laughs as Evan settles beside him. "Creating a rival gang? You must be out of your mind to risk my wrath like that, Brandr. Oligarch you may be, but rumor has it no one is safe."

His eyes fix on Edda with a small smirk. That's the Bertie Cerrick remembers. Always so sure he's right.

Brandr sighs, tired. "The Order of the Phantom's purpose is to bring hell upon Andor and Kryos as we know it."

All is quiet. Then Bertie leans forward, hands on his face, grinning like it's the greatest day of his life. Despite himself, Cerrick remembers how dizzying it felt to have pleased Bertie. "Ohhh..." His eyes fix on Cerrick. "The mighty Sun prince has fallen out with his boss?"

Cerrick swallows.

"Please tell me you're kidding," Bertie adds.

"We're not," Edda says, evidently tired of staying quiet. All eyes turn towards her. "Andor has betrayed every one of us. We want to lead the seventh rebellion of Kryos, and we need numbers to do it. Allies. We need you."

"No one has spoken as vehemently against the oligarchs as you," Brandr says. The two of them speak like a set, filling each other's sentences easily. "Edda has already been ousted for her bloodline because of a centuries' old law that needs updating. The sentiment of Krycs standing against Ressegalians has changed with the times, and—"

"Save me your political law speech," Bertie says.

Brandr spreads his hands. "I am going to be ousted soon, along with Eir and Solveig. They'll be replaced by Andor's own choices. He's going to turn Kryos into a dictatorial kingdom, the nature of which we haven't known for several rebellions, unless we do something about it."

Something prickles beneath Cerrick's skin at those words. *That was my research,* he thinks. *My work. Mine. And he's hearing it for free. We're offering it up on a platter.* Yet he trusts Brandr. He didn't know his opinion of someone could change so much in only a day, but it's undeniable that he'll support whatever Brandr's doing here. Cerrick just hopes it's not going to come back and bite him later the way so much else has.

He knows the business. He knows Bertie wouldn't possibly agree to help until he knows everything they can give. Cerrick has been the one interrogating petitioners under Bertie's orders before.

"And you want the help of my little organization?" Bertie asks, like he can't believe his luck. "What are we going to do? Storm the palace, emerge with Andor's head on a pike?"

"This operation will require a much more coordinated effort than that. Erika and Sigrid Thorpe didn't act rashly. They took their time making plans, gathering allies, determining what they would do once they had the government in their hands. All of this must be considered carefully, because we're not just destroying something—we're rebuilding in its place." Brandr glances at Edda, though he's speaking to Bertie. "You *will* help us."

Bertie leans forward, reddish brown hair falling in his eyes. "What do I get out of it?"

Cerrick snorts.

"It's not about what you *get*," Brandr says, "it's about what you owe us. We have paid the price. You have taken and taken and taken enough from us. Years of our lives." His voice shakes with barely restrained anger.

"You worked for my father," Bertie says stubbornly.

"Thanks to him, the Ice has carried on even after his death."

"Thanks to you," Bertie shoots back, "I had to take over."

Brandr pauses. "The point is that you don't get to demand anything more."

"So, nothing," Bertie says flatly. "I get nothing from this."

Cerrick almost hoped Bertie would listen, that he'd do better. That fear in his eyes, the hesitance, gave Cerrick some hope that things had changed even a little bit.

Bertie is charming, there's no question about it. It's how he's survived so long. He seems tamer now, though still as greedy and selfish and impatient as he's always been. Yet he's not as brutal.

Cerrick hasn't seen mania glimmering in his eyes and behind his grin yet. Cerrick always wished he could put a kinder man to the pretty face, but Njord Hagen claims that title. No one else deserves the honor of it.

Brandr growls out, "What you get is your life and your reputation intact. You get to keep your little organization running. What you *get* is this building not being blown sky high. You will follow us?"

All Bertie does is shrug and say, "Stay a while."

"Stay?" Brandr echoes.

"Stay. Andor has spent thirty years on that creaky throne without attempting a coup. He's not going to act so quickly."

Cerrick begs to differ, thinking of how soon Edda was ousted after Alfred's banishment. And then he registers what Bertie said. Stay.

Stay—stay here?

Cerrick looks up in despair, hoping it doesn't show on his face. No. Bertie wouldn't—

Bertie is smiling slightly. Cerrick knows that look, he knows it all too well.

Edlyn murmurs the Tailing words for *fucking bastard* under her breath, but it doesn't change anything. "Fine," she says.

"Yes, alright," Brandr says, trying for diplomacy now that he's pushed Bertie as far as he can with his bared teeth and brutality. "We'll stay a bit. We need a safe place to rest."

Cerrick barely bites back a scoff, both at the irony of referring to the Ice townhouse as somewhere *safe,* and the risk that comes with sharing their vulnerability. But Brandr isn't dumb. He knows what he's doing. Cerrick does trust him.

Cerrick knows he should've spoken more lest Bertie think him a weak puppet, but he's barely hanging on. Edlyn's hand finds his under the cover of darkness, warm and firm and strong. She hasn't wavered for a moment, hasn't shown anything but defiance and strength. Cerrick is a mess, and for a moment he's jealous of her.

Edlyn didn't need Bertie's influence to become the untamable fury. It's always resided within her. It's a sort of silent, building rage that leaves room for little else. Revenge lies on her mind; Cerrick knows that much. He's more focused on surviving his stay in this place than the thought of getting his hands around Bertie's throat.

Bertie too looks flabbergasted that Brandr would admit to such a weakness, but both men retain polite and empty smiles. Cerrick is surprised Bertie hasn't resorted to outright hostility yet. He hasn't ordered Evan to wake anyone else, hasn't placed a weapon against someone's neck. Cerrick prays to the heavens that this good luck will continue, if one can call it that.

Next step: staying in the Ice townhouse. He can do this.

Rising to his feet, he brushes Edlyn's hand as his legs threaten to give out. Edda shoots him a concerned glance as she rises with the rest of them, getting ready to discuss the specifics of what exactly the Order of the Phantom expects from the Order of the Ice.

Cerrick wishes to hell he could just walk into Edlyn's arms and rest there. All the rejuvenation he gained yesterday has evaporated from just a few short minutes in Bertie's presence.

"Would anyone here happen to be from Fura dukedom?" Brandr asks as they all stomp upstairs, probably waking the other occupants. The Ice members aren't morning people, if things haven't changed since Cerrick was here. More than likely, the people upstairs are still recovering from late night excursions. No one usually stirs before nine bells at the very earliest. They thrive at night.

"I am," Evan says before Bertie can tell him not to. Brandr doesn't supply an explanation to his question. Bertie doesn't ask.

Cerrick walks towards the front of the pack as they reach the hallway at the top of the dimly lit steps. The carpet is the same gaudy red, and the strong stench of ash hits him hard. He pauses in his tracks until Edlyn gently bumps him forward. This time, when they join hands, her fingers are trembling almost too much to capture his.

The thought of walking right past the people he laughed with, bled with, fought beside and fought against, is nearly what does him in. The temptation to run back downstairs and out the door and breathe in blessedly cold air is overwhelming, but Cerrick chokes through the stale air stinking with memories and pushes on.

He looks at the red walls, lit by yellow lamps in their dusty sconces, and remembers Edlyn slumping against that very spot on the wall the night she was stabbed. The two of them were frantic to fix it, though they had no idea how. There was so much blood. Cerrick's hands were shaking, sticky and red as they breathed harshly together. He thought—he prayed—he prepared—

A girl here named Kara was an ex student of healing at the University of Heynes across the city, and thanks to her, Edlyn survived. She still bears the scar on the left side of her stomach, long and angry. Seventeen months ago. Looking at these walls brings Cerrick back to that night like it was yesterday.

Bertie walks with only moderate concern for the sleeping, and they make it to the end of the hallway before they hear any thumps or complaints. A single sharp rap on a north side door makes Cerrick jump out of his skin. Thankfully, no one comments on it, though he can feel the judgment in Bertie's glare.

Bertie halts before the second to last door on the left. Cerrick would know it in his sleep. Nothing's changed—the scuffed paint on the red door, the gold handle that has always needed cleaning.

"I believe you'll feel right at home here." Bertie flourishes a wave like they're at the finest inn in the city as his esteemed guests. Edlyn smiles through her teeth, her knuckles white as she clutches the door handle. Cerrick touches her before she can open it. *Don't.* He can't face that right now. He can only take so much. She nods minutely.

"It's sunrise," Edlyn snaps, crossing her arms. "We don't need to nap now, Bertie. Take us somewhere we can talk. That war room of yours across the hall."

Bertie raises his hands. "Are you sure you don't want me to wake up the others so you can get reacquainted?"

"*No.* Straight to the war room, Bertie." She shoos him, ordering him about with all the bark Cerrick remembers. She used that bark the night she saved him from getting knifed in an alley a few blocks over. Cerrick sometimes forgets that she spent almost two years more in the Ice with Bertie than he did.

She claims she warmed to Bertie quickly and learned his tells enough to call him out on them. She fought back when he tried to do something about her. Cerrick wonders if she's always been this confident when dealing with the head of the snake. It doesn't seem possible, like dancing with your heels on fire.

Cerrick wonders if the others sleeping throughout the building can hear Edlyn's sharp voice, unique and recognizable. The hammer will be coming down on their heads soon. He just has to survive until, and then get through it.

Bertie knocks on another door as they pass and declares it'll be Brandr and Edda's room for the time being. Cerrick smiles deliriously as the two of them pointedly look away from each other. Good on Bertie for assuming. But they must—*be*, already. Cerrick never found the words to ask yesterday, but what seemed obvious then now looks more muddied.

As they get midway down the hallway, the first rays of morning light enter the window at the end of it. The darkness in the hall is banished for a few blessed moments. And then, a heavy knock raps against the front door downstairs. Cerrick doesn't jump this time, though it's a near thing.

"Who in the heavens is here now?" Evan mutters, one of the first things he's said this morning. They all troop back down the stairs, moving as a unit. Evan strides across the sitting room to open the door.

The man standing on the other side is not a man they were expecting. His braid is tossed about by the wind as he squints into the darkness. His fine blue cloak gives life to the dark street the way no Kryc could, and his Pointstaff gleams in his left hand. Cerrick's breath hitches, and he finds the time to say a prayer.

Njord.

CHAPTER FOUR

For a moment, all they can do is stare at each other, both their mouths open. And then Njord is moving, and Cerrick is stepping through the doorway to meet him. They collide in each other's arms. Njord is warm as always while Cerrick is frozen with shock.

He can't appreciate any of the sweet words Njord is murmuring in his ear, the warmth of his arms, the way he smells, the comfort he brings. Cerrick's too busy thinking about how he's going to explain this.

Cerrick forcibly pulls himself back, wrapping his thin brown cloak tighter around himself in the wake of the morning wind. The cloak Njord gifted him sits drying in Brandr's house, all those long miles away.

"How—how are you here?" he asks faintly, staring at Njord in awe, wondering if he's some kind of Saint come to haunt him. "How did you find me?"

"I knew this city is the only place you would go," Njord says in that rumbling voice Cerrick has missed so much. It's been only two days, but he's missed it so much. "I rode hard here through the night. I asked just now where you were, and the people said they saw you come in here."

The four of them were careful to hide their destination, or so Cerrick thought. "What people?" he says carefully. He fights back the wave of panic at the thought of what he'll have to tell Njord, the secrets he's been running from. He'll avoid that a few moments longer.

"The people over there," Njord says, gesturing vaguely. Njord's eyes stray into the darkness behind them, trying not to lock eyes with Cerrick' strange companions. "They told me that you come here once a month. That you disrupt the crowds and you piss them off with your nobility."

Cerrick's mind spirals downward. Folk across the street, taking notice of him like that. The lower class whose morning shopping he ruins every month when he has to pay his dues.

Fuck.

Leave it to Njord to wander into the most unsavory part of Rinnfell by accident.

"Cerrick?" Njord asks. "My love, what is wrong? Why did you disappear like that? Are you safe? I've been so worried about you."

Cerrick wishes that he'd learned to speak even a little Aeton during his time in Holbeck, so that they could have this conversation privately. His cheeks burn at the thought of what everyone behind him is thinking. *Please, Bertie, stay silent a little longer.*

Through the miserable ache in his chest, he says, "Let's—let's go inside. Out of the cold." The last thing he wants is to bring Njord into the townhouse, but they can't go anywhere else.

Njord was never meant to last. He was a daydream, the sunlight Cerrick could never stay in. He was always meant to come back to gray Kryos. The seventh rebellion—that's something that's designed to last, and he won't jeopardize it.

But damn if he doesn't want to fight to keep Njord too.

Cerrick leads him inside by the hand. His eyes adjust quickly to the dark, but he hates that he can't see Njord's face clearly. The faces of the others are just as well hidden. Cerrick swallows the lump in his throat and leads Njord upstairs. He'll let Edlyn carry their burdens a while longer.

On the stairs, he hesitates. This is probably his only chance to introduce them in a civil manner. Taking another excuse to stall, he says, "Njord, this is that friend I told you about. From Tailing."

Njord squints into the darkness. Edlyn steps forward to wave at him.

"Hello," Njord greets, bowing his head. Cerrick looks between them with a twinge of guilt. He hoped they would have a chance to know each other better.

Cerrick leads the way to Bertie's war room; second to last door on the right side of the upstairs hallway. He pulls Njord into it, shivering at the cold, and locks it behind them.

The window at the back looks out on a dark alleyway, but at least it provides some morning light. Cerrick busies himself going around the room lighting lanterns. It's something to do to distract himself, but thanks to the lanterns he can see Njord's face more clearly. He can't decide if he likes that better or not.

A round wooden table takes up most of the space in the sparse room. The white carpet has been made stiff and brown with dirt and stains over the years. Cerrick would be surprised if Bertie ever had this place cleaned.

"Sit down," Cerrick instructs. Like a doll, Njord wordlessly obeys.

Cerrick sits. They're doing this. Oh, Saints.

He takes Njord's hands in one of his own, swallowing at the sight of the silver and gold marriage bracelet on Njord's wrist. Cerrick still wears his own. It somehow survived the Gryting, even if the knots are loose and some of the beads are missing. He fights the urge to pull his sleeve up over it.

"Darling," Cerrick begins, hoping to minimize the damage before the storm has even begun, "I work—well, worked—for the Order of the Sun. As a spy."

"A spy," Njord repeats. His voice is low and detached, but he doesn't withdraw his hands. "Did you—were you spying on me?"

"No," Cerrick says immediately and laughs, already close to tears.

"Then who were you spying on?" Njord asks.

"I was investigating the theft of the Asger Archives." Cerrick has avoided thinking about this since he knew he'd have to have this conversation, but the words come easily now. He squirms under the hot-cold intensity of Njord's stare.

"And where are we now? Why did you leave so suddenly?"

"I—there's a whole nother piece to this. This place, these people...Njord, I used to work here. In this building."

Njord arches an eyebrow. "It's a rather dismal place to work."

"Yes, you could say that. I—I—"

"Were you a spy here, too?"

Cerrick laughs wearily, bending over their hands and resting his forehead on the table. "I need you to stop talking for just a moment. You're too wonderful. You're too distracting. You paint this in a better light than it deserves. You can speak as much as you'd like when I'm done—trust me, you'll want to—but just give me this for now. Alright?"

"Alright," Njord says, then winces and mouths *sorry*. Cerrick smiles with watery eyes. This is the most brilliant man in the world, and he's about to lose him forever. Saints, Cerrick is such a fool.

"This place is called the Order of the Ice," Cerrick begins. "It's—it's a gang house." He can't dodge and dance around the topic any longer. "I was a part of this gang. I did horrible things at the behest of one of the men downstairs. I threatened. Wounded." After a pause, "Killed."

Njord's eyes widen, and his hands tighten on Cerrick's.

"Edlyn and I," Cerrick says. "My friend. We did it all together. We took orders together, we slept beside each other, and at times, it seemed like we were one person of one mind. I'm not proud of what we did. In fact, I'm fucking ashamed. I—" He's stumbling, rambling, going about this in all the wrong order. "Saints, I'm not explaining well. Let me start at the beginning."

He describes the night he stumbled out of a tavern and nearly got knifed in an alley, how he was forced to join the Ice because Edlyn insisted Bertie not kill him. She claimed Cerrick was naïve, childlike, couldn't anyone see he was just a kid like them? Bertie said they weren't kids, none of them were, but that didn't matter. Every word spoken that night is burned into Cerrick's memory.

To pay off his impossible student loans, Cerrick took out a huge chunk of money from the Ice's stores. Edlyn had done the same thing years before in order to help her struggling family. He describes what he did in the Ice in the vaguest terms possible for Njord's sake. He doesn't speak of the parts he enjoyed. Njord doesn't need to know that yet.

The night Edlyn got stabbed. The nights after nights dealing with other gangs in other alleys, the endless nights in the sitting room with Bertie and Evan and Kara and all the others, standing in this war room and receiving orders.

The night Cerrick couldn't take it anymore and convinced Edlyn to escape with him. How they sliced their way through anyone who stood between them and the freedom of the streets. Bertie yelled after them, but Cerrick didn't care, because they were free. They were also left with a mountain of debt that they could no longer pay off by earning money for the Ice. That problem seemed small at the time, because they were so blessedly *free*.

They secured a meager apartment that was their *own*, rented out with what money they took with them. Bertie sent Evan along as a debt collector. He didn't need to describe what would happen if they refused to pay.

They spent a month or two drifting aimlessly around Rinnfell looking for jobs, and then they wound up at the Order of the Sun for an interview.

There, they began with small jobs at first, such as spying on various individuals around the city. Knowing what he knows now, Cerrick can only guess what kind of people they truly were.

They built trust with Andor, enough trust that he sent them abroad. Assassinating a Ressegalian councilman was the most important job Cerrick ever thought he'd pull off. Until the Asger Archives. Until Njord. But Cerrick never expected Njord to become such a big part of his mission. He was supposed to be only a means to an end. He was supposed to remain faint, like the background of a painting.

"And how do I fit into this?" Njord asks when Cerrick takes a pause. "Why did you marry me if you were a spy?"

"I married you because I was a spy," Cerrick clarifies. "I needed—I needed a discreet cover for my mission. The marriage was arranged upon Oligarch Andor's orders. No one would ever know." He winces at his own words. While he meant to blame Andor, he didn't mean to imply that Njord was uninteresting otherwise. That Cerrick only courted him because of orders.

"So it was all a lie?" Njord asks, his voice strangely flat. "Everything you told me? Everything we shared? Did?"

"No," Cerrick says, "no, no. None of it was. All of it was real. I love you. I still do. I never—nothing has happened to change that."

Njord puts his head in his hands.

"The outings," Cerrick says, "the cabin, the Middle Forests, the tourney—all of it was real."

"Then why did you run away?" Njord wails, the closest to despair Cerrick has ever seen. Oh, how Cerrick hates to be the reason. His heart shatters.

"I discovered all this bullshit about Andor, and Alfred, and the oligarchs, and—" He breaks off. "I was conducting an investigation about the Asger Archives, which turned into so much more than I thought it would. An investigation of my own government that unearthed its corruption. Now I'm on Andor's bad side, and Brandr and I and the girls are planning a rebellion. The person I snuck out to see when there were roses on our balcony was Edlyn, I swear on the Saints."

"Tell me more," Njord murmurs.

Cerrick shares his discoveries in Holbeck, what happened since he left Holbeck to lead him here. He doesn't tell Njord about Brandr's involvement with the Ice since it's not his place. When it comes to Edda, he eludes to a crime as simple and old as a bloodline.

Njord's face tightens with every word. Cerrick also knows how nervous the surrounding countries get when a new rebellion erupts in this land. The new regime of Kryos could have any agenda, any enemies, any goal. Any of Kryos' neighbors could be a sudden target for invasion. Countries like Aeton usually close their borders while Kryos fights their way to a new transfer of power. Even peaceful envoys are sometimes turned away.

"I know I'm hardly in a position to make demands," Cerrick says wearily, "but I'd appreciate it if you didn't spread the news of our rebellion far and wide. While we find our footing, secrecy is imperative. We don't want Andor so much as getting word we're alive."

"You didn't trust me to keep your secrets?" Njord asks. "Is that why you never told me the truth? You thought my tongue would loosen so easily?"

"It's not that, really it's not, it's just..." Cerrick bites his lip. "When we're on a job, we're instructed not to trust anyone. It's not a matter of loose tongues or tight tongues. We simply rely on discretion. And I wasn't exactly expecting to fall in love with you. To *want* to share the truth."

The ghost of a smile crosses Njord's face.

"We don't trust anyone," Cerrick adds. "And in my case, I didn't learn that lesson from just the Sun. I learned it from the Ice. I wanted to tell you. You have no fucking idea how badly I did, but it's not what we do. By the time I realized how deep I'd fallen, it felt like it was too late to tell you without irreparably damaging things between us. There was never a good time after that, and there never will be. I wasn't expecting you to—to show up here."

"You just ran away," Njord says, hollow. "I love you. I wasn't going to let you run away with no explanation and accept it. You make it sound like you intended on never coming back."

Cerrick's gut reaction is to say *no,* assure Njord in any way possible that he wasn't just going to leave him behind, but that is the truth. And Njord deserves the truth. That's what this is about. That's why they're here, even if it's not how Cerrick imagined it'd unfold.

His silence is telling.

Njord takes a shuddering breath and buries his head in his hands again.

"I'm sorry," Cerrick says, realizing he hasn't said it yet. "For whatever it means, I'm sorry."

"I'm—" For once, Njord seems at a loss for words. He shows his face, blue eyes despairing and agonized. The sight pierces Cerrick's heart sharply, consuming his senses with grief.

He chose this.

"I'm upset that you didn't trust me," Njord continues. Cerrick swallows his protests, his explanations. He tries instead to listen. Njord is hurt, and a bland excuse won't solve that. Cerrick hurt him.

The most precious man in the world, and he hurt him. His own husband, the greatest lover he could've ever hoped for.

He chose this.

"Did you know?" Njord asks. "That night you left, when you said you loved me. Did you know you weren't coming back?"

"No," Cerrick says, happy to supply another honest answer. "Edlyn made me go with her. *No,* I chose to go with her. I won't blame anyone else in this."

"That makes you better than most."

"Please, don't pretend like I am some Saint," Cerrick says. "I am not deserving of your mercy. Not right now."

Njord bows his head, deep in thought. "So this is what you were doing on all those nights when you snuck out. Meeting with your Edlyn. Piecing together the puzzle of your boss's corruption. It's nice to finally know. I thought—" He shakes his head, apparently thinking better of it.

"You thought I had a lover," Cerrick says quietly.

"That was one possibility. I thought—perhaps—" Njord takes on a sheepish expression. "Private visits to other people's homes. Assignations."

Njord thought him a whore?

Njord laughs a little, and Cerrick realizes he said it aloud. "I don't know. You're certainly handsome enough." He rubs the heels of his palms into his eyes, murmuring, "Sorry. I need a moment. You didn't *trust* me."

"I wanted to," Cerrick says quietly, standing up. "Saints, Njord, you don't know how much. But this is a dangerous business, as I've explained."

He doesn't want things to go back to the way they were. He doesn't want to live a lie while willfully blinding Njord to the truth, but he sure as hell doesn't want this either. He wants a future where he can be with Njord without issue, even if his current problems haven't been resolved.

It's a different life than what he thought he wanted in Holbeck, where the Sun and his past in the Ice didn't exist. Now he doesn't know what kind of world he wants with Njord. The Order of the Phantom has been formed, and the entire structure of Kryos is in jeopardy.

Cerrick just wants peace. He doesn't want to be running for his life, he doesn't want to be in debt, he doesn't want Bertie to haunt him every day. He wants to wake up with Njord and luxuriate in truth, with Edlyn close by and a government that doesn't loom over him. Impossible, unattainable. A dream.

Everything is gray. He doesn't know what he's allowed to hope for.

Cerrick hesitates with his hand on the doorknob, staring at the back of Njord's red-brown braid, his head bowed.

"At the beginning," Cerrick adds, figuring he has nothing left to lose, "I may have exaggerated some of my affection for you. But that changed. And even before it had, you always blew me away, Njord. From the first day we met, you were kinder, more thoughtful, and more respectful than I knew anyone could be. I thought people like you only existed in fairytales.

"I may not have told you everything, but I wasn't lying to you at every turn. I may have been living a lie, but I fell in love with you a little more every step of the way. Each time you held me or kissed me or whispered the sweetest things I've ever heard from anyone's lips.

"I told myself over and over I was *allowed* to get close to you, but it was exactly what I feared. Getting *too* attached. I didn't tell you the truth because I was selfish. I wanted to live in a dream with you. I knew it wouldn't last."

Cerrick opens the door but still hovers in the doorway. The peace and quiet of this room won't be found anywhere else, and Cerrick suspects he won't find such a peace with Njord again. This is the calm before the storm.

Njord speaks after a long moment as the gray morning light fills the room. "My mother always said there was something more to you."

They weren't the words Cerrick hoped for. He can already feel the air between them changing, the magic fading or perhaps just twisting. It's too soon to tell.

Cerrick slips off his marriage bracelet and places it on the table beside Njord. In some parts of Kryos, it would be a symbol of divorce, but Cerrick only means to give him the choice. Whatever Njord wants, he will do his best to acquiesce, no matter how much it hurts.

He waits, but Njord says nothing more. Cerrick finally slips outside, shutting the door between them with a loud click. The hallway lies empty.

Cerrick leans his head back against the door and draws a harsh breath, taking comfort in the small mercy that Njord is on the other side.

STAY, BERTIE ASKED of them, his only price for the moment. A small one.

So they stay.

They stay seven days in that dark and dismal townhouse, while Cerrick stews in memories and nightmares and doubts. During his first night there, he dreads to even open the door of his and Edlyn's old room. He can barely face the red walls, imagining blood splattered there.

The mattress is just as hard and uncomfortable as he remembers, and hates how easily he and Edlyn get settled, falling back into the same complaints about the room that they've always had. It's stuffy and thick and hot and dark, the bed is awful, the colors are gaudy, and the paint is chipped.

Predictably, Cerrick suffers nightmares. Some of the worst he's ever had, partly because he knows the privacy in this house is scant and the walls are thin. The greatest hope he can nurture is that in the morning no one will comment on it.

The contents of the nightmare are a blur that dissipates when he wakes—all the familiar faces sneering at him and drowning him and uttering ugly words. The truly haunting quality is the feeling that creeps over him after he's awoken—the hiccupping breaths, the pounding of his heart, the cold sweat dripping down his back.

Edlyn's touch drew him out of the nightmare. She places a hand on his neck and shoves his head down, bending him over as he gasps for air. Somehow, that breaks him out of it.

In the morning, Bertie keeps his needling to a minimum, perhaps at Edlyn's behest. Eating breakfast with that swine is just as awful as Cerrick remembers, but he tries to remind himself why he's here. Seeing Njord at the other end of the breakfast table is a particular degree of agony. He shouldn't be here. He never should've come here. Yet he doesn't indicate he's leaving anytime soon.

Edlyn refuses to wear anything but a mask of stone.

Cerrick excuses himself quietly.

In their gaudy old bedchamber, he kicks the wall. Once. Twice. Hard enough to feel it, hard enough to dispel some restless fury.

Edlyn, drawn by the noise, comes to the chamber with a hand on one of her knives. She stares. "What the hell are you doing?"

"It's all so *fucking frustrating,*" he growls, kicking the wall a second time. "Here playing nice with Bertie, watching him pretend to play nice with us. Smiles and lies and false niceties. I don't trust him for a second, and I sincerely hope Brandr is of the same mind. I'm questioning him. I'm questioning everything."

Edlyn sighs and lays a hand on his shoulder. "We're plotting a rebellion. I'd be surprised if any of us had a handle on it. We're not exactly in the most stable of environments. You know how this place fucks with your head. Just bear it a bit longer."

After a moment, he nods. "And don't go around kicking walls," she adds. "We need you. You can't afford to break a toe."

We need you. Her footsteps echo down these accursed hallways.

BRANDR AND BERTIE'S negotiations never make much progress, since Bertie refuses to give ground. Brandr's frustration radiates in droves that Bertie tactfully ignores. He still refuses to see why he gets nothing in return for what Brandr's asking of him. Brandr wears out his tongue trying to explain it, for all Bertie seems to listen.

Despite Cerrick's care to avoid Ice members, one morning he exits rooms at the same time Kara does across the hall. They both freeze, sizing each other up. She's grown out her hair since he was here last. Long black locs are piled up onto her head in braids.

She nods at him, and he notices a new scar on her left cheek, a long slash over her brown skin. "Been a while, Cerrick," she says in the smooth eastern Kryc accent that he always found charming. It has none of the harshness of southern Kryc accents. Friendly. Low. Intriguing.

"Yeah," he says, his voice caught thick in his throat. "How've you been?"

She shrugs. "You know how it goes. Bertie let me finish my degree at the University of Heynes after I scored a big win for us. He was so proud." She smiles. Cerrick knows what it was like to have Bertie's pride and approval. Like soaking in sunshine. Safety wrapped around him, all of his worries gone.

Bertie is charming and lovable, there's no doubt about that. If he weren't, how would he ever recruit? How would he get people to stay at his side? Fear is one motivator, but it can be circumvented, as can tyranny. Charm, however, is a different beast entirely.

"Good," Cerrick manages. "I'm—happy for you."

He remembers the quick way her fingers worked to stitch Edlyn back together, back to life, away from Saint Calith's clutches. There were other, happier memories he shared with Kara, too—they laughed together, they joked, they fell asleep on the stained couches downstairs when the nights grew late after a job.

She told him about growing up in Steinberg, the greatest city in Slairr, about falling into despair and crime when her parents died. The gang she joined in Steinberg wandered here, and she ended up with Bertie, as they all do.

They used to talk about making lives of their own. Getting free. Moving on from this place. Neither of them ever really believed they'd manage it.

Now, she says, "I wish you luck," and waves.

"Thanks," he says, warming a little. "You, too."

Everyone else he remembers has either died, escaped, or been disgracefully dismissed. In their place are a lot of young faces.

Sitting on those same stained couches one dark day, Brandr announces, "I am going to make Evan an oligarch."

Everyone in the sitting room *balks*.

My Saints, Cerrick thinks, *Brandr has finally lost his mind.*

Brandr smiles at Evan's gobsmacked expression and says, "You're going to ask how and why. Why you. Well, you're from Fura. I'm mere days away from being ousted myself, and Andor is wrong if he thinks I'm going to just run and hide with my tail between my legs. I am going to suggest someone new for appointment in my place."

"That won't do much good, as wonderful of an idea as it is," Cerrick points out. "Andor is the one with final say in replacements."

"I know. I don't know if he's going to give the real reason when he boots me out, or if he's going to make something up. He knows what he has over me. Yet I believe he'll hesitate." Brandr smiles. "I was in the Ice once. He knows what I can do to him. His imagination can run wild."

"You wouldn't be able to hurt him without bringing the whole weight of the government down on yourself. He'd call your bluff."

Brandr looks up, green eyes flaming. "Isn't that exactly what we're doing? Bringing the whole government down? Andor doesn't have to take my suggestion," he continues, leaning back in his chair. "But the power of the mind's suggestion is immense. I have a feeling he will at least consider what I have to say. He might appoint Evan for a short time, to placate and humor me. He'll waste no time devising a scheme to remove Evan and replace him with his own predetermined choice.

"A power hungry old man he might be, but he's still an old man. He's lived a long life, made a lot of enemies. If you think he's immune from fear any more than you are yourself, you're wrong."

"Why don't you explain to poor Evan what he'll have to do once he's made the Pristine Duke and Oligarch of Fura," Edda says, taking pity on the wide eyed, petrified Evan.

"Ah, yes." Brandr scoots forward to look at him. Bertie keeps trying to butt in, but Brandr won't let him speak. "You won't have to do anything close to actually running my dukedom, don't worry about that."

Some of the fear flies out of Evan's face. Cerrick knows how competent he is, but with an honest face like that, he wonders how Evan has lasted so long here. He reminds himself that being a good liar is not all it takes to make an Ice member.

Brandr continues, "You'll be a spy for the Order of the Phantom. Your duties will be nothing more challenging than anything you've done for this cesspit in the past. We need someone in the palace feeding us information about what the oligarchs are up to."

Whenever Solveig is ousted, Alfred Dalton will be her replacement and will take on the role of senior associate oligarch, if what Andor said was true. However, they haven't heard a thing about Alfred in the papers since returning to Kryos.

"They won't speak openly in front of the new appointees," Edda adds. Cerrick notices the gleam in her eyes and wonders if this was her plan. He and Edlyn exchange glances across the room. "But we have faith in you to bring us useful information."

Her tone is sweet, but her words hold a hidden pressure. *You'll do well because you must, and let your imagination provide the consequences if you fail.*

"Why not appoint someone from Burfell dukedom to be our spy instead, since that spot is already vacant?" Edlyn asks, still not giving poor Evan a chance to speak. "We could suggest two people...but no, Andor wouldn't allow that. He might follow his fears and appoint your choice, but not Edda's."

Brandr nods. "Not only that, but Edda has been effectively exiled in shame. If she hadn't left the palace and the public eye, if she had someone prepared to take her place when that vote was sprung upon us in the middle of the night, such a scheme might've worked. However, we weren't ready then. She couldn't go back now and expect Andor's leniency."

"So the vote was just as brazen and abrupt as we suspected?" Edlyn asks gently. "Did Andor bring up the secrets he'd learned about all of his oligarchs, proclaim their secrets would be used against them if they didn't vote each other out?"

"Yes," Edda says quietly. "In as many words."

Cerrick and Edlyn exchange glances.

"Edda, my friend," Brandr says, laying his hand on her knee, "I want to apologize again for the humiliation you faced. I wish I had the courage to stand in defiance of him and walk out with you at that moment, but I didn't. I'm sorry you were dragged through the city in chains like a common criminal." He shakes his head, sneering in anger. "Andor is an *animal*."

"Brandr, it's quite alright," Edda says. "Andor will be the one humiliated when we show up with an army of criminals, and everyone he betrayed comes to haunt him. We will drag him out in chains and parade him through the streets for all to see."

"Damn right," Edlyn says, clapping. "If I had a drink in my hand right now, I would toast to that."

During that lazy day at Brandr's house, Edda explained to Cerrick how she and Brandr wound up in cahoots. They'd been meeting in secret for months to discuss what Andor was doing and the possibility of fallout. They'd made a pact of alliance before that, but Andor brought them together. Ironic.

As soon as she was released from her chains the night she was ousted, Brandr slipped away with her to his house in Fura. She couldn't go back to her manor in Burfell, and she couldn't stay safely in Rinnfell. Brandr's home was the only place where she could be safe.

Brandr went back the next day to wait for Cerrick and Edlyn, no matter how long that wait might be. "He wasn't expecting to find you in the Gryting Sea," Edda told Cerrick with twinkling eyes. Brandr planned to lurk and wait, avoiding Andor unless he was directly summoned. Even if Brandr himself was ousted, he vowed to wait until Edlyn and Cerrick showed up.

At present, Brandr says, "You'll be fine, Evan," and pats him on the shoulder with enough force to make him shake. Evan has always been skinny as a stick. "And then after you've completed that duty for us, you'll be free. Free of this place."

"What?" Bertie sputters. "You barge in here, claim that I have no choice but to help you, and now you free one of my members just on your word?"

"You're the one who asked that we stay," Brandr says icily, ignoring Bertie's continued outrage. "I told you I could take over your organization in a moment if I wanted to. Freeing your members is the least that I could do to you. Evan gets his life back in exchange for giving it to us for a while. How does that sound, kid?"

Evan looks up wide eyed at Brandr as he stands, stammering, "Thank you. Yes, of course I'll do it." He avoids looking at Bertie, who's all but baring his teeth. Brandr just smiles brightly and shakes Evan's hand.

Cerrick is close enough to hear Brandr whisper, "You're gonna do fine," and slap him on the shoulder again. "Go pack." They've been here six days and are supposed to be leaving in the morning, the minimum amount Bertie insisted they stay. Cerrick's heart soars at the thought of escaping this dark place.

"So," Edlyn asks as Evan scurries away, "what's our next move beyond installing Evan as oligarch, Brandr?"

"We go to the Oslands."

Cerrick watches ten emotions flick across Edlyn's face in the span of a few seconds. He snorts.

"What?" she says, rubbing the heels of her palms into her eyes. "Why ever would we do that?"

"Because we have nowhere else to go, for one," Brandr says, counting off the reasons on his fingers. "The moment we step out of this haven, we're targets. I'd prefer to put a sea between ourselves and Andor, rather than simply fleeing to Aeton or Ressegal."

"Can't believe you're calling the townhouse a haven," Edlyn mutters, voicing Cerrick's thoughts, "but go on."

"Two, In the Oslands, I have—" Brandr purses his lips, choosing his words carefully.

"Connections," Edda supplies gently.

"Connections, thank you, dear. The Os have something that could be of great use to us. There is someone who lives on the coast whom I met during my time in the Ice. He's likely to help us."

Bertie gasps. "You mean—"

"Yes. *That* Os mission."

Cerrick searches his memory but can't recall any gossip about a job in the Oslands that Bertie's father pulled off.

"It was the equivalent of the job you two pulled off in Ressegal," Brandr tells Cerrick and Edlyn with a wink.

"You haven't been wrong yet," Edlyn muses. "About the Oslands, I mean. Killing an official in the Oslands sounds easier than killing a Ressegalian councilman and escaping with your life. That is, unless there are cliffs surrounding the Os palace as well."

"You killed a Ressegalian councilman?" Kara's voice rings out from the top of the stairs. She slowly makes her way down, arching an eyebrow at them. "You'll have to tell me about that sometime. I see your restless spirit hasn't dwindled, Cerrick." She crosses the room and exits in a blast of cold wind, making them all curse her name. Privacy and the illusion of it are impossible to find in this place.

"We won't be ready to make a direct attack against Andor for a long while," Brandr finishes. "We still have to contend with people like Gustav and Skad, the new oligarchs Andor is appointing to the council, all of their collective followings"—Cerrick thinks of his own parents with a grimace—"and it might even be a while before we're back in Kryos. While I wait for Andor to oust me, while I get Evan sorted, you should take care of whatever business you have left in Kryos for the time being."

Cerrick's biggest piece of unfinished business is hiding away upstairs. He doesn't know what he's going to do about that.

CHAPTER FIVE

On the morning of their departure, Bertie walks them outside. Cerrick does his best to ignore him, focusing mostly on Evan, who's sitting alone on a horse from the public stables down the street. He's avoiding Bertie's gaze, too.

Edlyn, sitting at Cerrick's back on the horse they share, squeezes his wrist. An admonishment or a gesture of support? She turns his head by grabbing his chin and says firmly, "We're going to be *fine*. Stop worrying."

He nods wearily.

Njord is seated upon another horse rented from the public stables. Cerrick told him this morning as quickly and painlessly as he could that he was departing for the Oslands, outlining every detail of Brandr's plan with Evan. Njord promised to see them off, but offered little more than that. Cerrick didn't dare ask what his plans were.

Honesty is the first rung on the ladder of Cerrick's journey back to Njord's good graces.

Bertie's voice draws Cerrick out of his reverie. "We'll be seeing you when you pay your dues," he says with a condescending little wave at the party. Kara stands uneasily at his side.

With a sudden burst of courage, Cerrick snaps, "No," before they can head back inside. "You won't be. Bertie, I am done with you. I am tired of living in fear of you. I refuse to be your plaything any longer—a toy to be manipulated and ordered around and fucked with. I'm tired of having you in my head, dictating my life, stealing every coin I make for myself. Tired of your threats. Tired of your ghost. Tired of *you*."

"Are you suggesting you won't pay?" Bertie demands. "Because then you'd be stealing from me. From the Ice."

"I won't speak for Edlyn," Cerrick retorts, "but yes, you're right. I won't pay. Even if you weren't richer than most nobles in this city, I would be happy stealing from you. You deserve to be stolen from. So you can take your demands for payment, your threats, and you can shove them up your ass. Fucking try to come after me and you'll see what happens."

For a moment, Bertie actually appears to be stunned into speechlessness.

"He and I both have been paying you back steadily, consistently, over the last year and a half," Edlyn adds. "Between that, you have more than half of what we borrowed. You won't get another coin of ours. Frankly, I'm sorry I ever gave you a coin to begin with."

Bertie's mouth opens, but no words come out. Beside him, Kara stands with her hand over her mouth.

"We'll be back for you," Brandr calls, "when we're back from the Oslands. You're not going anywhere, and you know what will happen if you attempt to escape from what I've ordered of you."

"Certainly, Lord Brandr," Bertie says in a tone of mocking respect, dipping into a deep bow. Saints, Cerrick can't wait to be rid of him.

As the riding party takes the first steps down the street, Kara pulls away from Bertie's side. She blurts out, "Take me with you."

Brandr turns his head. "That eager to be away from Bertie, hm?"

Kara, one of the fiercest girls Cerrick has ever met, meets his eye with an expression of stone. "Yes."

Behind her, Bertie sighs.

"Evan," Brandr says, "would you mind sharing?"

"No, not at all." And so Kara, underdressed for the weather and equipped with a blue duffel bag, hops expertly up onto the back of Evan's white horse. She settles herself and wraps her arms around his waist. "What are we waiting for?"

Edda and Cerrick exchange glances, both biting back laughter. They've decimated the Ice in every way, with now five of its members parading away before Bertie's eyes. If it weren't early morning and if he weren't presumed dead, Cerrick would whoop for joy until the whole city heard him.

Horse hooves on cobblestone streets give Cerrick a comfort he didn't know they could. He doesn't look back.

AS BRANDR PREDICTED, it doesn't take long for Andor to make a move. They haven't been riding long before a bone chilling horn rings throughout the city, waking up the entire population. Brandr's face instantly contorts into a grim mask of pain. "That'll be for me. Edda, swap places with Evan. Evan, are you ready? We're going."

Evan slides off his horse with the duffel bag he packed, taking deep breaths of frigid air.

Cerrick leans down to catch Evan's shoulder as he walks by. "I'm sorry," he whispers.

Evan shoots him an incredulous look. "Why do you apologize? I'm free of Bertie and this terrible place. I can see my mother again. I can rebuild my life. I have nothing but gratitude for you and Brandr."

"You might get caught. You don't have your freedom yet. This is a test. You have to survive it and prove to Brandr that you're worth the effort before he'll truly give you the freedom you deserve."

Evan shrugs. "I never have to sleep another night in his bed. That's good enough for me. After so long here, I think I can handle an undercover job for a short period of time." He clasps Cerrick's hand, thanking him again. Cerrick withdraws it and leans back into Edlyn's arms as he watches Evan join Brandr on a horse.

"All of you, go to this address," Brandr says, shoving a piece of paper into Cerrick's hand. "I'll be there in an hour or two. Call for Inge. They're a friend of mine and they owe me."

Evan and Brandr thunder away toward the palace to answer the summons. Cerrick sends a prayer to any Saint that will answer it for Brandr's good luck.

With their party down to five, they creep as quietly as they can through the back streets of Rinnfell. They avoid the people seeking the source of the horn, and the guards patrolling for Brandr. Silence falls over the party as Cerrick leads them to the northeastern tip of the city, near the waterfront, as the address indicates.

Trying to ignore Njord's presence behind him is a hard thing, but Cerrick focuses on the early morning crowds by the docks. At least it's not as crowded as it will be in an hour, two hours, five.

"This is better for all of us," Edda says quietly, rubbing Cerrick's shoulder. Perhaps she's guessed where his thoughts have strayed. "Brandr will be alright. Having his secrets aired before the oligarchy is certainly unpleasant, but I suspect he'll feel some measure of relief when he's no longer an oligarch."

"Really?"

"Mm. He enjoys representing his people, but it's difficult for him to bear the reputation of a grouchy recluse. It'd be hard for anyone, much less under Andor's thumb. Brandr had no intention of claiming another term as oligarch, even before this mess with Andor came to light." She sighs wistfully.

"Are you two together?" Edlyn pipes up. Cerrick turns his head to glare, but Edda just laughs.

"No."

"How?" Edlyn demands. "A blind man could see the attraction between you in a matter of minutes. That doesn't make sense."

"Don't I know it." Edda smiles sadly. "I have offered, but he has turned down my advances thus far."

Edlyn shakes her head. Cerrick is too busy thinking of Njord to reply.

A beat passes, and Edlyn shoves his shoulder and sticks the map in his face. "I don't need your melancholy ruining our perilous journey. C'mon, help me figure out where the fuck we're going. So, Gold Street turns into Moonlit Avenue..."

Predictably, the waterfront in the capital of Kryos isn't easy to navigate. They keep traveling east, searching for the address Brandr gave them, until they finally come upon something that looks like a shack. The addresses match, peculiar though they are.

Cerrick slides off his horse, determined to make himself useful after a week of struggling to so much as speak in the Ice house. "Inge?" he calls out, aware of his indiscretion but unwilling to get knifed by wandering into the shack unannounced. If they're a companion of Brandr's, Cerrick doesn't doubt he'd be welcomed in such a fashion.

"Yeah?" comes a voice from inside the shack. The door is yanked open, revealing an angry face with long hair whipping in the seaside wind. Cerrick shivers. He can't believe how cold it is here, despite having taken a dip into the Gryting himself. For a moment, he's thrown back in time to Holbeck, standing in the freezing wind in front of the house of Skad's informant.

"I'm a friend of Brandr Tofte's," he says, also reminiscent of that night. "He's going to be here in a few hours."

The face—a long nose, bright green eyes, pale skin, brown hair flowing—glares back at him. "What do you want?"

"To come inside. There's five of us, me and my friends." When they still hesitate, Cerrick says, "Brandr said you owed him a debt. He'll be around to explain everything, I promise. If he doesn't come, you're free to throw us out."

They swear and sigh and glare at him some more, but after an agonizing wait, they finally wave him inside. Cerrick beckons to the others, who quickly dismount and hitch the horses to the building outside.

"That little rat," Inge rumbles, slamming the door shut behind them as they all scurry in. Cerrick waits for them to elaborate, but they just set to wandering around the shack, seeing to various chores and mumbling to themself the whole time.

For a shack, it's not half bad. A window out the back overlooks the foaming white and green-blue sea, a view people pay fortunes for in fine manors and mansions along the coast. Western Kryos is generally too rocky on its coasts to have ports like this, but the Rinnfell docks are masterfully made to fit those limitations.

The window lets daylight in, and the floor on which the five of them sit is clean. The shack is too small to house furniture, but the cleanliness and light is more than can be said of many Kryc homes. Including the Ice townhouse.

There's barely enough space for them to sit and for Brandr's acquaintance to move around, even with their knees pulled up against their chests. Cerrick resigns himself to a long, uncomfortable wait, made doubly painful by how close yet far Njord sits.

They don't dare speak freely since they don't know the extent of Brandr's trust and friendship with this person, so they can do nothing but wait in awkward silence, breathing the stale but gracefully warm air of the shack. Only an hour or two. That's not so long. The sooner the better, what with the way this person is sneaking furtive glances at Cerrick when they think he's not looking.

An hour passes, and then two. No sign of Brandr.

The obvious explanation is that Andor is detaining him, perhaps even arresting him for his involvement in the Ice. The story of his ousting will be in the *Report* today, with or without the reason, depending on how much Andor reveals.

Cerrick's legs grow stiff, but he doesn't want to stretch and bring any more attention to himself than necessary. They all *could* wait outside with the horses, but Brandr told them to wait here. It's safer and warmer in here than outside, and he *will* be back.

Unless he won't be for reasons beyond his control. Unless this acquaintance of his gets fed up with them—rightfully so—and kicks them out.

More time drags by until the gray noon light is rising over the water. Cerrick's legs grow numb and then tingly from so long in one position. Finally, when he's about to struggle to his feet and summon Edlyn for a private meeting, a frantic rapping comes at the door.

Their strange host opens it to another blast of freezing wind, and sighs in exasperation. "I was beginning to think these fools of yours were lying to me. Do you know how many times people try to use your name on me? At least these ones tried to look convincing."

"They've done more than try," Brandr says dryly, stepping around them to face the five on the floor. "Sorry I took so long."

"Did it go well?" Edlyn asks, rising to her feet.

"Yes." Brandr's tired smile and cheerless eyes suggest otherwise, but he won't speak plainly here. "Inge, thank you for housing them."

"You're welcome, brother," they say fondly. At first Cerrick thinks it's just a figure of speech, an affectionate term, but the way Brandr rolls his eyes and swats at their arm makes him reconsider. That, and the way Edda curses under her breath.

"This is your sibling?" she demands.

Brandr winces. "Yes. This is Inge, who you've already met."

"You told them I owed you a favor?" Inge snaps. "You're the one who owes me. Money, days of room and board—"

"I paid that back! In hard labor! Who was out gathering firewood for you in the wind and snow?"

Edlyn and Cerrick exchange smiles.

Brandr sighs heavily. "Regardless, thank you again for taking care of them instead of throwing them out into the wind when I was late. We need to be going, I'm afraid. No time to catch up."

"You don't wish to tell your sibling that you were just ousted from the council of oligarchs?" Edda asks. Inge looks between her and Brandr, one brown eyebrow arched.

"That's a story for the future, when things are different," Brandr says stiffly, looking at Edda with a pinched brow.

"Will your house still be standing when you return to it?" Edlyn asks. "You're not the duke of Fura anymore. There's no telling what the madmen will do."

Brandr sighs. "I built that house from the ground up. If it gets sacked, I will rebuild. I have little other choice. That's what we're doing, isn't it? Rebuilding from the ground up?"

To distract himself from that uneasy thought, Cerrick studies the differences between Brandr and his sibling. The noses, their demeanor, the distrust in one and the honesty in the other. Cerrick never knew Brandr had a sibling, but he never knew anything about Brandr before meeting him on the shore of the Gryting Sea. By choice, he was rarely mentioned in the *Rinnfell Report*.

Each oligarch answers the press's relentless questions differently. Some like Duchess Skad overshare, overwhelming the journalists with details. Others like Solveig offer enough to keep them satisfied but not enough to build an accurate picture of their lives.

When oligarchs like Brandr don't share anything at all, the press hound them and resort to fiction if they must. Cerrick is glad he's getting to know the true man behind the vicious rumors. He wonders how he ever believed any of them.

Inge searches Brandr's face for any kind of admission, but he stares them down with a blank expression. Finally they shake their head in defeat.

"You owe me," they proclaim, slapping him on the shoulder. "The story and so much more."

"Yeah, yeah. Can you get us on a ship to the Os coast?"

They blink. "Shit, you really are serious. Running from the authorities? Same ticket as always?"

Brandr laughs. "Something like that."

Inge, it turns out, is not just a grumpy recluse stomping around their shack. They're at the seaside for a reason other than to torture themself with the wind—they smuggle people onto ships, forge tickets, change names on documents. Usually but not always for a good cause. Like brother, like sibling.

"I'll get you passage on a ship to the Oslands, no questions asked," they promise with a pat to Cerrick's shoulder.

The entire point of the Phantom is to fix the corruption in Kryos, not contribute to it, yet Cerrick can't help the comfort settling over him. How safe he feels around these people. He knows the monster lurking in all of them. He knows what they're capable of. Has seen it, in some cases. There's nothing more they could do to him that he hasn't seen, doesn't know.

He still has the knife Edlyn gave him the day they emerged from the sea, tucked safely into his boot. Cerrick is no less capable of defending himself than ever.

He breathes.

As Inge leaves to see about their passage, Cerrick belatedly notices the cloth bundles Brandr set down near the door. "What happened?" is Edlyn's first question, while Cerrick inspects the cloth. He realizes with a hitch of breath what they are.

"Evan is installed as oligarch," Brandr says with a shamelessly proud smirk. "Andor understood my message. It went just as well as we could've hoped for. We have to pray Andor doesn't vote him out tomorrow or have the poor kid killed, but unfortunately that's out of my hands. I gave Evan instructions for how to send us information without getting caught, not that he needed them after so long in the Ice. He assured me he knows how to defend himself if someone comes into his chambers in the dead of night with a knife."

His words are all but lost on Cerrick as he runs his fingers along familiar black fur. It's still damp, but impossibly lighter than the heavy mass it was a week ago.

"I'm sorry I was late. I rode to Fura as hard and fast as I could to retrieve your and Edlyn's cloaks, as you can see, as well as some clothes of my own. The less we have to buy in the Oslands, the less of a footprint we leave, the better."

As Cerrick pulls on the Njord cloak over his thin brown one—wearing two cloaks isn't a bad idea this late into a Kryc winter, by the windy seaside—he can't help breathing it in. Njord is watching him. Cerrick can feel the drag of his eyes over the fur resting against his neck, but he tries to ignore it.

Were it any other day, he would lean into it, show it off, encourage Njord to come to him, but he wouldn't do that now. He's been accused before of being insensitive and at times even emotionless, but he can be sensitive. He tries. He's trying harder for Njord than he ever has for anyone. It's hard to be aware that his words have impact, that even things like body language can affect a mood.

"Thank you," Cerrick says, smelling the inexplicable *home* past the stink of the sea clinging to the fur. Whatever the excuse, Brandr did this because he cares about the two of them, which is more than Cerrick can say about most. For Brandr to do something like this, delaying their journey just for Cerrick and Edlyn to have their own cloaks back, means a lot.

"Of course. Couldn't let my two best agents get cold." Brandr smiles and winks, pulling his green cloak over his own shoulders. Cerrick returns the smile, warmed through.

"You should go find some things to hang on your cloak before we leave," Edlyn whispers to Cerrick, rattling her own knives on her cloak. Cerrick sees in her face the beast lurking within. The fury. "You have to look like a true Kryc man once we're among the Os. I wouldn't mind some additions as well." Many of the hooks for her knives are empty, lost to the sea.

Cerrick opens his mouth to ask Brandr, but he's interrupted by the loud blast of a ship's horn. Human voices follow, asking workers to begin loading up, for the ship will be departing in half an hour's time.

"Why don't you go pick out something for me," Cerrick tells Edlyn, though he has eyes only for Njord. They need to talk. "Please don't make me regret asking that."

"It's tempting," Edlyn says, "but I'll behave, since we're going to be among foreigners who actually care what we look like." She slaps his shoulder and slips out of the shack in a bustle of black fabric, pulling up her hood against the wind.

"I need to see to our luggage, or lack thereof," Brandr says. "My friend in the Oslands will provide what he can, but not all of what we'll all need. Kara, Edda, why don't you come with me. I could use all the hands to spare."

The three of them file out, leaving Cerrick and Njord alone. Cerrick swallows and looks at the floor. He doesn't know where to start.

"Do you want to stay or come?" seems like a good place, though his tone is guarded and flatter than he'd prefer.

He doesn't know whether he wants Njord to say he'll come or stay. Njord coming along with them wouldn't aid the Phantom—foreign nations intervening in Kryc rebellions are how laws like the Ressegalian ban come about. Never mind the backlash Njord himself would face. Cerrick has already done enough damage to the man without involving his country. And his family—

"Where did you tell your family you were going?" he adds before Njord can answer his first question.

Njord gives him an odd look. "To find you, of course."

Of course. Because Njord doesn't lie to those he loves. The thought of the Hagens knowing Cerrick is missing and probably worrying about him breaks his heart for their sake.

Vi usha. Ice scoundrel.

He is a monster.

For a wild moment, Cerrick contemplates the other side of things without regard to the risks—Njord coming along. They'd be able to work out their marital problems, perhaps even make up with time. Cerrick isn't ready to give up on the dream of having Njord again, no matter how selfish and foolish it is.

He *will* find a way to work through this awful silence, whether it's now or in some distant future after the rebellion. Cerrick will fight through hell to make up for all the monstrous decisions he's made in his life, with Njord at the top of that list. Njord wouldn't have to participate in the rebellion, but he'd get to watch as Cerrick did what he does best.

Looking at Njord's face now, Cerrick realizes his fantasy was just that: a fantasy.

"I think it is better if we stay apart for a bit," Njord rumbles, his accent thick and beautiful and devastating as ever.

Cerrick bows his head, trying to hide his smarting eyes. That was the answer he expected, the answer he prefers, the answer he knows is best for both of them, but it still stings like hell.

"I wish you safe travels back to Holbeck," he mumbles, wondering if he's ever going to see Njord again in Kryos, or whatever it becomes. "You can use one of our horses."

He slips out of the shack, unable to stand the air in there any longer even if it means waiting in the cold.

Njord doesn't come out.

Brandr returns, Edlyn returns, the ship horn blares again. The ship is large and discreet, impressive in its bleak Kryc way. The workers lay out the gangplank, and Inge presses the documents of passage into Brandr's hands. Luggage is loaded. A flurry of activity consumes the waterfront.

The party looks upon the foamy green sea, all too reminiscent of the swim that birthed Cerrick anew.

Under gray clouds, Cerrick boards the ship without looking back.

CHAPTER SIX

Cerrick and Edlyn are assigned a small cabin together with a dirty porthole looking out onto the sea. It's clean and private, if not soundproof. That's good enough for him.

Edlyn doesn't remark upon his melancholy, though he can only guess at how gloomy he must seem. He took one look at himself in the reflection of a puddle on the ship and quickly looked away. He hasn't had a proper bath since Brandr's house, and his blond hair is in a constant state of worried disarray, but he didn't realize how tired his face looks. The dark circles nearly match the dark gray of his eyes. He's lifeless. He's Kryc.

Only the cloak Njord gave him, as bitter as it is beautiful, brings a hint of life back to him. The same brilliant blue of Njord's eyes, the fur softer than Njord's touch, lies finally dry next to Cerrick's skin.

Edlyn did well, buying him horns to decorate it with. He wore horns on his old cloak, the one he hasn't seen in months. That one is hanging on the wall in their Rinnfell apartment, but no cloak could be as beautiful as this.

The horns are beautifully shined, painted in red, blue, green, and purple. Much like Brandr and Edlyn, Cerrick's cloak will now rattle to announce himself as he walks.

It's then he remembers their pledge to stop paying Bertie. No longer do they have to carefully conserve every coin in their possession. They can spend their spare on things like cloak horns and not have to worry about being killed for it. Bertie will retaliate in some undoubtedly terrible way, but for now, Cerrick enjoys the newfound airiness in his chest.

For her own cloak, Edlyn bought herself chain links, to Cerrick's dismay and simultaneous amusement. Short ones, light enough to wear on a cloak, but *chains? Chains?* He won't stop needling her about it.

She takes it in stride, grinning like the little shit she is. "At first, I considered going for animal skulls, but I thought those might be too gaudy," is what finally shuts him shut up, albeit only in shock.

"I'm ashamed to have ever known you," Cerrick groans into his hand. Edlyn laughs loudly, drawing all eyes in the below deck common room. Inge did a wonderful job securing their passage—aside from the necessary crew, Cerrick and the others have the ship all to themselves. It's a bit jarring to walk the halls and hear so little.

The Gryting Sea is unpredictable and rowdy, so if all goes well and no storms bar their way, they should reach the coast in as little as a week and a half. Because of the close quarters and so much time at sea, however, Cerrick has nowhere to hide when Kara corners him to ask about his life after the Ice. *It could be Bertie,* he thinks as she hounds him about the Ressegalian mission he and Edlyn went on, the details of Holbeck, the extent of Andor's crimes. *It could always be worse.*

Reluctantly, he tells her what she wants to know. At first, he attempts to pawn off the duty to Edlyn, but she is enjoying his suffering far too much to take it off his hands.

Slowly, Cerrick unwinds. They're both different people now, but in Kara, he sees the version of himself he used to be. The powerful man in the Ice. Looking at Kara is like looking into the past, a disconcerting feeling.

No more secrets. Nothing more to hide from anyone. A new slate for him, an honest one.

Kara recounts her time at the University of Heynes—Andor's dukedom—with similar reverence that he regarded his schools with. She recounts that similar, strange sense of freedom they both felt for the first time in their lives. "I am an accomplished healer. If you or Edlyn are ever injured, I won't hesitate to lend my aid."

"Heavens forbid," Cerrick prays. "You know, you're free now. You don't have to answer to that bastard anymore. What are you going to do with yourself?" Some would say her choice to walk away was easy and quick, yet he knows it was anything but. He can only imagine the way her emotions have reeled ever since she stepped away from Bertie's side.

"Open the best damn free practice in the western side of Kryos," she says, snapping her long, colorful nails for emphasis.

"How are you going to fund it if it's free?"

She reaches for the small blue duffel bag she's had with her since leaving the Ice, always close to her person. Unzipping it, she reveals a hint of the gleaming gold contents.

"You didn't," he says, jaw falling. "Please tell me my eyes don't deceive me, and you're the third person in a row to steal from Bertie."

"Mhm." She sits with her chin in her hand, smiling.

"I'm glad to have you with us, Saints."

"I'm glad to be here."

Such a simple admission, said so casually. Stealing from the Ice is far from the worst they've done—it's a common and easy crime to commit upon leaving. But something about Kara's spirit, strength, and bravery sets her apart. Not even Evan would've dared to steal from Bertie, despite his hidden courage.

Cerrick wonders how he fares. The Ice never toughened him up like it did others. Evan refused to submit to the pressure of Bertie's harsh instructions—usually he stood frozen in place until he was yelled back into action.

His new position is equally challenging in different ways. Evan will be sending out the first of his first reports to the Phantom in a maximum of two weeks. Cerrick says a quiet prayer for him, wondering how he's faring—if he's faring at all. If he dies under Andor's hand, he'll be yet another failure at Cerrick's hands. He's not the one who asked Evan to be their spy, but he stood by and let it happen. Encouraged it.

Cerrick stubbornly rearranges his thoughts. *Not his fault.* Andor's. Cerrick is not the one who might be killing Evan, Andor is. Andor will be breaking another of Kryos' spoken and unspoken laws if he kills.

This is all Andor's damn fault. His fault that Cerrick had to leave Njord in the middle of the night and lie to him at all. His fault that Cerrick has never been able to grieve Orv with Njord the way he wished. His fault that Orv died in the first place, because of his order to Alfred.

It's because of Andor, says a little voice in Cerrick's head, *that you ever met Njord at all.*

Cerrick shakes off that disturbing train of thought.

No matter how many times they ask, Brandr refuses to tell them who they're meeting in the Oslands and what great boon they will receive for doing so. "None of us will say anything unwarranted," Edlyn argues, but Brandr doesn't budge. They turn to Edda, who refuses to reveal if *she* knows.

"Have you considered I'm not telling you not because I don't trust you, but because I want to see your faces light up when you find out?" Brandr yells, surrounded by people who could be his kids and a woman who could be his wife. She's watching from afar, hiding a laugh in her hand. "Let an old man have his surprises."

"Brandr, you're forty one."

"Oh? This leg makes me feel like I'm an old man." He stretches it out on the long seat beside him. He's merely joking. Between the lack of walking and the lack of stress on the ship, he claims his leg feels better than usual. Cerrick can attest to his own decreased stress.

"You should try those stretches I suggested," Edda says softly. Brandr scoffs, arguing with her about which of them can care for his leg better, which of them has dealt with the pain for more than a decade.

"I have my herbs, I have my cane, and I will be fine as I always have. You and your stretches are inconsequential."

"Even those at the forefront of rebellions have weaknesses, my dear," Edda says sweetly as she walks by and plants a kiss on his cheek.

FREEZING COLD.

Too cold for Cerrick's body to comprehend, so it goes numb instead. Falling under, his lungs filling with an unbearable pressure as he chokes and gasps for air that isn't there. Darkness. A bright whiteness interchanging, overlapping, blinding him.

Through the chaos and the panic, a voice. Andor's. It's not been long since Cerrick heard his voice, but it's so much more devastating now than he remembers. Cerrick is still fighting to the surface all on his own. There is no strong arm to pull him to shore this time. He's alone.

"Heartless," Andor says, invisible at first. Cerrick turns towards the sound of his voice and finds him walking on the green sea above him. He dips in and out of view as Cerrick's head bobs out of the waves.

Andor stands tall and regal with his cloak fastened around his shoulders, rings glittering in a sunlight Kryos doesn't have. He's perfectly put together as always, never smiling. He's without his Pointstaff. He doesn't need it to eviscerate Cerrick.

"Emotionless," Andor continues, walking in time with Cerrick's movements, getting ever closer. His eyes hold the power they always have, only amplified. "Traitor. Monster. Criminal. Incapable of love. You are nothing but the muck on my shoe, and you will fail to rise against me. I have the law behind me. You sealed your own fate when you joined the Order of the Ice. I will prosecute you as the law demands, and your friends with you. I will lay my hands upon that odious Brandr. You all will rot away in the lowest dungeons I can find for you. So low you could not imagine. Perhaps...perhaps underwater."

Cerrick thought he was making progress getting to the surface, but he's abruptly plunged under again as a wave crashes over him. He gasps, inhaling water. It burns like hell, stinging and choking, but it doesn't kill him. Andor's voice still carries clearly around the rush in his ears.

"Orv. Oh, how you failed him. Had he not associated with you, he would still be alive. We can only hope that Evan won't be your third failure. You are, of course, well acquainted with your second."

Njord's voice replaces Andor's when Cerrick breaks the surface again. He's staring into the bright blue sky of Aeton, and Andor is nowhere to be seen. Njord stands on the shore in his place, tall in brilliant blue, his red-brown braid hanging over his shoulder. Both of their marriage bracelets rest on his wrist.

Cerrick nearly sobs at the sight of him. If he had the capacity to call out to him, he would, but doing anything other than flailing and trying to stay afloat is laughable. Njord and salvation are so close, if Cerrick can just fight his way to the shore—but the water fights back, pushing against him.

"You walked away from me," Njord rumbles. "You just left me there. I left the fire burning all night, waiting and hoping that you'd return to me. You didn't."

I didn't want to leave, Cerrick tries to say, but he can't. It would be so easy to give up and let the water have him, but he can't. He can't relax, he has to keep fighting—

"All I wanted was you," Njord continues, bending down and reaching out a hand. Cerrick swims harder than ever, desperate to reach that sweet safety, but it's impossible. "But you ruined that. Now we can't live as the family I dreamed of."

I can fix this. We can fix this. All is not lost yet.

"Wait," he tries to say, really tries, and gets a mouthful of water for his trouble. Njord is standing up, turning away, disappearing into the mouth of the cave system Edlyn and Cerrick found salvation in that day. "Wait! Please."

But Njord either doesn't hear him or simply doesn't care, because he keeps walking until Cerrick is too far underwater to have any hope. As water fills his lungs, Andor's voice fades back in, piercing and strong. "Heartless."

Cerrick jerks awake, looking wildly around the room with a hand to his hammering heart. Edlyn is asleep in her own bed against the opposite wall of the cabin, undisturbed by his movement. But she'll be up soon. Their reflexes and instincts, not only for loud noises in the night but for each other, are too strong to ignore this.

Cerrick tries to lay back down as his heart calms, only to discover that he's lying in what feels like a puddle. He and his sheets are drenched in sweat, a rare and unpleasant experience.

He slowly swings his feet over the side of the bed, taking a moment to see if Edlyn's going to wake up. He's shaking. He feels half crazed.

Cerrick pulls on his Njord cloak for warmth, though the rattling horns are impractical and the sight of it almost makes him sick this time. So quickly has it turned from an item of utmost comfort into a visualization of something like the nightmare he just had.

Their cabin is dark but for the moonlight peeking through the clouds, leaking in through the porthole. Supposedly the weather in the Oslands isn't much better than in Kryos, though it's warmer. Here on the water, they haven't had too many cloudy nights. The Saints seem to be smiling upon them.

Cerrick makes his way up the steps, wincing at every creak of the wooden floors—Saints damn it, why did his cabin have to be so far within the bowels of the ship—until at last he's in the cold, open air of the night.

The air refreshes him. He looks up, and what lies in the sky makes him swear softly. An ethereal mix of color is painted across the sky, stunning greens and pinks. They rest in waves, sometimes static and sometimes moving. Cerrick is awestruck, and can do nothing but sit on the deck with his knees pulled up to his chest as the ship rocks.

He's heard of these before in passing, but Brandr didn't mention they'd have a chance to see them. Cerrick is tempted to wake him up lest the lights don't appear again, but he's heard they appear commonly on the coast of the Oslands. They'll have another chance. Cerrick isn't in much of a mood for company right now.

Sitting under the lights with a light breeze on his face, cloak pulled close around him, is the best remedy Cerrick could've hoped for. He hasn't been sitting there long when he hears heavy bootsteps and the rattles of those fucking chains that can only belong to one person. He doesn't say anything, just waits for her to sit down beside him.

"Sweet Saints," Edlyn breathes, looking up at the sky.

"I know. It's more beautiful than all of Kryos."

"So colorful. The green reminds me of Tailing."

Cerrick looks at her profile. "Aside from the flag," she says, while Cerrick admires the way the colors reflect onto her black hair, "everything wild in Tailing is green. The bamboo forests, the grass…Saints, I need to take you there."

She only takes the name of the Saints when she's feeling especially reverent or angry.

He knows she heard him rise from his bed. She waits patiently for him to find his words instead of pulling them out. Cerrick is loath to ruin their first moment of calm since his last night in Holbeck, when he thought their meeting at the embassy would be like every other.

It doesn't take long for the words to come spilling out. "I had a nightmare."

"I know. I'm pretty sure everyone sailing the Gryting knows."

"How?"

"You were screaming," she says. "Screaming for Njord, for Andor, screaming for someone to wait."

His face heats. He's in for an awkward breakfast. "Oh."

"Yes, oh. Tell me what it was about." She scoots closer.

A few weeks after they escaped the Ice, Cerrick dreamt of Bertie's face every night. He felt the phantom pain of a knife as it slipped between his ribs—a knife that had never been there, not that it mattered. Every night, he wound up holding back tears in Edlyn's bed while she ran cold fingers through his hair, calming him enough to choke out the words and let her banish the horrors.

The nightmares didn't truly fade until he and Edlyn took their jobs at the Sun, though walking back to the apartment alone at night always gave him a fright. Cerrick would glance furtively down the alley that led to the townhouse, glimpsing the light in the upper window even if all else was dark. *You have nothing to fear, not anymore,* he tells himself, for all the good it does.

Edlyn doesn't say much, she never has. What is there to say? Cerrick isn't a child in need of coddling. She prefers to assuage the source of his fears or pain and end it by whatever means necessary.

Cerrick endeavors to do the same. However, Edlyn can't fix it in this case. The business with Njord is completely out of her reach, and dismantling Andor's regime isn't going to happen in a few turnings of the day.

So Cerrick speaks, filling the air instead. "I'm consumed with this burning rage whenever I think about Andor. I'm furious at him, but I'm even madder at myself. I thought I knew him, but—" He breaks off. "I did know what was lurking beneath the surface. On some level, I must've known about his treachery, and I should've done something about it." He slams his fist into the ground. "I've been a blind idiot."

All that time spent admiring Andor, thinking to himself that perhaps this time things would work out and he could put his full trust in someone. What a fool he was, just a pawn in Andor's game.

He's having the same doubts about Brandr, but the man is an open book, and Edda vouches for him. Cerrick has never known Edda to lie, and her moral compass is strict—although that's the problem, isn't it? Knowing? Thinking he knows someone's philosophies and loyalties only to have them flipped on their heads. Each time he tries again, he can only hope he'll be right. Only the Saints truly know.

"We had no way of knowing about his corruption beforehand," Edlyn insists. "We've discovered the lengths to which he went to keep it quiet."

Cerrick shakes his head. "I should've listened to my instincts. I should've noticed how suspicious Andor's secrecy was. He kept you so far from me. He's never done that before. We're partners. A stolen biography about Alfred Dalton isn't inherently damning. I should've realized that."

"What would it have changed?"

Cerrick looks at her, incredulous.

"Are you saying you wish you'd never met Njord?" Edlyn asks. "Because that's the only thing that would've changed if you'd have found out in Andor's office the day he gave you that assignment," she says, rubbing his shoulder. "You still would've fought him. He still would've turned on you, and we still would've been forced to flee. We'd still be where we are now. You wouldn't have any memories of Aeton or Njord. Is that what you want?"

Cerrick sighs as those very memories plague him again. This time, the plague is Njord's warm arms and warmer voice when Cerrick needed comfort. Njord provided it without Cerrick even needing to ask—he always seemed to know. Cerrick yearns for his silent support now, the warm arms that could solve international conflicts.

"I just wanted to save myself the humiliation of being led along and then exposed like a fool. I wasn't even thinking about Njord until you brought him up." *For once.*

Edlyn squeezes his arm. "You will see him again. You will get the chance to fix things. Until then, can you survive off memories?"

Cerrick considers a variety of other, sadder replies, but goes with, "I have you. That's all I need."

She smiles. "Don't you ever believe that I'm going to be one of the ones who betrays you, is that clear? I'd sooner die."

"I'd sooner die than let you rip out my heart like that," he says, pulling her closer with an arm around her shoulder. "I'll kill myself before you could knife me."

That's not true. He would die for her, with her, to her hand, a thousand times over. She could hand him the knife and command he do it himself, and he would. He knows she would do the same for him.

"Perhaps the sky lights are affecting me," Edlyn says haltingly, "but I—I'm not going to say this often. I know you don't need me to say it aloud, so I don't, but I do know it's nice to hear. I have no one in Kryos. When I fell into the Ice, I found more than a source of revenue for my family. I found people who were willing to have more of a relationship with me than that of a polite shopkeeper.

"That night I saw you, something immediately felt different. You looked at me, your eyes so wide with an innocence I hadn't seen in that part of Rinnfell in years, and I thought, there's something worth saving here. Bertie didn't speak to me for a week afterwards, if you remember."

"I do." Bertie's silence gave her more time to acclimate Cerrick without his interference. Cerrick began under her wing, and their relationship evolved into an equal partnership.

"You're the only one who's ever cared for *me*," Edlyn says. "Not what I can do or what I can bring. You actually care about how I feel. You want to be around for the sake of being around me. I'm the one who puts a barricade in our communication, and you respect that, but I am communicating to you now. I love you. I'm glad you're in my life."

Cerrick has been subject to Edlyn's spontaneous rants before, but never one quite as sweet as this. He's shocked to find himself tearing up, nightmare forgotten under the moonlight. "We're going to get through this together," Edlyn promises as he squeezes her shoulder. "Whatever it takes."

Looking up at the lights, Cerrick believes her.

CERRICK HAS THE NIGHTMARE again. And again, and again, night after night of their journey.

Each time he startles out of bed, he climbs the steps to the deck to look at the lights, but Edlyn doesn't follow him outside again. If he needs her, he'll go to her during the day, but sitting under the lights and breathing in the cold air is enough to clear his head. He grows somewhat used to the nightmares. It's been a long time since he's had such consistent and consecutive nightmares, and the bone deep exhaustion and numbness that come with them are familiar.

The nightmares differ slightly. Sometimes Edlyn is the one on the bank, naming all his faults. The promise she gave him about betrayal isn't quite enough to keep the dread from overflowing in his heart like ink from an inkpot. Sometimes she's bleeding out in his arms while water rises around them both. Sometimes his parents are there on the bank instead, dark and terrible.

During the day, the others are kind enough not to mention the nightmares, though he's sure he continues screaming. He suffered his share of sleepless nights in the Ice because of someone else's screaming nightmares. With four ex-Ice members on board, he feels a bit better about it.

The fourth night of this cycle, he stumbles up the steps to the deck and makes his way towards his usual spot on the floor, only to stop in his tracks. "Hello, Cerrick."

He turns and finds Brandr and Edda sitting side by side. Their hands rest on their respective armchairs, almost touching.

"Hello," he says, voice still rough from screaming and sleep. "I didn't see you there."

"You haven't, the last few nights," Edda says. Cerrick raises an eyebrow. His reflexes are evidently not as sharp as he hoped. He's more focused on banishing the thoughts of Andor, Njord, and Edlyn than he is on checking his surroundings.

"We come out here for peace, too," Brandr says kindly. His face is difficult to see, cloaked in shadow, but the moonlight illuminates his eyes. His gaze is directed towards the colors in the sky. "You remind me so much of myself, you know. When I was your age.

"So angry, so hurt, looking for an excuse to lean into the monster just so I wouldn't have to think about what I could be without it. Without the monster, I thought I was nothing. I thought I had nothing except the crimes I could do, the money I could steal, the goals I could achieve in the Ice. Rising up the ranks. Look at me now, the hypocrite, starting a rebellion with a band of criminals.

"It's because I have hope for all of you. I want you to lead better lives than I did. I know it's not too late for you to leave behind Bertie and the Ice and heal from Andor's betrayal. There is more for all of us.

"Looking at these lights reminds me of a simpler time. They help me dream of a time where I can be happy again."

Edda takes his hand and squeezes it tight. Brandr smiles, the only indication that he's not lost in his own mind. Watching their hands is safer than watching their faces. "Edda has made me believe in the possibility of a better world."

Cerrick can't fathom why Edda is also awake. Does she have nightmares, insomnia, troubled sleep, or does she rise with Brandr? They're not sharing a room to the best of his knowledge. Perhaps she has a sixth sense about Brandr in distress like Edlyn and Cerrick do for each other.

Brandr says nothing else. Cerrick leaves them be, still holding hands, and takes his usual place on the floor to pull his arms around his knees and watch the lights. To coexist with them brings him more peace than ever before.

He doesn't have the nightmare again.

CHAPTER SEVEN

As promised, the beautiful phenomenon of land comes into view quickly. The farther north they've climbed, the calmer the waters have been, offering a peaceful transition. The first look they have of the Os coast is one of pure white snow, muddy gray clouds, and a clearness in the air Cerrick didn't expect to find so far north.

The closer they get, the easier Cerrick can see the igloos lining the coast. He's heard endless stories about them, how they've supposedly been here for thousands of years. Cerrick has never seen anything quite like them before. The circular white structures stick out of the snow like arms out of a creature.

On the ship, Brandr told them numerous stories about the creatures of the deep, taking on the role of a father trying to scare his kids. His dramatics didn't stop Cerrick from peering over the rail to check for creatures with eight arms and a mouth wide enough to swallow men whole. Edlyn hit his arm.

"Welcome to the Oslands, my friends," Brandr says, standing with them at the rail. "You're visiting a land most Krycs never visit in their lives."

"What recluses we are," Cerrick says, thinking of how many Krycs will never leave the city they were born in despite having the money to travel. How many Krycs will never see the light of the sun despite it being just a few hours south.

He thinks of how quickly and easily they were able to get to the Oslands, while also recognizing the unique treatment they had by getting a ship to themselves. Still, as they dock in the port where workers bustle to and fro, he pities the people who will never get to see this.

"I'm setting foot on land across the Gryting before I've ever seen Aeton or Tailing," Kara laughs.

"You've now been everywhere on the map," Cerrick says to Edlyn.

She scoffs. "Everywhere on a Kryc map, maybe."

"Can you put a positive lilt in your tone for once? Pretend that you're anything more than gruffly pleased to be here?"

She swats at his arm before Brandr reminds them to look professional on their way in. The ship brushes against the dock with a rough scrape that makes Cerrick wince, but the dock workers and their ship's crew work quickly to fix things.

"The Os speak good Kryc," Brandr says, "so you won't have to worry about that. We have envoys to thank for that. Here we go."

Edda insisted on carrying bags alongside the crew. She manages well, even swathed in a thick fur coat. The coat reaches her feet almost like a cloak, providing glances of a pale fabric underneath when she walks. Between that, her shining hair, and her lips painted red, Cerrick has a feeling she's wearing a dazzling gown underneath. Always one to make a good impression among strangers, she is. He wonders how Brandr's going to react to that.

Their cloaks and corresponding adornments speak for the rest of them, except Kara, who doesn't have a rich cloak like theirs. Cerrick doubts the Os will care—anyone Brandr would willingly associate with wouldn't care about clothing decorations. But Brandr did say he worked here under the Ice's orders, so perhaps it wasn't a willing association after all.

Brandr is fidgeting with his gloves and smoothing down his clothes needlessly as they walk off the ship, thanking their crew while assuring them they look forward to the return journey. Cerrick isn't eager to return to everything waiting for him in Kryos, but he won't have to face that for a while. The ship will transport cargo up and down the coast while the crew waits for them, as private passenger ships often do to generate money.

Cerrick takes in his first true glance of Os countryside. The ground is flat and endless, stretching and fading into the distance. Their boots make a satisfying crunch on the snow underneath, a thick layer spanning Saints know how deep.

As they walk past heavily cloaked groups of people, Cerrick spots buildings in the distance past the igloos. Scientists and historians have been living on the coast of the Oslands for as long as people can remember, observing the igloos and trying to uncover their history. Who built them, who used them, when they appeared out of apparent thin air. Since the large cities lie far inland in this huge, barren country, scientists have had no choice but to build settlements on the coast.

Everyone waves and greets them in Kryc, which is far cry better than what Cerrick is used to in Rinnfell. Brandr waves back merrily. Cerrick shakes his head. If you tried that in Rinnfell, you'd get an odd look at best, a shove and a curse at worst.

"Brandr Tofte! I'll be damned," comes a strange voice, cheery and thickly accented. They turn to find a man approaching them, swathed in white furs and a thick black beard framing his face. His skin is light brown, his eyes dark. He grins as he vigorously shakes Brandr's hand, pulling him into a hug. "I almost believe I am seeing an apparition. Do I expect to pick up a fresh shipment of pots and find instead my long lost Kryc? No. It bring me such joy to see you here. It is long time no see, friend. I have missed you."

Brandr smiles, withdrawing his gloved hand to the safety of his cloak again. "I missed you too, Ivan."

"What are you doing here now?" this Ivan asks. Cerrick and Edlyn exchange glances.

Brandr waves. "We'll get to that later. First, I would like to introduce you to my companions." He goes down the line one by one, saying their names instead of their titles.

Ivan recognizes Edda and smiles more for her than he did for the rest of them. "Duchess Edda," he says, bowing before her. "Your kindness is famous even here. It is an honor to meet you."

"A flatterer," she teases, looking at Brandr. "I'm familiar with those."

"It is no flattery, Madam."

Cerrick keeps his guard up and his words scarce, not knowing how much Ivan knows about them. He can feel Edlyn's tension beside him, the urge she has to put one hand on a knife. The only time they like working with strangers is when they can burgle them first.

"I would trust this man as I would trust myself," Brandr says to all of them in a low tone. "You can speak freely."

"Welcome to the Oslands," Ivan says, spreading his arms and gesturing at the great expanse of snowy nothingness.

"We're happy to be here," Brandr says smoothly. "Is there somewhere more private we can talk?"

Ivan laughs heartily. "My friend, the Os mean you no harm. We do not care to eavesdrop into the lives of others. You must leave your twisted Kryc mentality behind."

Brandr holds his ground.

"Yes, yes, alright," Ivan concedes, though he doesn't sound truly peeved. "Follow me."

They follow him across the plains of snow, their fur blowing in the light wind. These winds don't bite with icy teeth like they do in Kryos, nor do they whip as hard. The cold here is no worse than that in the heart of a Kryc summer. Foreigners make jokes about their Saints disliking Kryos enough to give them the world's saddest weather, but fuck, it seems to be true.

"You don't see many white furs in Kryos," Kara mutters beside him. Cerrick nods. The snowy animals who provide them aren't as commonly found in the urban city streets, and the southern Kryc forests yield orange, brown, black furs. Here, Cerrick sees small white rabbits running freely in the snow, a few disappearing into dens underground. Cerrick also notices the distinct lack of factory smoke. The fog here is natural.

They pass several small groups of scientists crouched in the snow around the igloos, getting their dark green and blue uniforms wet. All their dark hair is braided back tightly, and a scribe scientist sits a few feet away with a quill and ink in hand with a stack of paper in front of them. The scientists all have the same symbol pinned onto the front of their jackets, a silver shovel digging out white snow. Cerrick assumes it's the insignia of the organization they represent.

There's no road to guide them, so folks walk wherever they please. When people bump into each other, they don't swear at each other, and when someone drops something, someone else picks it up and gives it back to them. Everyone is civil. Cerrick knows he's lived in the most unsavory part of Kryos, that his home is not all ugly, but this—he's never seen anything like this.

"What's that?" Kara asks, pointing to something off to the right.

Cerrick shifts to see what she means just as Ivan starts speaking. "They are our prized jewel here," he says, referring to a red flower so huge it's almost comical. All its petals rest on the ground, and it has no stem that Cerrick can see. It has a silver center, and it gives off an ethereal glow, letting off glittering particles into the air. "They provide heat to us in this freezing land. Go on, step closer, it's okay."

Kara cautiously approaches and gasps in surprise. She stretches her hands over the heat and rubs her palms together. The rest of their party join, and Cerrick feels the flower's radiating heat like a campfire. He warms his hands with great relief, shuddering as the warmth takes hold.

"They are just another anomaly," Ivan says with a shrug. "Like the igloos. You'll find them everywhere, not just on the coast. Come, we have better heating inside. Let us go."

They follow him toward a great stone fortress. Cerrick could only see the faint outline of the building from the shore, but now he sees the intricate carvings set into the stone, black wrought iron lines balconies a few stories up. The fortress appears unshakable, immovable, rising high into the sky as far as the eye can see. Little ovular windows line the outside, providing perfect cover for an archer.

Folks are milling about in the courtyard, bickering good naturedly in their own tongue. It's the first glimpse Cerrick has had of it, a flowing, rapid language with hard words and power behind them. Despite the threatening nature of their voices, they smile and wave to Ivan and the Krycs as they pass, calling out greetings in Os. Cerrick recalls his knowledge of Os pleasantries as they shuffle through the low pair of double doors inside.

Cerrick is greeted by a long hallway lined with bright chandeliers, all hanging over long dining tables of pale gold wood. The whole room smells fresh like pine, like dried fruit during the holidays. Cerrick is taken back in a flash to his childhood home, to the warm scent of the servants cooking for Sven's Day.

The floors are made of solid stone, but the room is warmer than Cerrick expected. He searches for the hearths needed to make that possible.

"We need no fires here," Ivan says proudly, as if reading his mind. "We extract the syrup from our red flowers and use it to keep our drinks warm since it has no taste. We dry and crumble the petals to warm a room by keeping jars of them throughout."

"Saints, how many flowers does that take?" Edlyn asks, toying with the clasp of her cloak and bringing Cerrick's mind back to those fucking ridiculous chains.

"Only a few. I run Greenhouse Three. I oversee the making of these products." Ivan grins proudly.

"What's Greenhouse Three?" Kara asks tentatively. Brandr is getting antsy, shifting on his feet, but he lets Ivan ramble on with a smile.

"Another branch of the science we do here. Those scientists out there study the igloos, but they do not sustain us here on the barren coast. Someone has to tend to the plants and the flowers that keep us all from freezing and starving. That is me. This building is here for us all to live in. Well, is more of a compound." He waves, mumbling to himself in his thick accent beneath his breath. "I talk too much. Come with me."

The hall is relatively empty. Ivan leads them to a secluded chamber at the end, an office of some kind with a round table and a window looking out into the white world.

They all find their seats around the table, Ivan taking the head with his back to the window. He flicks his long black braid away from his shoulder and says to Brandr, "My friend, I cannot thank you enough for what you did for us all those years ago. Whatever you need, I will be happy to provide it."

"How's Timur faring?" Brandr asks as he sits on Ivan's right side, giving Cerrick a glimpse into a world of which he knows nothing.

Ivan laughs. "Ah, good, good. He's moved back north, but when he was still here, he always talked about you. Missing you, and for more than just the aid you gave us with the gemsha. You are still just as good looking as I remember, my friend."

Cerrick raises an eyebrow at Edlyn.

Brandr notices them all staring and smiles. "Yes, I know, Brandr the peacemaker," he says with a wave. Cerrick barely holds back a snort—does he not know what Ivan just implied? "How surprising. I was here on a mission from the Ice, and my goal was to stir up the conflict that was brewing here. I was in hot water with Bertie's father for months."

"You have never told them?" Ivan gasps. "My friend, you must!"

"It never came up," Brandr protests, running a hand along the back of his neck. "I wasn't ready to admit I'd betrayed the Ice for anyone's sake."

"I am not just anyone," Ivan says proudly, boldly.

"I'll drag the story out of him later," Edda promises. "I would love to have dinner here. It's such a beautiful building."

"Oh, Madam, you have not even heard of the best part of dinner here." Ivan sighs. "They are a treat. A feast for the eyes to go with the feast for your body."

Brandr chuckles. "Enough of that," he says. "You said I could ask for anything?"

"Anything."

"Lend me the gemsha."

Ivan's eyes widen, and he slowly starts shaking his head, then his finger. "No," he says. "No, no, no, no."

"You said *anything*."

"I did not think you were going to ask for the gemsha!" he yells, eyes flaring with not quite anger.

"For Saints' sake, what is a gemsha and why do we want it?" Edda demands, the only one of them brave enough to interrupt and ask.

Brandr looks at her, eyes wild. "Oh, darling," he says, "it's the biggest fucking cannon you've ever seen."

Cerrick and Edlyn exchange glances.

"It is not cannon," Ivan says with the tone of someone arguing a long debated point, slamming the side of his hand on the table to illustrate his point. "It is drill."

"It can be both. And more."

"The hybrids are rare, and are called gemshi. The individuals are much smaller, and they are the gemsha. We only called it a gemsha when you were here last because we weren't paying attention when our sergeant told us the difference. But I am wiser now. I know."

Brandr leans back in his chair, exuding confidence. "I want the cannon I helped you take back. The very cannon, whatever you want to call it."

Ivan shakes his head. "Why could you not ask for jars of red flower dust to warm your house instead? You do not have *them* in Kryos."

"Because I can't win a rebellion with flower dust."

Ivan stares. "I always thought you were slightly out of head, but now I am sure."

"My companions can vouch for me. We have all been betrayed by Andor Estensen, the Head Oligarch of Kryos, and we want our revenge."

"And we want to build a new era in its place," Edda adds. "A new legacy. The same piece of land, a new name, a new way of governing."

"I always knew you were destined for big things," Ivan says, "but not with my gemsha."

"I thought no one could own a gemsha," Brandr says, grinning like a schoolboy who's caught his teacher in a lie.

Ivan scratches his beard and gestures between him and Brandr. "*Our* gemsha."

"Brandr?" Edda asks, apparently not content to let this play out.

Brandr sighs. "About twenty years ago, there were rumors of unrest in the science camps along the Os coast. Bertie's father sent me to investigate them. An opportunity to exploit a brewing war in another country? You know the Ice's interest in that."

Bertie himself held lofty dreams of organizing an operation abroad. Cerrick wonders now how much was his own desire and how much was a legacy he wanted to live up to.

"I was stationed here for a while, undercover, supposed to be stirring up the unrest. I soon found out the cause. These gemshas, gemshis, they're used to mine ice deposits underground."

"They mine through the ice to get to the gold," Ivan corrects. "The ice is useless, much like in your country."

"Yeah, yeah. However, an inevitable problem arose among the miners, because the drills can sometimes double as cannons or tanks—for defense of the precious gold they carry. They're portable, rideable, and valuable, so humans fought over them."

"Our military provide them," Ivan says. "Only a few to the people who need them. They post guards to look after it, night sentries and everything."

"People fought over them down here," Brandr says, the words flowing easily like he's reliving that day. "There were rumors of a civil war brewing over these tanks. A few were stolen. The Os have a history of peace, not violence. Mere rumor of this was huge. It should've been easy to exploit, as I was sent here to do. So where did I go wrong?"

"You befriended me," Ivan chuckles.

Brandr nods. "He was fighting to get the stolen gemshas back where they belonged, without any glory for himself. And Saints damn it, I couldn't help where my thoughts strayed once I'd seen him. He and a miner named Timur and I all became friends, and I eventually broke down and revealed my cover. They weren't angry. They were understanding. They remained my friends on the insistence I help them retrieve the stolen gemshas."

Cerrick swallows, thinking of Njord and broken cover.

"So I did. Civil war was averted thanks to us, and Bertie's father nearly killed me after I went home. I was prepared to face those consequences, but I remained in the Oslands far longer than I should've. I was determined to avoid it as long as I could."

"Still too soon," Ivan says. "You were only here for four months. Not enough."

"I told you I'd someday return when I was out of the Ice and could come freely," Brandr says. "I left the Ice and joined the Kryc oligarchy."

"I know. No one was more surprised than me to read your name in the newspapers—and for something good."

Brandr swats his arm, and Ivan laughs. "Let us not forget that you asked me for the gemsha, you animal," Ivan growls with a swat of his own. "I cannot give it to you."

"Why not?"

"Because it is madness!" Ivan yells, gesturing wildly. "You cannot steal, transport, or conceal a gemsha discreetly. That is what we learned twenty years ago. Crazy man."

"We have a private ship. We could cart it off through the snow in the middle of the night."

"My friend, you forget"—Ivan gestures out the window—"we have no trees here. Nowhere to hide if someone sees. A gemsha is the largest moving object in the Oslands, and we would be moving it out in the open. How would you explain that?"

"Smoothly," Brandr says. "I've improved my variety of excuses since I was last here. We'll find a way. We must. That gemsha is the reason I'm here."

"You sailed here after twenty years to ask for a gemsha?"

"Well, for that and recruitment. If you know of anyone who's voiced opposition to Andor and the Kryc oligarchy, or anyone with a general desire to overthrow a government, please point me in their direction."

Ivan rolls his eyes. "You know us. We don't care much for foreign politics. We don't care much to criticize people who don't concern us."

"What if we're not criticizing, but celebrating?" Brandr tries. "A rebellion is a common cause to rally around."

Ivan laughs. "You might convince someone with that philosophy, but it will not be me." He stands up.

"I will win you over on at least one point," Brandr says fondly. "Even if I only leave here with the gemsha, I'll be happy."

"*Only* the gemsha? What do you need with a gigantic drill overseas?"

Brandr shakes his head. "Those gemshas are not just a bragging prize and a good way to get gold, they're deadly weapons. You forget that. We're lucky no one took advantage of that in the unrest."

"You warmongering Krycs," Ivan grumbles. "I will never understand you. Is it not enough for you to live among those beautiful, legendary southern forests?"

Cerrick stifles a laugh.

"They are as legendary as you, Madam Holman!" Ivan says as they all slowly shuffle out of the office. Cerrick realizes as Kara slips out that she hasn't said a word this whole time. They were all enraptured with Brandr, but that's no excuse. Cerrick didn't mean to exclude her. He touches her shoulder on the way out, and she gives him a soft smile.

"I do not understand it," Ivan says.

"Clearly I didn't teach you all about Kryos that I thought I did, my friend," Brandr says, wrapping an arm around his shoulder.

CHAPTER EIGHT

Amidst the chaos of being shown to their rooms, Ivan boasts of an entertainment feat shown at dinner. Brandr laughs whenever he brings it up but refuses to spoil the surprise for the rest of them. Edda grows fed up, insisting they go to dinner and see what all the fuss is about.

The red flowers in the hall provide a warmth enough for them all to take off their cloaks, and Edda is indeed wearing something stunning underneath her furs: a suit of deep purple with sleek trousers, jewels shining about her neck. Brandr walks into a wall staring at her.

Ivan brings them into the dining hall, where the tables have been shifted for the evening. In place of the long communal tables are small round ones scattered throughout the room. The rest of the stone floor is left strangely empty. "You'll see why," Ivan says with a wink.

Cerrick had no idea what to expect from Os food, and all Brandr will tell him is that it's wonderful and he mustn't worry. Brandr proves right once again—servants wearing white and gold bring out bowls of soup made with the very vegetables Ivan proudly grows, loaves of fresh bread sprinkled with brown sugar, pristine cuts of venison spiced with herbs. Cerrick stuffs himself full. Kara says it's the best meal she's ever had.

Edlyn sits beside him dressed in the same rumpled gray robes she's been wearing since they left Kryos. Between the gray and the chains on her cloak, she looks rather dreary and intimidating all at once. Her only saving grace is the intricate white embroidery on the sleeves of her shirt, but none of them could ever look as dazzling as Edda. The Os appear quite comfortable in the warm room—most of them keep their furs and cloaks draped around the backs of their chairs.

"What is this supposed dinnertime marvel?" Edda asks for the umpteenth time. "When is it?"

"Patience, Edda," Brandr says. "They come out once we're finishing."

"Your food would get cold if they came out while we ate," Ivan says.

"*Who are they?*"

Finally, the plates of fruit tart made with the flakiest pastry Cerrick has ever had are taken away, and the Os shift their chairs to face the empty floor. Cerrick follows suit.

Without any announcement, a line of people come filing in through a wooden side door. The Os instantly erupt into cheers. At first glance, the newcomers are all ordinary people presenting in a feminine manner, dressed in matching gold and orange. Their clothing styles vary from ballgowns to sharp robes to trousers and half tops that show off their stomachs and shoulders despite the cold. They all line up and bow before the audience, then split off into pairs.

They're not Saints here to perform miracles. They're not glowing like heroes of legend. What is their secret?

Ivan leans forward. The girls join hands, and music playing begins from somewhere unseen. Cerrick searches the room for the source, but it seems to bleed from the very walls of this fortress. "That is part of it, my friend," Ivan says, noticing his stare.

The girls begin their dance, one hundred of them or more crowded into the space. The girls match the fast pace of the music with practiced ease. They twirl in perfect synchronicity with each other, moving faster than Cerrick's eyes can process.

Ivan laughs, clapping his hands like a little boy. "Magnificent, magnificent!" Kara's eyes dart between them, her mouth agape.

Colors flash before Cerrick's eyes. The gold on their sleeves and hems glitters under the lights. The music matches them perfectly, as they seem to glide over the ground like they're floating on air. Cerrick's head spins as their feet move. The music chases them like a mortal might chase the wind.

The women finish by lifting their partners into the air and spinning them around, their feet fluttering as the music soars. The crowd's screams are thunderous even for Cerrick's ears, and pink paper money goes flying towards the women's feet.

They take a collective bow and smile gracefully, picking up piles and piles of money as it comes. A few flowers are thrown here and there, some jewelry from the patrons' own necks, but the women ignore those.

"They do this for the money," Ivan yells amidst his own applause. "The only gift they'll accept, the only reason they have stayed here so long. I have been blessed to have seen them in four locations in my life."

"One would think you follow them around," Brandr teases.

"Oh, not like that. They are simply a majesty of the artistic kind that needs to be appreciated. Some people claim they have heavenly blood, or at least a heavenly blessing on their feet."

"Who are they? What are they?" Kara asks as the women shuffle out through the same door, taking their glitter and their money with them, leaving the floor a mess. Even Edlyn watches with rapture.

"They have no name," Ivan says with a shrug. "They are the wandering warriors, dancers, lovers, to us."

"Lovers to you?"

"No, to each other. Mostly, anyway. They were in those pairings for a reason. They take in any woman who holds similar affections for her fellow women, or one who holds no affection at all. They turn away the men and those who keep men as lovers, but anyone else is welcome."

"How did they find each other? How recently did they band together?" Kara asks.

"They're nothing new. They've been legend in the Oslands for centuries. They never stay in one place long, a true tragedy, in order to take their talents to all of the Oslands."

"Are you sure you're not just making that up?" Brandr says. Turning to the Krycs, he adds, "They don't reveal details of themselves or their nature to anyone. They answer to no one. They set up camp wherever they go, perform, collect their money, stay a bit, then move on. That's all we've known about them for centuries."

"I—well—yes," Ivan concedes.

"How close is their camp?" Kara asks.

"Just out the back. I can take you there later if you like."

"Do they let men into the camp?" Edlyn asks, undoubtedly thinking of Tailing's similar customs.

"Oh, sure. The men who enter are subject to some friendly mockery, but nothing more. They'll appreciate you more if you bring money."

"Speaking from experience?" Brandr asks wryly.

Ivan hits his arm. "Idiot. Stop mocking me like you weren't just as enthralled with them when you first saw them. I believe we saw them…hm…every single night when you were here."

Brandr lowers his head with a blush.

"Warriors?" Cerrick asks belatedly.

"Oh, yes!" Ivan's eyes light up; he could talk about these dancers all day if he had the chance. "That's another aspect of their brilliance.

Some women live lives of war and abandon them when they join the troupe. Others who grow weary of the troupe leave to become a warrior who fights on her own terms. However, I've heard that no matter your stance on war, when you join, you're trained to be a warrior. When the time of battle comes, all of them fight together. They are dancers in peacetime." He grins. "The Oslands haven't been involved in any wars in a long time."

"Except the war of the gemshas that almost was," Brandr notes.

"Indeed." Ivan gives him a look. "That's exactly why I'm not giving you one—we don't want another war!"

"I would die to meet them," Kara says with the same stars in her eyes. All eyes turn to her, to her mind still fixated upon the dancers. "Can you take me to their camp tomorrow?"

Ivan nods. "Of course! I take all of you. It is always a pleasure to have an excuse to visit them. I think they're getting sick of seeing me alone—they will welcome new friends."

BRANDR CLAIMS THEY can stay in the Oslands as long as they wish, as long as it takes to secure that gemsha, as long as it takes to gather recruits. The nagging thought of Andor is ever present, but he'll have a difficult time hunting them down in the Oslands if he finds out Cerrick and Edlyn are alive.

He can replace Eir and Solveig on the council of oligarchs and further poison the people's minds with lies, with false dreams of a greater future. At least Cerrick can't be killed. The Phantom will not die.

Either way, Brandr seems unconcerned with convincing Ivan of their plight immediately. He's content to let Ivan come to them.

True to his word, Ivan takes them to meet the dancing warriors the next day. Cerrick and Edlyn sleep restfully beside one another in a large bed of golden wood, the headboard carved with rich scenes of the Os countryside. The windows face east, providing a brilliant light through the curtains come morning. The Oslands don't get direct sunlight either, but the skies are brighter and cheerier than the gray of Kryos.

Their breakfast is a warm bowl of mush warmed with sugars and fruits heaped atop it. Ivan brags again about his greenhouse, the things he's grown here, how he's turned the coast into a land of plenty.

When they step out into the morning air, the deathly cold makes Cerrick reconsider this errand. Still, it's nowhere near as bad as an early morning in the Kryc winter. Cerrick's face hasn't yet gone numb, a welcome change.

The dancers' camp is on the northeastern side of the fortress compound, a little city of tents and campfires. Some of the women are huddled around them, drinking coffee and eating in heavier cloaks than they wore last night. In the bold light of day, the luster they wore last night has faded.

A frozen pond lies to the east of the camp, where a few dancers are skating with the same bladed shoes Cerrick used in Aeton. His heart seizes at the sight of a pond like that. It's smaller than the lake in Aeton, but the same color, and the women here are as skilled as the finest skaters in that little Aeton coalition.

Mist comes to his eyes. Sweet Saints—if staring at a fucking pond is enough to make him cry, what will the bigger reminders be? A pool of blood? He's sure he hasn't seen the last of those.

The mere sight of an ink jar? Any blue cloak other than the one Njord gave him, the one currently resting about his shoulders? Sometimes even that cloak threatens to pull his emotions to the surface. Every day, he works a little harder to hide them. The longer he shoves them down, the longer they'll take to return.

Heartless, he hears before turning his gaze from the pond. *Emotionless. Traitor. Monster.*

He is all of these and more.

"Ivan," says one of the dancers, rising from her fireside seat. Her dark skin and red hair shine brightly against the backdrop of white snow, and her blue eyes sparkle as she shakes his hand. She says something in Os, and Ivan laughs and replies in kind before gesturing to the Krycs. Surprise flickers across her face.

In perfect Kryc, slightly accented, she says, "My apologies, my Kryc friends. Welcome to the Oslands, and welcome to our camp." She looks at the women in their group when speaking.

"I'm from Tailing," Edlyn says, "but thank you. Your camp is lovely, and your performance was—"

"Life changing," Kara finishes, stepping forward to clasp this dancer's hands. "Stunning, beautiful, enrapturing. Everything about it was perfect. I look forward to seeing it again and again."

The dancer smiles. "Your first time seeing us, I assume."

"Yes."

"Our power dwindles over time, don't worry," the dancer says, patting Kara's shoulder.

"Oh, I would beg to differ, Sofia," Ivan croons. "Your power increases every time I see you."

Sofia ignores him, turning to Brandr. "You're the man who kept the gemshas in their proper place a few decades ago, weren't you? My older sisters have told me about it."

"I am," Brandr says.

"Would you like to dine with us?" she asks. Cerrick's eyebrow rises. He was expecting a lukewarm reception at best. The Os are full of surprises.

Even though they just ate breakfast, Ivan says, "Of course."

They step through the quiet peace of the camp, moving past groups of five or six sitting in front of their tents. Most of them are clad in white fur coats, leaving Cerrick to wonder just how rich they are.

Kara's starry eyed expression never fades with each step she takes, waving to every woman who will so much as glance at her. Her joy is unique and infectious, so rare after so long in the dark hole of the Ice townhouse.

Sofia sits them down at an empty campfire, heedless of the disappointment on Kara's face. She calls for someone inside the nearest tent behind them to bring them food—Cerrick would recognize the meaning of her snappy tone anywhere, in any language.

A younger girl comes scurrying out of the tent with a plate of food, bowing politely to her guests.

As they eat delicate pastries that almost crumble in Cerrick's hands, glazed in sweet honey, a woman passes by who looks vaguely familiar. Perhaps it's the clothes, the gait, but something compels Cerrick to turn his head to get a better look—and stops short, the pastry falling from his fingers. The woman stops in her tracks.

Looking back at him is the same girl who he cornered at the scene of Orv's death. She's dressed for battle instead of dance, and her hair is pulled up taut onto her head.

"Cerrick?" Edlyn asks, noticing his distress. "What's wrong?"

Cerrick takes a while to muster up the words, "Who is she?"

Sofia answers, "That's Anya, Anya Borkova. She's one of us. Have you met?"

"You might say that," Cerrick says, too shocked to offer more. The floor is shifting beneath him. Anya seems to be in a similar state of shock, and luckily her Pointstaff stays in her hand.

She turns and stalks off before he can think of what to say to her. Cerrick turns back to the group and their questioning looks, but does his best to ignore them.

Questions fill his mind. How is she here? Do these warriors double out as assassins for hire? How does she know Alfred? Was she just another of his victims, forced to work for him under threat of her life?

He shakes his head and attempts to distract Sofia with compliments about her pastry. She squints suspiciously, but offers thanks and introduces their chef. Cerrick doesn't hear a word she says, too busy thinking about Anya Borkova.

IVAN TAKES THEM TO Greenhouse Three. They don't really have a choice in the matter.

The hour is far too early. Cerrick follows the others to the line of greenhouses in the snow, blinking sleep out of his eyes and breathing in the crisp morning air. It's not too harsh, nothing in the Oslands is, and the cold is almost pleasant. Just sharp enough to wake him up—that, and the thermos of coffee in his gloved hands.

"The plants are best viewed in the morning, before the sun catches a glimpse," is Ivan's explanation for why they're here at the crack of dawn, ignoring the fact that the Oslands don't receive the sun directly.

At this hour, it's almost too dark to see them, though light slowly filters through the thick white clouds. Cerrick is growing used to Ivan's strange phrases and odder antics. They're as endearing as the man. Ivan has never had a bad word to say about anyone or anything. Even his grumblings about the strange ways of Krycs are affectionate comments directed at Brandr.

Greenhouse Three is a long, narrow structure of glass and green detailing, surrounded by many others of its kind. It's a long walk from the fortress hub, out of the way enough for the fog to hide the greenhouses entirely from the fortress.

Outside each greenhouse is a wooden table piled high with tools, soil, seeds, and empty clay pots in every color. The greenhouse walls are fogged up, hiding the plants inside from Cerrick's curious view. Out of all the tables, Ivan's is by far the messiest.

A few sleepy attendants in green are already moving within the greenhouses. A scant few stand in Three. Ivan holds the door open for his guests with a cheery grin.

The inside is blessedly warm. Ivan leads them down a long central row with tables to either side. Every space that's not for walking is covered in plants—hanging plants, potted plants, tiny plants that fit between the spaces of larger ones. A lot of them are red flowers, but there are many other types, too, like plants with long green leaves that drape over the sides of their pots, down from their hooks in the ceiling.

Ivan tells them about each and every plant like they're his children. Cerrick prays no one will ask him a question and keep them here longer. Not that he doesn't enjoy seeing the simple joy on Ivan's face, but he's looking forward to the breakfast inside the fortress. No one should be awake at this hour, let alone this cheery. There's a reason the Ice members rise no earlier than nine bells.

"My husband would love this place," Cerrick says idly at a break in conversation.

"Oh? You have a husband who is a gardener?" Ivan pounces.

Cerrick bites his lip, wishing he hadn't spoken. Ivan is good natured but nosy, and Cerrick doesn't want to have to talk about Njord if he doesn't have to. "Yes," he says. "He is from Aeton, where the gardens and foliage are truly magnificent. The Middle Forests took my breath away."

He wonders if Njord is as enthusiastic about Aeton's plants as he seems, or if he was just eager to show off the wonders of his country. Cerrick may not love Rinnfell, but he's lived there for years, and it's still a point of pride for him to brag about it. *This is Kryos.*

Ivan scoffs and waves a hand. "The gardens in Aeton are nothing compared to this. Do they have red flowers to heat their houses there?"

"No, but they have white trees with the brightest red leaves. They have these underground, underwater caves that supply light crystals. Those crystals are the light source of many Kryc houses."

Still, Ivan rolls his eyes. "Crystals are not a plant."

"Have you ever even been to Aeton?" Brandr asks with a wry smile. Ivan flounders, waving his hands again, grumbling about cold addled Krycs. Cerrick chuckles, watching Ivan show Edlyn how to harvest the dust from the red flowers and store them properly. From what Cerrick can see, there's no technique other than crushing the petals in your fist, but Ivan swears there's an art to it. Too much moisture or too little will melt the powder and destroy the petals.

Throughout all of this, all the days in the Oslands that seem to blend together, his mind wanders to the rebellion, to Njord, to Kryos, to the gemsha. Brandr remains of the opinion that they have all the time in the world, but Cerrick counts every second that ticks by. He doesn't say anything, though Edlyn confides in him that she's having the same anxious doubts. Cerrick doesn't know how to proceed other than to follow Brandr's lead.

They visit the dancing warriors' camp several more times, in the mornings after viewing them at night. Ivan was right, their power doesn't diminish over time, it only grows. Kara in particular falls more and more in love with them every day. Cerrick sees it on her face long before she announces to them at the breakfast table, "I want to join the troupe of dancing warriors."

Silence, then, "You're free to do as you like," Brandr says, though he can't quite hide the disappointment in his voice. "Saints know you deserve a life of your own choosing after the life you've led. We'll miss you. We'll be losing a great fighter and an even better healer."

"They'll be gaining one," Edlyn says, slapping Kara's shoulder.

"There are advantages to having an operative in the Oslands," Brandr says, a gleam of genius entering his eye. "If you'd be willing to continue serving the Phantom from your position here, Kara, we could use all the information we could get. Send us an encoded letter every once in a while to update us on the opinion here regarding our rebellion.

"Continue recruiting for our cause, both Os and the Krycs. I'd try the docks. Visiting Krycs will be more willing to speak freely in this foreign safe haven. They'll be emboldened by the distance between here and Rinnfell. We're far from the only ones with a grudge against Andor."

She nods. "I'd be honored. It's the least of what I can do to repay what you've done for me."

They all toast her with their water and fruit juice, reminding Cerrick of Aeton's *bura* with a sharp pain in his chest.

The next morning, Kara takes them along to support her as she breaks the news to the warriors. Sofia, who's used to hosting them by now, welcomes them with a smile.

Kara is more forward than Cerrick expected. After exchanging pleasantries, she asks in a breathless and eager tone, "Madam Sofia, I ask humbly if I could join your troupe. Will you allow me?"

Cerrick has never seen Kara so passionate about anything, The light in her eyes is new and unique. He watches, grinning, as Sofia raises her eyebrows in pleasant surprise.

"I would count towards your requirements," Kara adds. "I only take women for lovers, though it's been years since I've had any. I'm not a dancer, but I'm a good fighter and a healer. I know you have no need of a fighter in these times of peace, but—"

"Kara."

"I would do whatever you asked of me, I promise. I follow instructions well—"

"Kara." Sofia lays her hand on Kara's mouth to shut her up. Kara's eyes go wide.

"I would be happy to have you," Sofia says gently, smiling with mirth. "There is no need to be so frantic. We live a very easygoing lifestyle. That's a good first lesson for you."

"Yes, yes, of course," Kara breathes. "Thank you."

Sofia looks at Edlyn. "And you?"

Edlyn shrugs. Cerrick glances at her with muted panic, wondering how foolish he's been to think Sofia would never ask. "Would I be allowed to join you? I have never felt a love like poets describe. Not for anyone. My only lover was a coping mechanism and a poor one at that. I do not need the sort of love you describe, nor do I want it—nor do I experience it at all."

"The only ones we turn away are the men and the ones who take men as lovers," Sofia says gently. "All others are more than welcome. You are one of us."

Cerrick sucks in a breath. *Don't,* he prays. *Please, don't.* He would respect whatever decision she made, but he can't do this without her. The moments she takes to respond removes years from his life. He doesn't let out his breath until she speaks again.

Despite the pause, Edlyn's words flow with ease. "I qualify, but I will never be one of you." She speaks kindly. "Even if I desired to become a dancer, I would not abandon my cause. I have a rebellion to lead."

Sofia bows her head. "I respect that. We all have our strengths." She beckons to Kara, and the two of them fade into the camp.

Cerrick touches Edlyn's hand once they're far enough away. *Thank you. I love you.*

She squeezes his wrist with icy fingers. *It was never a question.*

"You're not romantically interested in anyone?" he says, trying to lighten the mood. "Carr helped you realize that?"

"Indeed. I was trying to fill a void—a Bertie shaped void. The void I perceived in my heart had nothing to do with it. My heart is full and not lacking in the slightest. I am content. Plus, I get to avoid all the shit that lovers go through. Just look at you and Njord."

Cerrick sighs through that wave of pain. He squeezes Edlyn's hand again.

CHAPTER NINE

Evan's first letter arrives just over a week into their stay. Brandr gathers them all into the office they used to discuss the gemsha before reading it aloud for them all. "Eir has been ousted," it begins. Brandr sighs and leans back in his seat. "Fuck."

The anticipation and excitement that had filled the air only moments before falls like snowflakes.

"That didn't take nearly as long as I hoped it would." Brandr shakes out the yellow parchment and continues, "She's already been replaced. Edda's replacement has finally been installed."

A bang from behind Cerrick makes him startle. They all turn their heads to find Edda—sweet, silent, smiling Edda—examining the hole she just punched in the wall.

"Sweet Saints, Edda," Brandr says, though he sounds impressed rather than angry. Even a bit breathless with awe. "How will we explain that?"

"It's no matter," Ivan says cheerily. He comes over to inspect the hole himself, bending his head to peer into the darkness behind the gray wall. "This happens all the time."

"Really?" Cerrick asks. "You're such—"

"Happy people, exactly," Ivan says. "We need an outlet. Now, Brandr, I believe you were reading about your kind colleague's replacement?"

"Apologies for interrupting," Edda adds, shaking her hair out of her face. Between her delicate necklaces, bright red lips, and the flowing skirts of her gown, one would never guess she's clenching her fist to deal with the pain of punching a wall. Her face is flushed, but that could be explained away by the cold. Altogether, she makes quite the innocent picture, deceptively gentle.

Cerrick stares at her, pondering how they could use that to their advantage. She has a fierce warrior's heart beneath her skirts and smiles, a fighting spirit.

"Quite alright," Brandr says, looking more than a little flushed himself. He shakes his head and gets back to reading. "Andor replaced Eir with the Lysa born daughter of his former colleague, as Cerrick discovered. Andor released Eir from her services with every disgrace possible to assign someone. One would almost think he's making them up, except for the evidence C discovered."

Brandr glances Cerrick's way. "I wish I could bring better news," Brandr reads, then scoffs. "This kid makes it sound like he's never served in the Ice before. We were expecting bad news. We don't want sweet lies to cloud our vision so that when we sail back into Rinnfell, we find some unpleasant surprise awaiting us because this kid was too afraid to upset us with the truth."

"I know Evan," Cerrick cuts in. "He might suffer a world of guilt for it, but he'll never lie to us or omit a thing. Bertie trains that into all of us."

The annoyance on Brandr's face smooths out. "His father did the same," he says gruffly, and straightens the letter once again. "I fear for my position, my mission, and my safety. Perhaps even my life. Please hurry back. Even if you mean to keep me here, I would feel safer just knowing you're on Kryc soil. That's closer than across an ocean I've never set my feet in. Be safe and victorious, sincerely, your friend." Brandr shakes his head and puts the letter away. "Damn kid. Gonna keep me up at night worrying."

Would Andor openly violate the laws to remove Evan in a permanent way? At this point, Cerrick doesn't know what Andor would and wouldn't do.

That thought brings with it a sharp fear that makes him want to remain in the Oslands forevermore. Yet he yearns to get back to Rinnfell if only to see to Evan's safety, make sure he'll find some semblance of happiness.

A somber air settles over the room. "One more step in Andor's plan is complete," Edlyn says quietly. "His remarkably easy, genius, and foolproof plan. No matter what, the Order of the Phantom will be made to look like criminals. We'll be the mindless rebels, the ones to hate."

"Try to forget about Andor," Brandr says gently. "He's an easy worry. Our greater worry is the people of Kryos. Ultimately, they're the ones who decide who stays in power. Not just for one year, or two, or thirty, but for centuries."

If Andor is the easy problem, Cerrick can't fathom the road ahead. That thought follows him to bed with Edlyn, worrying when Alfred Dalton will replace Oligarch Solveig. The last of Andor's first steps.

Sleep evades him that night. He tosses and turns restlessly under the moonlight until his frustration gives way to resigned sighs. Edlyn grumbles that he's driving her mad, that he should take a walk and burn off some restless energy. He whispers an apology and slips out to get them both glasses of water.

During times like these, he wishes he could sleep next to Njord instead. When Edlyn and Cerrick get on each other's nerves, when she has patience for nothing more than snapping at him, Njord would listen. Sweet, sweet Njord would simply roll over and ask Cerrick what's wrong. He'd stay up as long as Cerrick needed to spill every word, even if he was teetering on the edge of sleep himself.

Like most people, Edlyn doesn't have the tolerance for such things late at night. Njord has given Cerrick unrealistic expectations for real people, because surely that's not what Njord is. Surely he's a Saint, sent down to torture Cerrick into fucking up the perfect life he had, make him want that which he is not deserving of.

Saints are martyrs, and they deal in misery. Calith of death and Renalie of hell, the most powerful. Lotis of the light, Irena of heaven, and Kaseir the hedonist often fade into the background. Perhaps it's a human trait to focus on the misery before the joy. Maybe other homes keep statues of the better Saints on their hearth mantles instead of shrines to the two darkest ones.

Cerrick doesn't make it more than a few steps out into the moonlit hallway before he catches a snippet of Brandr's voice, clear and strong instead of muffled by a door. Cerrick pauses behind a corner and peeks out at Brandr, facing Ivan under the bright white light of a chandelier.

They haven't noticed he's there, and Cerrick almost forgets to breathe as his fingers wrap around the cold wall. He slides back into spy instincts quickly, making his whole purpose to not be seen and to hear every nugget of conversation he can.

Brandr is saying, "What will it take for you to give me the gemsha? Name your price."

"I have no price," Ivan says lowly. "The Oslands are not like Kryos, man, how many times do I have to tell you? We refuse your deals not because we have a price you cannot meet, but because we want no part of your games."

Brandr smiles knowingly. "You keep insisting that this is a Kryc ideal, a Kryc flaw. These qualities go beyond borders, Ivan. In our hearts, we are all people with a little seed of greed in our hearts, just waiting to be watered and tended. Everyone has a price. I mean to find out what yours is."

Ivan sputters, muttering *you're crazy, let me go*, but Brandr keeps him there with a hand on his chest. "Stay," he says softly. Cerrick shivers. He's not meant to be seeing this. He's shaken by the power in Brandr's voice, by the calm manner in which he tilts his head, as if he's never felt more comfortable in his life. "I am not leaving until I have that gemsha. Let's work something out."

The air chills.

"Fine," Ivan grumbles after a long moment, muttering curses under his breath. He hovers with his hand on his bedchamber door. "I thought you were a man of peace, Brandr."

Brandr barks a laugh. "Me? I was in the Ice for five years. I came here to stir up a war. I came back to win a weapon of war. What gives you that idea?"

"Your actions may not reflect your inner feelings. The Order of the Ice leaves no room for rebellion in the minds of its members, from what I've heard. You could have done those things under the orders of others."

"I rebelled against them when I was here last. To join you."

"Exactly. And now you are rebelling again, and your kids with you. My point is that you aim to secure peace, yes?"

Brandr frowns. "Only after we have dethroned and thoroughly humiliated Andor and his circle of allies. After we've disrupted the legacy he means to make for Kryos. We are going to burn him down and sweep away the ashes to start something new."

"And you need a gemsha to do that? Could you not do what it is that you Krycs are so fond of in theory—use the law?"

"Andor has used the law, and that's precisely the problem. He uses it as a weapon against the rest of us by ousting Edda and Eir and I, and likely Solveig in the near future. Nothing says rebellion quite like a gemsha."

"Gemshas have the capability to tear apart worlds," Ivan says gently. "My friend, I worry that—that you will use it for the wrong purpose. That you will go overboard. Do not let your quest for revenge shed the blood of innocents. That is my price. I will give it to you, but I will come with you back to Kryos to ensure that you do not use it on anyone who is not deserving."

"I swear on the Saints," Brandr says, "that I never will. I never intended to use it to kill anyone. I promised myself I would never take another life after leaving the Ice, and I have not broken that promise yet. I am going to use it to intimidate, to clear crowds, to bring about change, but I am not going to spill blood. Would you like me to spill my own blood on that oath? I will."

"No, heavens, no. You crazy Krycs with your dangerous rituals. Is there nowhere in the world you have traveled where the honor of a word given is enough, without the need to shed blood to prove it?"

Brandr laughs softly, melting into the gentle lantern light as he follows Ivan into the bedchamber. The last Cerrick hears before the door shuts is Ivan's gentle, "I was planning on going with you back to Kryos no matter what, you know. I don't know if I could stand another twenty years without your infuriating company. My apprentices can take care of the plants sufficiently. I only wish we…"

Cerrick lets them be, slipping back to the safety and warmth of his room.

BRANDR ANNOUNCES AT breakfast that they'll be stealing a gemsha and leaving the Oslands that very night. Cerrick and the others are surprised, to say the least. Only Edda appears to have been given the news in advance.

"You fools are not considering one thing," Ivan says after the initial clamor of *how, why, what* dies down.

"Just one?" Brandr supplies.

"How are you going to unload a gemsha into Rinnfell harbor without attracting any notice? How are you going to get it where you need it to be without attracting any notice?"

Edda thinks for a moment. "We'll use two ships. One for the gemsha, one for us, and hide the one with the gemsha far from sight of the main harbor. We'll deliver it onto Rinnfell soil sometime when all is empty and quiet, in the middle of the night. It won't be a problem."

"Where will you acquire a second ship?" Cerrick asks.

"I have connections in this place," Brandr says, not for the first time. "I know where to find people who won't ask any questions as long as they're compensated for it."

"Your life savings will be depleted from bribes by the time this rebellion is over," Edda teases.

Brandr grins. "Ah, but then we'll be in the palace, my dear Edda, and I'll want for nothing."

Ignoring all this, Ivan says, "I'll ride with the gemsha. Even after twenty years, I'm not sure I trust you with it."

Brandr huffs. "You're the one who agreed to give it to me, you buffoon. Make up your mind."

"I will protect the gemsha with my life. I will protect it for your sake, but also for my own sanity. I will keep it from all others who wish to take it."

Brandr shakes his head. "Fine. You ride with the gemsha. We'll shout at each other across the ships over the roaring sea. That sounds pleasant, hm?"

"I didn't say you couldn't join me," Ivan gripes. "Just that I don't want you riding with it alone."

"I'm perfectly fine being on the other ship. I trust you to guard it."

Ivan nods. "I asked around for the volunteers you wanted, but I could find no one to join your cause. The Os are pacifists, my friend, just as I told you."

"I see." Brandr can't hide his disappointment, his mouth pinched and his eyes hollow. "Well, thank you for trying. Kara will carry on the work. Perhaps she'll have better luck as a foreigner." He sighs. Cerrick leaves him with Edda.

That day, they say goodbye to Kara in the camp of dancing girls. Kara claims she's never been happier. She hasn't danced in the hall yet, as Sofia says she needs a lot more training before that's possible, but she has become Sofia's partner. In dancing, in fighting, in culture education. Judging by the way Kara looks at her and the smile in Sofia's voice when she speaks about Kara, they might become partners in another sense.

Cerrick wonders yet again about what could've been had he stayed in the Ice. Had he left later and followed a different path—a path like Kara is following now. She is a map of endless possibilities, the *what if*s and *I'll never know*s. He and Kara led very different lives. He's only glad that now, they're both out of the Ice to stay.

Cerrick never saw Anya Borkova after his first visit to their camp, for which he's glad. For all his unease, he has a sinking feeling he'll be seeing her again. All she brings to mind are flashes of Orv and blood and ink spilling over the floor. He prays only that when he sees her next, he'll be better equipped to do so. Orv's death still feels like a raw wound he doesn't know how to heal.

Kara hugs Cerrick and wishes them all luck in Kryos. Cerrick makes her promise this isn't the last time they'll be seeing each other. "Perhaps someday, the troupe will venture to Kryos," she says with a smile and a wink. Out of the two of them, at least one will be happy, safe, and cared for. Cerrick sees the glint of a knife in Kara's hand as she runs off, and laughs.

Cerrick and the others have to wait for nightfall before they can strike. For the first time, Cerrick finds himself with nothing to do.

While preparations are being made, Cerrick stands at the wall of the fortress, watching the Os go about their daily business. He stares up at the sky. Sadly, the rumors were false—one cannot see the breathtaking colorful lights in the sky from the Os coast. The clouds and fog are too thick.

Cerrick watches the groups of Os researchers carry packs of tools, food, and supplies into a tidy circle before venturing out into the snow. The Oslands are magical. The red flowers, the dancers, the food, the igloos and their devoted scientists, Ivan's greenhouse, the white fur cloaks. Cerrick will miss it all dearly. It hasn't' yet sunk in that they're leaving tonight. Saints know if they'll ever return.

He wonders idly what it'd be like to live in one of the coastal houses here, reminiscent of the colorful houses of Holbeck. Fuck. He hangs his head. He's having the same thoughts he once had about Holbeck.

This is his second chance to run away, forget it all. Abandon his problems and responsibilities for a life of easy routine, in exchange for abandoning the rebellion and every step on his path forward.

Then he remembers the absence of the bracelet on his wrist. Yet another thing he'll have to face upon his return to Kryos.

That delivers an ache in his chest, brief but powerful enough to make his breathing stutter. He closes his eyes.

Cerrick wishes he had some stability to lean on, that he wasn't having to make the world's hardest decisions left and right.

He does have stability. Her name is Edlyn. But a tall building can't be stable with just one post underneath to hold it up.

As if summoned by his thoughts, Edlyn floats to his side, the edges of her black cloak fluttering in the wind. She says nothing, hands clasped on the barrier beside his, staring blankly at the people moving about in the snow. Her eyes shift to his profile, but he doesn't speak either. He can't seem to gather his words or thoughts enough to even look at her.

"Thinking of running away?" Edlyn asks, the gentle breeze carrying her voice.

Cerrick smiles. "How do you always know?"

"You know me just as well. Now, tell me, what is it you're so afraid of that you want to stay behind?"

"Everything you should be afraid of, too. Bertie. Andor. Getting caught, dying in prison, not having anyone believe that we're on the right side and that Andor's guilty. Watching you die before my eyes. Any of you. Anyone I care about coming to harm. Njord never wanting to look at me again."

She puts a hand up. "Saints, alright." There's that gruff fondness, the rough way of handling him he's come to love. Edlyn doesn't sweeten her words to make them more palatable. That roughness is ugly, brutal, but it's what Cerrick needs, what he thrives in.

"Any remedy for such fears?" he asks. With that roughness, he wants a bit of comfort, too. His fingers twitch with the urge to pull her into a hug. Being parted from Njord has left him starved of contact after receiving more than he ever has in his life.

"You're going to come back to Kryos." She doesn't demand it—rather, it's a simple fact. She says it as matter of factly as if they're discussing the weather. "For the same reason you came back to Kryos with me the first time. Because staying here and not coming back would drive you mad with the possibilities. You're not that much of a coward. Even if it wouldn't kill you to hear of the rebellion ended through secondhand news, you wouldn't leave us behind."

I would love you regardless.

Cerrick swallows and looks at her, finally. "You're right. How are you always right? It's so unnerving."

She smiles. "You're easy for me to pick apart. Now come here. I can read every bit of longing in your shoulders. When you go too long without a hug, you get antsy. That's why Njord should be here, the damn fool. You're both fools."

Cerrick bites back an uncomfortable retort in favor of the open arms she offers. She's not usually one for open affection in the view of strangers, but she squeezes him as if they're alone. He's mortified to feel tears forming in his eyes, stinging and harsh. He can't afford to do this in public. Edlyn's chin rests on his shoulder, her warmth radiating powerfully through their cloaks. She encourages him, rubbing her warm palm over his back.

She's the most comforting thing he's had in the Oslands. What kind of fool would he be to leave her behind for these lands of barren snow and cheery people? She is a fury, a danger, but he'd rather stick by her side in her good graces than live in fake bliss anywhere else. She did exactly what she came out here to do, he realizes—show him that he'd already made his decision to come with her. He just needed the firm kick to remind him sometimes.

"There will be time for tears later," she murmurs into his ear as he breathes through the force of the onslaught, pushing the tears back again. Her hair is so striking, so shiny, and she smells fresh and lovely like a field of springtime flowers. Nothing could ever dull her brilliance.

"Thank you," he whispers. "Let's go steal a gemsha."

She grins, pulling back. "Let's go steal a fucking gemsha."

They must wait another six hours before they can steal said gemsha for the cover of darkness. Coordinating the theft of a gemsha is just as difficult as Brandr and Ivan made it out to be, and five minutes into the process, Cerrick finds himself wondering if they can abandon their plan and pull off the Phantom's mission without it.

Brandr began by clasping his hands and giving an awkward speech. "Tonight, we capture that gemsha. No one will be the wiser."

"Heavens help me if this sparks another civil war in my country," Ivan grumbles.

"Hey, you'll be in Kryos with us if that happens. Nothing to worry about." Brandr slaps his shoulder with such force that Ivan stumbles back. Ivan glares at him and shoves his arm.

"Boys," Edda says tiredly, like she's scolding schoolchildren.

"Sorry," Brandr mutters, thoroughly chastised. He clears his throat and tries again.

"Save your speech," Edlyn snaps. "Let's just get to work. The nights are short here."

Murmurs of assent echo through the group. Brandr, now twice chastised, sighs and shakes his head. "Lead the way," he says to Ivan with a smile too bright to be true. Ivan picks up the little bag he's been carrying since they left the warmth of the fortress.

"What's in there?" Brandr asks.

Ivan stops abruptly, nearly making them all crash into each other, and bends down to retrieve whatever's in it. "This is my plant," he says proudly, showing them a potted green plant with leaves hanging over the sides. "I bring to Kryos."

"That's not wise if you want it to live," Brandr says. "Nothing that bright ever survives."

"That is the point," Ivan says. "It has not been a good plant. I take it there to teach it a lesson." He stoops and pulls out another plant from the bag, hefting it into the crook of his other arm. This one is smaller, not as bright. "This one needs the shock of cold to wake it up. I will hold a funeral for this one if it dies. It is my favorite plant."

Cerrick and Edlyn exchange glances. Taking one's favorite anything to Kryos is bad luck.

"Isn't it plenty cold enough up here?" Brandr asks hesitantly.

"No," Ivan says, and that appears to be the end of it. He smiles, stows the plants back in the bag, and resumes walking with his soft bootsteps in the snow.

They walk to the east side of the fortress, past the dancing warriors' camp—Cerrick's last time seeing them perform tonight drew a few tears, he admits—to the rise of a hill. "I was convinced there wasn't a bit of texture in the Oslands," Cerrick says.

Ivan laughs. "You have seen only the boring part, my friend. The north is hemmed in by mountains. The capital—my heavens, you must see it someday. The whole thing is lit up and golden at night. The nights are prettier than the days."

"I'm eager to get back there someday. Did you know the king summoned the three of us to the capital to personally thank us for what we did with the gemsha war twenty years ago?" Brandr says, throwing an arm over Ivan's shoulder with an easy smile Cerrick so rarely sees.

In the Oslands, it's appeared often, when he's not reading Evan's letter or arguing over whether he can control himself with the gemsha. Yet another reason Cerrick isn't looking forward to going back to Kryos—Brandr's stressed, tired frown will return. "I'm sure the rest of my Phantom would delight in it too."

"I still can't believe you took twenty years to get back to me," Ivan says. "At least you brought your wife. I tell you, it's a true shame you're spoken for, but I'm glad to see you so happy."

Brandr's face fills with color faster than Cerrick has ever seen. His own eyes dart to Edda, finding her hiding a wide smile behind her palm.

"She's not my wife," Brandr says, finally finding his voice. His arm slips from Ivan's shoulder.

Ivan laughs and gives Brandr a hefty slap to the back, though he's so much shorter it doesn't have the same impact. "Keep telling yourself that, my friend."

Brandr shakes his head and goes back to business. The night's darkness hides Cerrick's smile.

A glint of silver, illuminated by the distant fortress lights, draws Cerrick's eye beyond the line of the hill. To his utter shock, he spots a giant silver machine closely resembling a tank sitting in the snow at the base of the hill. "What is that?"

"That's our coveted gemsha," Brandr breathes. He rubs his hands together like one does when they're plotting something.

Cerrick edges closer and inspects the gemsha. It's taller than him and then some. The height and the darkness make it difficult to determine the details, but on the base, Cerrick can see switches and levers and buttons. He runs his fingers hesitantly over a few of them, wary of turning anything on by accident.

A cloth seat rests at the top of the great bulky machine, in the center of all the controls. The focal point is the huge cannon neck at the front, round and wide enough to fit a person inside. It's silver like the rest of the gemsha, as glowingly bright as the moon. The cannon looks powerful enough to blow a hole in the moon, taller than any horse Cerrick has ever seen. Metal rungs are bolted to the outside to help someone climb up to the seat. It's truly magnificent, equal parts showstopping and terrifying.

Cerrick tears his eyes from the gemsha and scans the land, planning ahead in his mind. He spots their two ships—Brandr worked fast and used his former connections to secure them a second one—in the harbor, alone at the dock. Awaiting them and their burden.

"That's the ship which will carry the gemsha," Brandr says, pointing to the closest one, which has a ramp extended down to the shore. "We're going to push it from here to there, up the ramp and onto the ship."

"Push?" Edlyn asks. "Sweet Saints, does the thing have to be pushed everywhere? No wonder it wasn't stolen twenty years ago."

"No, no, it can be driven. But it's loud as hell, louder than you'd believe. And very distinct. Every Os within five miles would know what we're doing immediately. We can't afford to start it, but luckily we don't have to push it far."

Looking between the giant, monstrous, silver machine and the distance to that ship, Cerrick would classify it as *far*.

"Ivan," Brandr calls, just loud enough to make Cerrick wince and glance back towards the fortress.

"You have no idea the hell I had to go through to get the gemsha here," Ivan says. He always has a complaint at the ready, but never one he truly means. "No one has trusted anyone alone with a gemsha since twenty years ago. I got approval from my friend's supervisor—my friend who has authority to drive one of these things for its intended purpose—and snuck it out of the warehouse right before dinner. Hopefully it will not be missed among the dozens of others until morning. We're lucky nothing keeps my people from their dinner."

"We have the dancing girls to thank for that."

"Mm, indeed." Ivan sighs wistfully and rests a hand on the gemsha. "I've known someone who could push one of these alone. We'll make do with five."

"I think only a Saint could move one of these alone, Ivan," Brandr chuckles. "Enough dallying. Let's get moving." With the calm, sure air of an oligarch, Brandr directs them all into position against the back of the gemsha. Cerrick is worried about navigating the snow, but Brandr assures them the gemsha will cut through the thick layer like paper.

The gemsha is cold against Cerrick's back, his feet braced awkwardly against the ground, his arms flat on the gemsha beside him. Brandr and Ivan bracket him. Edlyn and Edda have the more unfortunate positions of pushing the gemsha on either side.

Cerrick braces himself, unsure whether to tense or relax. "Heave!" Brandr says, and then they all take their first push.

Cerrick can't *believe* how heavy the gemsha is. He's bearing only one fifth of its weight, but it pushes back against his shoulder and fights back as powerfully as it's rumored to do in battle. It's not silent, either—it scrapes through the snow easily, but loudly, and their collective groans could probably be heard from Kryos. Cerrick grits his teeth, willing his feet not to slip, and keeps at it. His eyes are screwed tightly shut.

"Stop," Brandr calls, and they all go limp. Cerrick opens his eyes, breathing hard, and observes the trail they've made through the snow.

"We made it that far?" Cerrick asks in pleasant surprise. Twenty feet isn't a lot compared to the distance they have to go, but it's better than the five feet or so he was expecting—if that.

"We have a long way to go," Edlyn says, pessimistic as always. They all fall back into place and push again, and again, and again.

Cerrick's shoulders and arms burn, the gemsha digs into his back, and his feet struggle to find purchase in the snow. He doesn't glance towards the ship once, unwilling to see the amount of ground they still have to cover. When Brandr says, "Okay, last push before we're on the ship," Cerrick says, "You're joking."

He picks himself up and observes they're only inches from the ramp. The others chuckle at his disbelief.

They heave a final time and finally shove the gemsha up the ramp. Cerrick's limbs have long since gone numb, from both the cold and the effort, but they have this ship's crew to help them now. The captain overseeing them is a dark haired woman with an accent Cerrick struggles to understand, a voice that's strong and piercing.

The gemsha struggles up the ramp, but when it's finally over, the sight of it on the ship is so glorious Cerrick collapses back into the snow. His legs and arms give out.

"Holy shit. We have a gemsha," Edlyn laughs, somehow still on her feet. "We stole a gemsha where not even people twenty years ago could."

"There is indeed a gemsha on our ship," Brandr says with a wide, boyish grin. Cerrick has seen people who derive joy from nothing more than holding a massive weapon in their possession, but no one has ever looked quite as happy about it as Brandr.

Cerrick flops onto his back on the snow, welcoming the relief against his exhausted muscles. He'd be quite happy never having to move again. "You will have to carry me onto the boat," he groans, draping an arm over his eyes. The others laugh.

THEIR JOURNEY HOME is peaceful. On the ship without the gemsha, Cerrick isn't plagued by nightmares. He gets to watch the beautiful lights cascade across the sky every night at a normal hour. Edlyn even joins him.

Brandr fills their days with more news of what he and Ivan got up to twenty years ago that makes them all clutch their stomachs in laughter.

Cerrick can finally breathe out. He doesn't dread going to sleep every night.

Brandr cooks with what meager supplies they have, turning the dreaded but necessary meals into something to look forward to. Brandr's only demand of payment is the praise they're all too happy to heap on him, Edda in particular.

Brandr preens, chin in hand, covering a grin as she groans and describes just how decadent the apple tart he made turned out. Cerrick agrees wholeheartedly.

Brandr switches from mellow to happy to melancholy with an unnerving ease. Cerrick sometimes doesn't know which version of Brandr he's looking at, which he'll find when he glances over next. The unabashed joy he showed in the Oslands is fleeting now. Through it all, Brandr wears his familiar melancholy smile.

One day, Cerrick is standing at the rail of the ship, watching the spray of the ocean fan out behind them. Brandr joins him in peaceful silence, standing beside him with his forearms braced against the wood.

"How does it feel?" Cerrick asks, caught up in his head enough to forget Brandr can't read his thoughts.

"How does what feel?"

"This," Cerrick says, gesturing to the majesty of what they've accomplished all around them. "Leading the rebellion against Andor."

"I'm not leading it. I thought I told you that."

Cerrick rolls his eyes. "Leading it with us," he amends. "After having to wait so many years in silence, dreaming of revenge, now it's in your hands. The power to have it, anyway." He gestures towards the mighty gemsha on the other ship. Even from here, he can see Ivan pet it and speak to it like he would one of his plants. *The gemshas and the plants,* Ivan said once. *Better company for me than any man might be.*

Brandr is busy staring into the foamy green deep. At first, Cerrick isn't sure he heard him. "It's incredible," Brandr says at last. "A bit surreal, though I don't think it'll truly kick in until I see the look on the old bastard's face when I approach his palace from a gemsha. I'm doing everything he made me believe I couldn't."

"Soon you're going to take over his country," Cerrick says with a grin. "I'd love to see his face then."

"Edda and Ivan have cautioned me against losing myself to the bloody edges of this rebellion. I caution you to do the same."

"I think Edlyn needs that warning more than I do."

"Well, the both of you heed it, then. It's surreal to me that I'm actually here. I never thought I would be. Not really. The odds were too impossible, as was the chance of finding others who were willing to oppose Andor openly.

"I never realized the solution was right in front of me. His greatest enemies would be the people once closest to him, the people like me whom he wronged. To feel such fervent hatred and betrayal, one first had to feel love and admiration for him."

Cerrick closes his eyes and imagines the power of an army of Andor's biggest enemies come to haunt him. Cerrick wants Andor to know their power, to know and feel in his bones that he can't outrun his wrongs forever. Cerrick can only hope Njord, the biggest crime he's ever committed himself, won't haunt him for the rest of his days.

Amidst the horrors he unearthed in Holbeck, Njord was the saving grace. Njord was the sprout that rose from the fire, refusing to be sullied no matter how much the world tried. He's a Saint of heaven, and Cerrick is just a criminal bound for hell. They will not change.

CHAPTER TEN

The seas are no rougher than when they set out the first time, and their captain assures them that this journey will take only eight days. Cerrick goes to sleep the night of the seventh with a knot in his stomach at the thought of returning to Rinnfell, returning to business. They won't be safe under the international blanket of the Oslands anymore. All he can do is pray to the Saints that Andor still thinks them dead.

Cerrick does want this rebellion badly enough to make him ache at times, he only wishes he could project himself forward to the day when Andor has already been overthrown, where they're already victorious.

Edda's insistence about creating something new in place of what they're destroying—what will that look like? What does she envision? None of them yet know.

Cerrick, at least, doesn't want Kryos to descend into chaos and anarchy. He remembers reading about the disastrous third rebellion. Its leaders fell into the same trap that the Phantom is hurtling towards; rebellion without a plan for what comes after. In that time, the land and its people fell into disorder. Only the fourth rebellion soon after achieved order again.

The leaders of the third rebellion rest in shame, their names stamped out of many books, executed and buried in unmarked graves—the worst offense possible for the dead of this land, to taint the earth with one's remains instead of dispersing them on the winds, traveling to all their loved ones through the air.

Cerrick doesn't want to end up like the leaders of the third rebellion, killed by those who had to step in to save everyone.

He'll talk to Edda about her plans in the morning, he decides, since he has no good reason to put it off any longer.

He drifts off to the sound of Edlyn's breathing, and he wakes to the heavy pounding of footsteps overhead. Cerrick cracks open his eyes, groggy in the total darkness of the cabin, and throws off the blankets. The cold air hits him like a sword, and he fumbles to pull his cloak around his shoulders. In the dark, in his rush, he knocks over the cloakstand next to his bed.

"The hell?" Edlyn murmurs. The footsteps overhead don't stop, they only grow louder. Low voices accompany them.

Cerrick says nothing, just stumbles into his shoes and fastens the cloak, wincing at the rattle of the horns.

Edlyn grumbles her way out of bed, clinking her daggers together. Cerrick waits for her as Brandr's voice rings out above the noise, the muffled roar of the sea outside. Brandr is frantic and upset, and the sound sets Cerrick's blood thrumming.

They crack the door and creep out as silently as they can, mounting the creaky steps to the deck. They find Brandr there speaking with Edda, the former drawn and worried while the latter frowns.

"Did I wake you? I'm sorry," Brandr says, running a hand through his disheveled hair. He and Edda are both in their cloaks and boots, as if they too were suddenly awakened. Gone are the days when they would sit on the deck to watch the lights.

Cerrick looks at the lights fleetingly, longingly. The sense of peace he derived from watching them is gone before he even knew he could miss it. "Not to worry. What's going on?"

"See for yourself," Edda says, pointing east. Cerrick goes to the rail of the ship to see what's so interesting.

"Oh, Saints," he breathes. Another ship looms in the distance, its shape piercing the fog, dipping in and out of sight. "That's...what manner of ship is that?"

"I don't know. It's not marked, but it's not a warship. It could be a freighter. It's been trailing behind us for the last thirty minutes. Saints know if it sees the gemsha ship with Ivan."

Cerrick shivers, hardly daring to look back. The gemsha is far too visible for his liking with that unknown ship so close.

"We're just keeping watch on it for now," Edda says. "To see if—"

An arrow whines through the air and embeds itself in the deck floor behind them. "Holy shit!" Edlyn shouts. "Get down, everyone!"

The four of them dive for cover as more arrows fly over their heads. Cerrick cranes his neck, trying to find the gemsha ship in the foggy night. Edlyn shoves him back out of sight with a forceful grip on his shoulder. Panic rises in Cerrick's chest.

"We can't worry about them right now," Brandr says, though his voice is shaking. "We're powerless ourselves. We have to help ourselves before we can help Ivan."

Cerrick nods, though his eyes still search the night. He's braced, tense and waiting for something to happen. Arrows continue to pour onto the deck, sticking out like little white trees in a forest. The four of them are trapped. Cerrick looks at the stairs down belowdeck, so tantalizingly close.

"Here's what we're going to do," Brandr says, pulling himself together. "We're going to make a run for portside and take cover there."

"What?" Edlyn demands. "We're not going belowdeck?"

"No. I have an idea." Brandr draws a deep breath, grasping for Edda's hand. "It's a crazy one, one that might end in our deaths, but you have to trust me." He meets Cerrick's eyes in the near darkness, searching for trust. "Can you do that?"

"Of course," Cerrick says. "I trust you."

"Good. Everyone ready?" Brandr ducks as another arrow flies over his head, too close. Pressed up against the portside wall, they'll be twice as exposed. Cerrick's heart hammers fiercely.

"Yeah," Edlyn says.

"Okay." Brandr takes another breath, leaving a suspended moment in time before he releases it. When he does, he moves, beckoning the others after him. The unseen archers rain down a fresh flurry of arrows.

Cerrick keeps his head down, cloak hood pulled up, not wasting time or breath by stopping to look over. Arrows whistle and whine through the air, but no cries of pain follow. Cerrick sees all four pairs of their feet as they make it to portside. He rolls to the side, banging his shoulder against the wood. He's hidden behind a crate. Edlyn squeezes in beside him. Brandr and Edda find their own cover a few feet down.

An arrow lands beside Cerrick's feet. He squeaks and tucks his feet in, heart pounding, breath coming short and freezing in the air before him.

"Are we all intact, unharmed?" Brandr asks. The others nod.

"Now what?" Cerrick asks as the arrows cease to fall behind them. He peeks over the edge of the wall to glimpse Ivan's ship, ignoring hissed warnings from Edlyn. The gemsha is still lying in the open, and Ivan stands protectively in front of it. Ivan, bless him, is going to get himself killed.

"You have to trust me again," Brandr answers, though his nervous tone doesn't inspire confidence. "Apologies in advance for your ears." He faces Ivan's ship and yells at the loudest volume he can manage, "Ivan!"

Ivan turns towards them, wide eyed and frightened. He yells something back, but a sudden rough wave falls between the ships and drowns him out. Arrows land beside the gemsha inches from Ivan's feet. He scoots farther into cover, both arms spread across the gemsha like a mother protecting her young.

Brandr gives up on trying to communicate through speech and instead uses gestures, which aren't much easier to see through the fog and sea mist. He makes a few sharp hand motions that Cerrick interprets as *come hither*, and whether Ivan understands them or not is unknown.

Another wave of spray flies up between them. Cerrick glances at the clouds rapidly moving in, covering the moon and the colored sky lights. The clouds are dark and ugly, spelling impending doom.

When the seas calm down again, Ivan nods and smiles cheerily at them. Then, to Cerrick's horror, he runs out from behind cover.

Brandr is the one to shove Cerrick down this time, more gently than Edlyn did. "He's fine, lad. Just watch." He speaks calmly even as Ivan dodges flying arrows left and right. He's sprinting towards the captain, who's busy shouting orders. Ivan slips and falls face first into a puddle. He quickly scrambles back up. Cerrick's heart is in his throat until Ivan reaches the captain, standing at the steering wheel.

At least get down, Cerrick prays, watching anxiously as Ivan converses with her. She nods and starts shouting new orders to her crew. Slowly, the ship pulls in closer to theirs. Ivan turns to Brandr with wild, victorious eyes. Brandr smiles. Cerrick doesn't ask, just waits.

Cerrick watches, fascinated and confused, as the ships draw perilously close. Arrows still fly, but from his place of cover Cerrick is able to ignore them. Cerrick realizes far too late what Brandr intends, well after Edlyn's gasp of surprise.

When the ships are close enough to touch, Brandr leaps from behind the cover of the wall and shouts, "Jump!"

Oh, fuck. Edlyn grabs Cerrick's wrist and spurs him into movement, springing up from safety and leaping across the narrow gap between the two ships. He glances to the right as they all sail through the air, when he swears time slows for a moment. When the arrows that fly their way have no chance of finding their mark.

He finds the foreign ship much closer, peeking through the fog. He makes out the shape of archers on the deck, standing in a line.

The four of them land safely on the deck of Ivan's ship, and Cerrick barely has time to worry over the fate of their own before Brandr is picking himself up and saying, "I told our captain what I feared before you joined us. Don't worry. Worry for us. Worry for him." He gestures towards Ivan, who's crouched behind the gemsha wearing an expression of fear for the first time Cerrick has ever seen.

"What's your plan, Brandr?" Edlyn asks as arrows chase them. Sweet heavens, how many arrows does the enemy have? Are they Os, here for the gemsha? Is this Andor's orchestration? Is it a random attack in the heart of the stormy Gryting?

Cerrick stows those questions and pulls Edlyn to safety with him, plastered against the side of the gemsha. Before Brandr can answer, the foreign ship begins careening toward them. The creaking slowness with which it moves, Brandr's useless shout, the water spilling onto them and soaking Cerrick to the bone—all are slow markers of their inevitable doom.

Cerrick can only watch and helplessly brace himself as the foreign ship crashes into theirs. The impact sends him flying across the deck, crashing into the floor behind him as their ship tips downwards. Brandr is swearing, pulling Edda against him when she starts to fall away. Edlyn has a good grip on the gemsha and doesn't move as the ship slowly rights itself.

As soon as he can find his footing again, Brandr begins climbing the gemsha's built in ladder. "Time to test this thing out," he says with a wild grin, dodging arrows as they fly his way. Edda shrieks in a way

Cerrick has never heard, trying to pull Brandr back down. It doesn't work.

"Ivan," Brandr yells.

Ivan yells back instructions Cerrick doesn't bother trying to understand. Surely Ivan and Brandr went over this twenty years ago, all the intimate details of operating a gemsha. Cerrick says a quiet prayer to the Saints just in case.

Brandr pulls the tallest silver lever back, and the gemsha fires. Cerrick watches a ball of roaring flames fly through the air with a pop so devastatingly loud, it can probably be heard from the Kryc shores. The force of it knocks the gemsha back, but Brandr quickly scrambles back to position.

Cerrick prays for the flaming cannonball to hit the other ship, but achieving perfect aim would be impossible in these conditions. It misses, though not by much, grazing the other ship's stern. It takes with it a chunk of wood before crashing into the sea.

Cerrick swears in tandem with Brandr, sick with disappointment. Cerrick's heart hasn't stopped thrumming since this other ship came into view. Perhaps in the Ice he would've savored the thrill, but now he just wants this to be over. The sea tosses them like they're children, thunder rumbles in the distance, and a light rain drizzles down.

"Duck!" Brandr yells as the foreign ship recovers and fires more arrows. *How many fucking arrows do they have?* Cerrick wonders before ducking to safety.

He feels so helpless, pinned down with no way to fight back, nothing to do but sit and wait and hide. They're not close enough to throw knives that would hit. Cerrick risks taking a peek over the edge of the rail.

He watches the crew of the foreign ship rush around in chaos. He squints, trying to pick out any sort of clue about who their adversaries are, and widens his eyes when he spots one familiar face among the mass.

"Is that—is that Bertie?" he gasps.

"By the Saints," Edlyn breathes. His form is clearer now—skinny and auburn haired Bertie is shouting orders with a blond man at his side. Their clothes are dark, not fine. The way they move, the way command flows effortlessly to their fingertips, is too remarkable not to notice. "And Carr, too."

Cerrick swears. Bertie betrayed them and the Phantom, ignored Brandr's demands. The thought that he ever would've done otherwise seems ludicrous now. Cerrick feels abruptly foolish. "We put too much faith in him."

"Our fault was ever putting any faith in him," Edlyn says in disgust, kicking the deck. "What kind of idiots were we to think he would wait for us in Rinnfell, shaking in his boots simply because Brandr served his father?"

Cerrick says nothing, filled with the same boiling rage—at Bertie and Carr, yes, but himself most of all. He can't imagine the burning within Edlyn at this moment, the guilt she must be harboring. He touches her shoulder lightly.

The other ship rears back, preparing to do Saints know what. Cerrick turns towards Brandr, knowing Edyn's rage will have to wait. She hammers on anyway. Her voice shakes with the power of restrained fury. *The* fury.

"I don't want Bertie or Carr to ever lay eyes on me again after this. I am going to drive a chisel into the heart of the Ice and break it apart. I want to watch it shatter on the ground in pieces it'll never fit back together. I want to watch it slowly melt. I want to pick up a shard and run my fingers along the edge, endure the temporary burning cold to know the burn it feels is far worse. I want to watch it dry up before my eyes. I never want to see or hear of it again."

Cerrick looks at her, finding the same fire in her eyes as in her voice. She has a white knuckled grip on the edge of the railing. He can imagine lightning crackling along her skin.

"We will do so," he says, "but first, let's get back to Rinnfell alive." She nods.

Brandr is fiddling with the lever of the gemsha, preparing for another attack. Cerrick suspects that most of the room within the enormous machine is taken up by the enormous cannonballs. Ever since he first laid eyes on one, Cerrick has been idly searching for the hatch to load the cannonballs in. Only now does he remember something Ivan said in passing in the Oslands, slapping the side of the gemsha; "These things refill themselves."

Cerrick didn't know then and doesn't know now what that means. Hopefully it means Brandr doesn't only have three cannonballs to fire at their enemy. Cerrick says a silent prayer for his accuracy.

He risks a peek around the side of the gemsha to watch Bertie draw back the string of a bow and release. Cerrick quickly ducks back into safety as the sea tosses them yet again. He locks gazes with Edlyn. When did Bertie learn to use such a weapon? The thought that Bertie knew he couldn't defeat them with words alone is flattering, but not enough to overtake the maddening image of his smirk playing behind Cerrick's eyes.

Cerrick and Edlyn never learned archery, after all, who'd need a long range weapon for close combat in Rinnfell? How foolish. Andor recommended learning archery once, or at least a weapon other than the knife once it became obvious Cerrick had no skill with the Pointstaff or sword. He wishes now he'd listened.

When Cerrick risks his next peek, Carr is the one staring him down. He looses another arrow, and it lands in the wet wood beside Cerrick's palm. Edlyn swears colorfully. "Brandr, how much longer?"

In answer comes another cannonball pop that nearly bursts Cerrick's ears. The ship rattles like creatures of the deep have taken hold from beneath. The sea lurches, sending another splash of water over the side and into Cerrick's face. He grimaces and spits it out.

He watches the cannonball hit, striking Bertie's ship clean through the starboard side. Cerrick can't contain his whoop of joy as the cannonball connects in a shower of wood splinters, painting the sky with them. That ship disintegrating before Cerrick's eyes is as beautiful as the colored lights.

With Bertie, Cerrick won't hold back. The monster in him delights to watch his maker suffer.

Bertie and Carr stand on opposite ends of the ship when that glorious cannonball hits. The ship splits in half, loose boards sticking out to the sky like arms reaching for help. Bertie and Carr run back and forth, shouting to one another with their crews in tow. Cerrick's laughter is lost in the myriad of sounds on the Gryting.

Bertie and Carr search for cover as splintered pieces of their ship sink into the water. Fire spreads from the cannon's crater, licking the edges of the wood, shrinking their field of safety even further.

Cerrick watches with rapture as they scramble uselessly to and fro. He pictures this moment immortalized as a painting. The gray skies, the foaming green seas rising up to claim the ship and drag its passengers down to a fate unknown. The brilliant orange flames, the dark wood as a dull background, the billowing black smoke, the pale forms of Bertie and Carr as they scream across the rift to one another.

Cerrick would hang that work of art in every office, every bedchamber he ever inhabited, so that it never had to leave his sight. He would remember it with reverence each time he glimpsed it.

"Your bows aren't so useful now, are they?" Cerrick murmurs.

The sound of swearing and pained moans from behind draws Cerrick out of his heavenly reverie. Edlyn is leaning against the gemsha with one knee pulled up to her chest, both hands clutching her abdomen and her face torn in agony. Edda is kneeling beside her, trying to staunch the bleeding. Red still overflows from the gaps between their fingers. It's like trying to hold in a waterfall.

"Sweet Saints. What happened?" Cerrick gently replaces Edda's hands. The screams from the foreign ship dissolve into background noise instead of the symphony they were.

Edlyn moves her hand enough to unfurl one bloody fist, showing him the long bloody splinter clutched in her palm. It's still embedded in her skin. Only the sharp, jagged tip of it pierced her, but it went in deep. Cerrick quickly presses down on the wound. He doesn't dare lift up her clothes to see how much damage was done. His heart is pounding again.

"That's what happens when a ship explodes," she gasps. For the first time, Cerrick notices the splinters littering the deck of their own ship, covering it like a deadly rain. Those splinters are Bertie and Carr's final parting gift, a more lethal weapon than any arrow than any they could loose.

The sound of the cannon's impact must've drowned out Edlyn's scream. Cerrick curses himself for paying more attention to the glorious spectacle than her safety. Cerrick shakes out his hair, watching bits of Bertie's deck fall from the blond strands.

"You're going to be fine," he says, firmly holding down her wound while Edda leaves to check on Brandr and yell for help. Cerrick's world narrows to Edlyn's bloodsoaked black cloak, the red coating his fingers, and the harsh sound of her breathing. The burning ship is all but forgotten.

The wild waves carry Bertie's half of his ship perilously close to theirs. Cerrick scoots closer to Edlyn, ready to shelter her body with his if Bertie decides to try something outlandish like jumping. Cerrick reluctantly tears his eyes from her as Bertie screams, "I'll meet you in Saint Renalie's hell, the both of you."

"Fuck you," Cerrick growls, hardly recognizing his own voice. He searches for something to say, but he's said it all already. Cerrick lets his eyes do the talking. With any luck, they'll be glowing with the very flames that ignite Bertie's ship. Said flames are hot enough and close enough to make Cerrick shiver.

Bertie is sweating from the proximity of the fire, ash running down his cheeks like Saintly tears. His teeth are bared, his arms bloody as he clutches his bow. Cerrick only wishes he could retrieve it from Bertie's cold corpse, soon to be claimed by the sea. Cerrick allows himself a moment of smug satisfaction in knowing Bertie's ashes won't float on the wind. He'll be condemned to the depths.

Cerrick turns back to Edlyn, who's staring at Bertie with a blank expression. All the fight has gone out of her.

They let Bertie pass without another word, watching his ship burn while his crew sit slumped against the wall, his quiver empty of arrows.

Carr's half of the ship is sinking faster thanks to the damage from the first cannonball Brandr fired. The winds and roaring seas carry it away from Cerrick, but he can hear Carr screaming their names across the sea regardless. Carr's voice is laced with agony and rage, regret and apology, furious pleas for help all rolled into one.

Cerrick doesn't dignify the bastard with a glance. "I suppose I ought to thank him," Edlyn says tightly, "for enlightening us to Andor's true nature. Without Carr, we wouldn't have had cause to start a rebellion."

Both halves of the burning, wrecked ship drift away into westward fog and rough waters. The fire fades from the distance as the ships sink into the deep. The creatures of the deep, legend or no, will feast well tonight.

As the ship drifts out of sight, Cerrick focuses entirely on Edlyn. Brandr climbs down from the gemsha and pulls Ivan out of hiding, and both of them quickly work to find a more comfortable place for

Edlyn to rest. He tears up one of his spare shirts to make a makeshift pressure bandage around the splinter. They don't dare remove it.

The other ship they've been sailing with emerged from the battle unscathed, gone quiet and dark in a cloud of fug until Bertie and Carr passed by. Now, the two ships maneuver close together again so they can carry Edlyn back.

Brandr clambers over first, receiving her in his arms. Cerrick holds his breath as he passes her over, her eyes closed. She's deathly still other than the rise of her chest. Cerrick doesn't again draw a full breath until he too is on the other ship, soon followed by Edda and Ivan. The captain of the gemsha ship veers west, to anchor in Rinnfell harbor well out of sight of the shore until they have need of the gemsha again.

"Captain says we'll be back in Rinnfell in minutes," Brandr says, softly enough not to grate on Cerrick's oversensitive nerves. He seems to have lost his own capacity for speech. Silently, he lifts Edlyn onto a makeshift stretcher. Thus begins the waiting.

Cerrick faces south so that he may have the first glimpse of Rinnfell shores the moment they come into view.

"Stupid kid," Brandr grunts, standing at Edlyn's side with a gloomy worry in his eye. He smooths her hair off her face. "Should've known she'd get herself injured. At least she knew not to remove the splinter. She's lost enough damn blood as it is."

Cerrick blinks and sees the image of Saint Calith of death. He just as quickly shoos her away. He won't let her feast on his doubts for even a moment. Doubts fester just like wounds, and wounds they have enough of.

Finally, after an eternity, land comes into view and the ship anchors in the harbor. Cerrick doesn't dare leave Edlyn's side—even if he wanted to, he's afraid of what might happen the moment he turns his back.

What he wouldn't give to have Kara with them. Why in the Saints' name did they leave behind the only one of them capable of healing?

"Hey, kid," Brandr says, touching his shoulder. Cerrick nearly jumps out of his skin. "We're here. You need to let her go so the professionals can tend her."

Cerrick's lip curls into what might be a sneer, what could be a soundless sob, but what ends up being nothing. Very reluctantly, he takes his hands off her, keeping his hands in front of him so that he doesn't get blood anywhere. Most of him is covered in her blood, anyway.

Brandr presses a towel into his hands, and after a moment, Cerrick takes it.

As they anchor, the ship dissolves into chaos. Their crew shouts over the dock crew, drowning each other out in the familiar song of the harbor. It grates on Cerrick's ears as the ramp is lowered. Brandr shouts for a healer.

Cerrick scans the typical seaside crowd for a healer, but no healer comes forth. There are only crew and passengers bound for other ships. No healers.

Panic closes around Cerrick's throat, threatening his breath. Only Brandr's hand on his shoulder grounds him, and Cerrick slaps a hand over his wrist to keep him there.

Brandr pauses for a moment when Cerrick truly can't draw breath, where he's back in the Gryting in his nightmare with Njord, Andor, Edlyn standing over him with nothing kind to say. Edlyn's blood is still staining his hands.

Brandr says, "Edlyn is going to survive. Do you hear me? Edlyn is not going to die."

His words have the effect of a parent slapping their child harshly on the back; it punches air back into Cerrick's lungs and he takes a heaving breath doubled over.

Brandr's hand lingers uncertainly, but the touch suddenly becomes too much and Cerrick pushes him off. The world slowly fades back in. The yelling, the rush of people, the sharpness of the air, the sea smell. Those become grounding instead of grating. Cerrick remains doubled over for another moment before righting himself, deeming himself finally strong enough to do so.

Knowing Brandr will follow, Cerrick jogs off the ship, eager to have his feet back on solid ground. He doesn't know where Edda and Ivan are, but he watches the captain and one of the crewmen carry Edlyn's stretcher off the ship. Soon Brandr's sibling Inge is there among them, directing them to shelter in the seaside shack.

Cerrick's instincts prickle at the chaos of a docking ship, a process he hasn't often witnessed. Before he can ponder it further, Brandr gasps and points, touching Cerrick's shoulder to turn him around. "Cerrick."

Cerrick looks down the street, locking eyes with someone who makes his breath catch.

Njord.

His husband is standing just beyond the edge of the chaos, a slight smile on his face, his hair loose around his shoulders. He's the only one wearing a cloak that's not covered in adornments on the front—his cloak is bright purple today. His Pointstaff leans against the wall of a house beside him, gleaming and bronze.

"Go," Brandr says with a gentle shove to the small of Cerrick's back. Cerrick needs no encouragement more than that. As torn as he is about letting Edlyn out of his sight, he knows he would only be in the way of whoever's trying to help her. Njord is right here. Still, he hesitates.

"I'll look after Edlyn, I swear on the Saints," Brandr yells, jogging towards the shack. The last of Cerrick's hesitation fades, and he runs into Njord's open arms, where the noise of the docks fades and time seems to slow. He collides with Njord's broad chest, and Njord is right there to wrap his arms around him, lift him up a bit.

Cerrick falls into Njord's warmth and the welcome smell of Aeton he brought with him. Cerrick is exhausted to his core, and Njord catches him, holds him in strong arms. His strength is endless and unshakable.

"Njord," Cerrick says, too exhausted to act or speak as he should. "What the hell are you doing here? You're supposed to be in Holbeck."

"Shh," Njord murmurs, and cradles him closer. "That doesn't matter right now."

Cerrick wants to argue, but he can't help but savor this the way he wants to despite all his misgivings. He needs to know Njord isn't mad at him, that he means this, that he feels this the way Cerrick does. But he's right, they have time for that later. To melt against Njord's chest, his love, his column of strength, is all Cerrick needs and more. All else can wait.

"I am glad you're home safe," Njord says, completely enfolding Cerrick in his arms. Cerrick couldn't hope to be warmer. The warmth of south Kryos and Tailing couldn't ever compare to this. "I missed you."

"You are the nicest surprise I could've come home to," Cerrick says, unable to wait any longer. His feelings and words come spilling out. This is everything he missed so desperately in the Oslands, everything he needs. He doesn't know the right words to get it back. "Do you forgive me?" he asks, hoping it's enough.

"Yes," Njord says instantly, like it's the easiest thing in the world to do. "Yes. Yes. Whatever it takes to have you back. We will work through it."

"We will," Cerrick says, and the thought isn't even daunting. Anything, any conversation will be better than separation. No matter what he must weather with Njord, he will weather it *with Njord*.

"You said you worked for the Sun," Njord rumbles right into his ear, so warm, the epitome of simultaneous sunshine and storm power. Cerrick wants to sob. This storm would never hurt him. "Well, you are my sun." He says it like it's the simplest truth in the world, like stating the sky is gray in northern Kryos. A plain fact. Nothing more.

Cerrick does sob then. Njord clutches him closer, kissing the top of his head with a strong arm around his waist. Cerrick has been awake for so long, through battle and stressed over Edlyn and worried out of his mind. Njord's gentle touch, so familiar and given so freely in front of all these people, is more than Cerrick deserves after everything. Njord doesn't seem to care.

Cerrick doesn't deserve this. He's hurt Njord too much for this, however wonderful it might be. People like him, those who make choices like him, don't get things like this. They can't be hell and have heaven.

"Cerrick, Cerrick, hear me," Njord says as Cerrick begins to fall back into his head. "Hear my voice. I forgive you." Njord speaks through the noise and the chaos. He is the center of the storm, calming and strong. "I forgive you. I forgive. I would rather have you hurt me than not have you at all. We will work through it, like I said."

"No," Cerrick is saying, placing himself back in that night where he left, that nightmare where Njord walked away from the bank while Cerrick drowned, the very real Edlyn bleeding out in his hands, guilt guilt *guilt*—

Njord kisses him.

The noise of the docks, the cold wind on the back of his neck, the nauseous worry in Cerrick's chest all slowly melt. Njord doesn't let him go, both arms strong around his waist with Cerrick pulled close to his chest.

Cerrick can do nothing but hang on. His thoughts fly away under Njord's ministrations. Saints, he's missed this, all of this, right down to the way Njord's beard tickles him.

When he lets Cerrick a little bit of slack, he's aware enough to realize they're not alone.

Plucking that thought from his head, Njord says, "No one cares." Docks are always chaotic, and the arrival of a new ship with a wounded passenger leaves no room for wonder about two people kissing.

They haven't kissed since the night Cerrick left Holbeck. He wraps a hand around the back of Njord's neck to pull him down for another. Njord's hand moves down to his wrist, what Cerrick thinks is an idle desire to touch until he feels something slide over his hand. His own marriage bracelet. Njord is giving it back to him, marrying him anew. A fresh start.

"How are you here?" Cerrick finally asks, separating from those addictive lips. "How long have you been here?"

"I never left," Njord says, smiling. "I've been coming here every day to wait for you."

Cerrick is rendered speechless. The sound of horses' hooves draws his eye and mind away, buying him time to think of a reply.

None other than Oligarch Solveig Salverson comes thundering down the crowded street on a horse as black as the night. Her dark hair is pulled up into a braided knot on her head, dark brown skin popping in the dullness of the gray day. A joyous fire resides in her dark eyes.

No one except Njord wears blue as well as she does. The color of Slairr is a dark, rich blue that shimmers before the eyes, captivating. It's currently presented in the form of the cloak draped around Solveig's shoulders.

Hers doesn't have a fur lined collar, and it's not as bulky as most Kryc cloaks, letting her arms peek out easily as she waves to one and all, showing the metal breastplate she wears underneath. Slairr natives are commonly healers, but also skilled soldiers. An academy for said soldiers resides in the eastern mountains where Andor himself attended in his youth.

Solveig attended both the soldier's academy and a healer's school, and is well accomplished in both fields. Cerrick has never spoken to her, but the legends of a woman with commander's blood sewn into her so far prove true.

Behind her are a group of riders in the same blue cloaks, some on black horses and some on stark white horses. Most of the riders are dark skinned, as people from Slairr tend to be, and most of them women. Solveig waves merrily to Cerrick. A Pointstaff with the spearhead attached is propped up on her right foot, clutched in her right hand.

"Cerrick Montef. Or Cerrick Hagen, I should say. How delighted I am to meet you after hearing so much about you. I must say, your husband is a joy. If I weren't married to the prettiest girl in Kryos I'd be jealous myself." Solveig smiles down at them, and Njord smiles back.

Cerrick stares between them, flabbergasted. "W—what is going on here?"

"We have been in company while you've been gone," Solveig says. Cerrick looks at Njord in alarm, wondering how much she knows, but he shakes his head minutely. Cerrick breathes out.

"I have been staying with her," Njord says, "in her mansion in Slairr."

"You'll have to tell me that tale sometime," Cerrick says with a raised eyebrow. His attention drifts again to the shack. Worry for Edlyn returns, if it ever left. "I'll be with you in a minute, Lady Slairr," he says, using a rare term for the oligarchs.

"Take your time," she says. "I'm not going anywhere."

Cerrick runs with Njord into the shack. Putting his eyes on Edlyn again helps him breathe, though the sight isn't pretty. She's still motionless and covered in blood, though he sees the rise and fall of her chest. He takes in the other occupants of the cabin with a glance. Brandr. Inge. Edda. Ivan hovering in the doorway. All of them wearing grim expressions.

"There's not enough room for all of you in here," Inge growls, "especially with someone who needs air."

"I'm not leaving her," Cerrick says.

"We still need a healer," Brandr says, and the worry in his voice sends a chill through Cerrick's bones.

"Solveig is a healer," Njord says quietly.

Cerrick calls himself ten kinds of fool and pushes back out into the street.

Brandr's call of, "Solveig is here?" follows him out.

"Solveig!" Cerrick calls. His desperation must show in his voice, for she turns towards him instantly. "Could you come in here? We need you."

"As a soldier or as a healer?" Solveig asks, though she's already climbing off her horse and handing the reins to one of the other riders.

"Healer." He holds the door open as she gathers a medical pack from her saddlebags. A small kit, but hopefully enough to save Edlyn.

Inge and Edda slip out to make room for Solveig, but Brandr doesn't take her subtle encouragement to follow. He keeps looking at Cerrick. "It's alright," Cerrick says softly as Solveig rummages through her medical pack. "I'm alright." He squeezes Njord's hand.

Brandr's eyes rest on their hands. "I'll say another prayer for her," he says softly, clapping Cerrick's shoulder and ducking out. Cerrick is happy to let him handle all that awaits them outside. In here, he only has to worry about Edlyn and be with Njord. That's more than enough.

"Tell me," Cerrick says. "Is she going to live?"

Solveig takes too long to answer for his liking. She's bent over Edlyn with a razor focus. Cerrick shoves down his impatience.

"She should," Solveig says finally, rolling up her sleeves, taking off her cloak, getting her hands bloody. She's moving at a speed that is both relieving and worrying—relieving that she understands the urgency, worrying that this requires such urgency.

She finally takes mercy on him and looks up. She's smiling. It's a calm smile, not one plastered on for his benefit, and it sets Cerrick's heart at ease more than anything else. "Having you here worrying over her is going to help no one. It breaks my focus. I know you care a great deal—"

"She is my everything," Cerrick cuts in. "She is woven into my soul. If she dies, I lose everything. I lose myself."

Solveig's smile fades a bit, and she nods. "I will do my best," she says, all he can expect of her, all she can do. All any healer can do. Only the Saints can perform miracles.

"Thank you," Cerrick says. "I'll—I'll go." Still holding tightly to Njord, he pushes back out into the world of cold air and the stinking sea.

He hasn't made it more than a few steps out the door when a great series of booms make Cerrick clamp his hands over his ears. Brandr swears and yells for them all to get down.

The ground starts shaking, and then another series of booms strike the air. They're piercing, whistling, and Solveig's horses start whining. Everyone is shouting, and suddenly the world is hot. Njord's arms are around Cerrick again as his vision goes dark, as he's knocked to the ground. He's trying to shout for Solveig and Edlyn, but the ground is shaking and the world is hot and black and formless. Njord is screaming his name, but he can't think.

CHAPTER ELEVEN

"Heartless."

Cerrick has been here before.

The salt of the sea fills his nose again, but it's the air, not the water. Cerrick is standing on the deck of the ship he just departed, facing Brandr this time.

"You weren't fast enough." Cerrick knows somewhere, somehow, that this isn't real, but the wind whipping through his hair and cloak certainly freeze him like they're real. Brandr's voice is icy enough to be real. "You should've told her to get down sooner. You're the reason she's bleeding out on that table."

Cerrick looks at his hands and finds them stained in red. He scrubs at them fruitlessly until they're a shade redder from the irritation, until he has blood stuck under his nails like tattoos. He looks up again and finds Brandr gone. Bertie's ship is split in two before his eyes, framed beneath storm clouds, drifting away on the rough seas.

Good fucking riddance, Cerrick thinks bitterly.

When he looks down, Edlyn's body is leaning against the side of the ship. Her head is slumped, blood pouring out of her abdomen and staining her shirt. This time, her chest isn't rising and falling. Cerrick sinks to his knees beside her, staining his trousers with her blood.

"I am dead because of you." Her voice travels around his head in waves, fading out slowly like an echo. He swivels his head and finds her standing behind him, tall in all her glory. Head to toe in black, her cloak adorned with chains and knives. She glares at him with her mouth set in a thin line.

This is not real. She promised you she would never betray you. That reminder, the effort it takes to pull forth the memory of her oath, are not enough to pull him out. His breath slips out like a whistle, and he can't gasp enough to get it back.

"You will scatter my ashes on the wind like you did for Orv," Edlyn says, "dispose of my remains, but you will never get the blood off your hands." Blackness closes in around him, smoke and fire and fog, the whistling whine and booms and the coppery taste of blood.

He wakes up gasping in a bed that's not his own with a splitting headache. It's eased only by the softness of the pillow under his head. Cerrick groans quietly, letting his hammering heart come down.

He rolls over, away from light, and bumps into a warm body. Cerrick's eyes fly open. Njord. He's the first thing Cerrick is fully aware of, groggy and disoriented as he is. "Oh, thank the Saints," Njord breathes in Aeton.

Cerrick opens his eyes wider, adjusting to the world around him. He's in a room painted in low golden light. The bed beneath him is wide and white. Njord lies on his side to Cerrick's right. The décor is sparse and impersonal, with only a few lamps placed throughout to cast in that dim golden light. Cerrick doesn't recognize this place. Such cluelessness spikes a momentary panic in his chest, but Njord's heavy hand pushes him down when he attempts to rise.

"Welcome back," Njord rumbles, caressing his cheek. His eyes shine, and a smile of relief graces his face. "You were screaming. Thrashing. I—I held you down, but—"

"It's okay," Cerrick whispers, discovering his throat is dry as sand. He's rarely heard Njord's voice so harrowed, and as unsettling as that is, it does provide him an opportunity to comfort him.

Cerrick scoots closer, wincing at the pain in his head and the sudden aches that erupt in his chest, his back, his legs. He pushes through the pain and musters up a smile. Memory slowly returns—the ground shaking, the explosions at the docks. Njord. Brandr. *Edlyn.* "I'm okay. See? You are too." Cerrick takes Njord's cheek in his hand. "I'm fine."

"You're injured," Njord grumbles, but the helpless despair fades from his tone.

"What the hell happened?" Cerrick asks, rolling onto his back and closing his eyes again. He's dressed, he realizes, not tucked beneath the bedcovers. He's warm all over, and when he gains the strength to move his hands again he realizes he's not wearing the cloak Njord gifted him. It probably needed to be washed. Whatever's been switched out is soft under his fingers.

"There was an explosion. An entire section of the harbor was destroyed. We don't know who or how or why yet."

"Where are we?" Cerrick's eyes fly open again. "Is Edlyn okay?"

"We're at Solveig's mansion in Slairr." Njord draws a long breath. "Yes, she is. Everyone survived and made it out. It was all thanks to Solveig," he adds. "I don't know what we would've done without her. She figured out what was happening quickly and evacuated Edlyn from that little shack before it was blown to bits."

Cerrick shivers at the very image. He throws an arm over his eyes to block it out, which of course has the opposite effect. Njord tugs it down again. His face and the light in the room are grounding. His bright blue eyes are striking.

"Everyone is okay," he says, and while he means well, that's not what Cerrick needs. He needs to lay his eyes on everyone. Edlyn herself has undersold the severity of her injuries in the past for his sake. Now he doesn't trust her word. Only thorough patting her down will satisfy him. When he tries to get up, his muscles scream in agony, and Njord's heavy hand keeps him down.

"I've been instructed under pain of death by Solveig not to let you out of this bed at least for today," he says, kissing Cerrick's cheek in apology. Cerrick turns his head so that Njord catches his mouth too.

"Mm. Keep doing that and you'll keep me here easily." He tests his agility by stretching his arms over his head. His muscles burn, but not as badly as the rest of his body. What happened to make him so sore?

"You were thrown to the ground by the force of the blast," Njord says. "I tried to take the fall for you, but I wasn't fast enough."

Cerrick is touched. "You didn't have to put yourself in danger for me. I'd in fact very much prefer that you didn't."

Njord hums like he's considering it even though Cerrick knows he isn't, propping his chin up in his palm.

Cerrick draws a breath. "How is Edlyn?"

"You lasted longer than I expected to ask that question. She is alive," Njord says. "Solveig got her out of there quickly. We all rode here on horses and carriages, and Solveig operated in one of them—as much as she could under those conditions. I handed her things. Helped her hold Edlyn down."

Cerrick shudders. "Is she conscious? Can I see her?"

"You're not leaving the bed, and Edlyn is certainly not leaving hers. You'll have to wait at least until tomorrow. But," he quickly adds at the scathing look Cerrick gives him, "I can tell you that she's still unconscious for her own good. Solveig gave her something to ensure she stays asleep a while longer.

"She's lost a lot of blood, but it could've been worse, believe it or not. She's going to live. She's had blood from everyone here who was able to give it, and she'll continue to need it for a while longer, but she won't die from the blood loss. Solveig was very thorough. I swear on the Saints, she'll be up again, though Solveig says she must be ginger about her movements for a while."

Cerrick doesn't care if she emerges with four limbs or three, the ability to walk or not. All he cares about is that she's alive and going to stay that way.

"That's good. Thank you. I'm glad *you're* alright," Cerrick says, reaching for Njord's hand and kissing the back of it.

"There were many people in that explosion who weren't. Everyone in our party escaped with us, unscathed but for you and Edlyn, but Brandr is still badly shaken." Njord frowns. "So many innocents lost to the rubble. How tragic."

"We have no idea who did this?"

"I think Brandr and Edda do, but they're unwilling to speak freely, especially in front of me. Their two prime agents have been unconscious for the better part of two days, after all. There's no one they trust more than you two."

Cerrick bites back a sigh. Which one of their enemies could it have been? Was it a last ditch effort to retrieve the gemsha? Did word somehow get out that they were carrying one home from the Oslands?

"I can bring him to you, if you want," Njord offers. "I can bring you food, and drink—"

"Bring me Solveig," Cerrick says, "so I can have words with her about letting me out of this bed."

"She's not going to let you up," Njord laughs, but slides off the bed anyway. Cerrick admires the way his hair shines in the light as he exits the room, shutting the door with a soft click. Cerrick glimpses only a dark hallway beyond him. It's amazing, how Njord's hair seems to glow a different color in every different type of light, sometimes favoring the gold highlights, sometimes the red, sometimes the brown.

Cerrick hopes he can reach a day where the greatest things he has to consider are the shades of his husband's hair.

Cerrick dozes comfortably while he waits, not having had a chance to do so since the Oslands, and not in nearly as nice a bed as this. He can do nothing but lie on his back, since he soon discovers all other positions upset his aching muscles. He's warm, the room is warm, and his worry over Edlyn unravels slowly. He takes some much needed rest, knowing it will come sparsely in the near future.

The door creaking open again stirs him. Njord has Brandr, Solveig, Edda, and a tray in the hand not holding the door open. They all file in, dressed in casual clothes that make them appear smaller. Much easier to digest.

"Good that you're finally awake. How are you feeling?" Solveig asks with a warm smile, pulling a stool close to the edge of the bed.

"Directly proportionate to how Edlyn's feeling."

She snorts and rolls her eyes.

"I told you," Njord says. That's another story Cerrick means to drag out of him; how he and Solveig met and became so close so quickly. They laugh like they've been close for years. What transpired in the mere weeks Cerrick was gone?

"Edlyn is fine and going to remain fine," Solveig says. She drags his arm out from under the folds of his cloak to inspect it. He winces when that jostles the other parts of his sore body.

Still, he asks, "How soon can I be up, Pristine Lady Slairr?"

"Using nice titles isn't going to get you out of this bed any sooner than tomorrow. You got quite lucky. There was no tissue damage, no broken bones, but you're badly bruised. I don't need to tell you how tender your back must feel. Besides that, you've been through a terrible ordeal of stress. Your body is crying out for respite."

He groans and flops his head back. Solveig chuckles.

"You don't know what I'd give for a day in bed," she says. "You have the added advantage of being ordered not to move around. All you have to do is sleep."

Cerrick bites back another sigh, placated by the tray of food Njord places beside him before climbing back onto the bed. Cerrick likes that. He likes having him casually close.

Pulling himself upright takes far more effort and pain than he was expecting, and he doesn't hide his cry of exertion as well as he hoped he would. The moment he can go limp and rest his muscles is a much needed relief.

"Rethinking your desire to be up and about?" Solveig asks dryly. "You're not missing anything, don't worry. The rest of the house is quiet as can be. Terribly boring, I assure you. The only event of remote interest is Brandr. He's been entertaining himself by planning logistics—our food and supplies once we return our base to Rinnfell, paying off the crews of those ships you used to keep them quiet about your journey. That sort of thing."

"It's not that Cerrick's afraid of missing something," Edda says. "It's that he wants to be exploring, mapping everything out in his head. Escape routes, points of interest. Old Sun habits die hard."

Cerrick looks at her sharply; she's smiling. It's at least nice to know that Solveig's been filled in on the Phantom's activities. She can only offer them and the rebellion good things.

Instead of dignifying Edda's accusation with an answer, he turns to the tray of food. Gulping down a glass of water soothes his aching throat, and he doesn't even bother with a spoon for the bowl of soup. It's rich, hot, and nearly goes down his shirt as he realizes how weak his arms have been rendered. Njord and Solveig watch with twin expressions of amusement. The bread that goes with the soup is hot and fresh, slathered in butter.

"I don't mean to spoil your meal," Brandr says, scratching the back of his neck like many do when they're nervous, averting his eyes, "but would you like to discuss—you know—"

"Yes," Cerrick says, swallowing quickly so he can answer. "I need to know."

"Okay." Brandr takes a seat in the stuffed armchair right next to the door, sighing as it eases the pressure on his leg. He clutches his cane like Andor would his Pointstaff.

Their eyes meet when Brandr looks up, green piercing gray. His hair is messy, but Cerrick only puts the pieces together when he sees the choking exhaustion in every inch of Brandr's face. He's had to carry the brunt of their collective worries for so long.

Cerrick absorbs a moment of his exhaustion just from that quick glance into his eyes. It's staggering. Edda's hand clasps his shoulder, and Brandr leans into it gratefully. Good. At least he has her.

"I've already told Solveig everything, you don't need to worry," Brandr says. "Oh, I'm glad you like the soup. I made it."

"Of course," Cerrick murmurs.

"I'll start with the most pressing matter, the one we unfortunately can't avoid any longer: Bertie betrayed us, and he was more than likely responsible for that attack on the harbor. Inge swears on their life and the honor of our parents' ashes that they didn't see anything to indicate Bertie and that other man interfered there."

"Carr," Cerrick says. "Edlyn's ex. That was him with Bertie on the ship."

"How he got in contact with Bertie, and how Bertie decided to trust him is beyond me. Well, no, I take that back. Whatever Carr promised him, whether it was money or loyalty, was clearly better than what we were offering."

"Nothing," Cerrick says dryly.

"Indeed." Brandr sighs and runs a hand through his hair. "Well, at least he's dead now. At least they both are. Those poor, innocent souls in the harbor, though. I wish to the Saints they hadn't been victims. Yet another thing Andor will be all too happy to blame us for."

"How could Bertie and Carr have orchestrated the failsafe attack on the harbor after their ships went down?"

"They must've prepared in advance in case we survived their ambush. Speaking of the ambush, I've been thinking about why they might've attacked, and I highly doubt they knew we had the gemsha. I doubt they even know what a gemsha is. I'd wager they'd always planned to attack—that they hung around with agents in the harbor for weeks waiting for us. With Ice connections and threats, they could've easily secured a ship while keeping things quiet. Perhaps even during the time we spent with Bertie, while he cast us fake smiles and petty insults, he was already planning our deaths."

Cerrick's chest tightens, more so now than when he got to bare his teeth at Bertie and watch his burning ship sail away. The ocean has them now. Cerrick will never have to see either of them again.

He'll never have to see Bertie again.

That concept is too daunting to grapple with. Cerrick sighs. "Andor? Did he have any involvement in this?"

"No sign of him yet. Let's pray it stays that way."

Cerrick is inclined to agree, though another part of him dreads the prospect of two of their enemies united against them without any intervention from Andor. He thought Carr was Andor's man, but evidently the bastard simply allied with whoever would likely pay him the most.

Cerrick sighs again. "We'll figure it out," Brandr says quickly. "We don't need to do so today. Solveig promised we can stay here as long as we'd like. Rinnfell isn't safe for us right now. Slairr is the safest place we could be."

Cerrick nods. The sad, sorry faces of Brandr and the others are replaced by Ivan and Inge, who come to Cerrick bearing gifts. The former brings plants that definitely do not belong indoors, the latter brings a begrudging frown. Cerrick appreciates the cursory check in.

Ivan's enthusiasm could of course light up a whole room. Solveig scolds him for getting soil on her carpets, but she's smiling. He looks up at her with thinly veiled awe—Kryc women are tall, and Ivan is short. They make quite the picture next to each other.

Recovery is a slow thing. Cerrick can't imagine what it's like for Edlyn, but even after his first day of mandatory bed rest, sleep only seems to worsen the insistent aches in every part of his body. He suspects, and Solveig affirms that he's not only sore from being thrown to the ground at the harbor—getting slammed against the wall of the gemsha ship when Bertie's ship rammed it is also partly to blame.

Cerrick was too high on adrenaline at the time to notice the pain, but now he's paying for it with days spent groaning in bed. There's no relief to be found other than herbs that wear off quickly, and interchangeable hot-icy cloths on his skin.

Njord watches him with obvious distress. He asks dozens of times what he can do to help, asks Solveig if there's anything stronger she can give Cerrick. She shakes her head, giving Cerrick more leaves to chew on. "His body just needs time to heal itself. The wounds are not ones I can do much for."

Despite his fervent wish to rise from bed, Cerrick can't find the strength to drag himself out of bed until the dawn of the third day. He only manages that with Njord's help. It's more than a little humiliating to need help even getting out of bed, but no one judges him. Only Edlyn would dare, and Edlyn isn't capable of that at the moment—or so he's been told.

His first task out of bed is to familiarize himself with the house, as Edda teased him for. He sets foot into the tight hallways of

Solveig's mansion, the maze they make up. Observes the colorful paintings hung throughout the walls, the breathtakingly high ceilings. Solveig proudly says her wife painted each one, giving him a detailed explanation. Cerrick then searches in vain for a window to look out. His room doesn't have one, the hallways neither.

Struggling to the stair landing finally provides him with a view of Steinberg from high up in the mountaintops, a bittersweet image of Trygg that he hasn't seen in four years. It brings unexpected emotion welling to his eyes. Njord doesn't comment about that either, bless him.

Cerrick's first stop after that is Edlyn's room.

He tried to go there first, but Solveig insisted he walk around first to see how much he could handle. Now that he's proven himself to her, he limps to the room in earnest, ignoring every twinge and sore spot that ignites when he moves. All his pain evaporates when Njord pushes open the door for him and he sees Edlyn laid out motionless in bed.

Immediately he's back on that ship, struggling to convince himself Edlyn is ever going to move again while Brandr tries. He hasn't heard her speak, seen her move since that moment. Cerrick doesn't realize he's swaying until Njord catches him.

"Edlyn, you have a visitor," Solveig says, calmly going to Edlyn's bedside. Njord pulls up a wicker chair for Cerrick, then quietly slips out of the room.

To Cerrick's immense relief, Edlyn finally stirs. She sits up slowly, groaning and groggy, while Solveig fusses over the white bulge of bandages covering her abdomen. "Edlyn," Cerrick breathes. Her eyes land on him, squinted with sleep, but a grin of relief slides onto her face.

"Cerrick."

He's moving before he can think better of it, and Solveig lets him wrap his arms gingerly around his other half. She's warm and alive, clean and bloodless. When he pulls back his hands aren't stained red, and his soul is lighter. Seeing her, touching her has just the effect he knew it would. It's invigorating just to see her smile and know she's okay and going to remain that way. She's a bit ashen, but wouldn't anyone be?

Solveig fusses over Edlyn a bit more, then leaves them alone. "How are you?" Edlyn asks. Cerrick takes in her bedchamber—hers has a huge northern facing window, but otherwise their rooms are the same.

He shrugs. "Sore, achy, but otherwise fine."

"How's your heart?"

"Better now that I know you're okay. I believe my worry over you is what would've done me in, rather than getting slammed against the wall of a ship and the Rinnfell streets."

She scoffs, withdrawing her hand when he goes to grab it. "Sap. I meant with your husband."

He raises an eyebrow. "That's what you want to talk about right now?"

"I want to hear about something other than Brandr's grim report of what happened and see something other than his sad, restless face. Njord has been in and out of here, and I've tried prying anything out of him, but he just smiles and says that's something for you and I to talk about. It's maddening. He's too much of a Saint for his own good."

"Agree with you there."

She hits his hand lightly. "Well? You're already moving about, and I've been confined to this damn bed since I woke. Tell me something interesting so I don't go out of my mind."

"I've only just gotten up myself," Cerrick says defensively. "I wasn't ever on death's doorstep."

She sighs and flops her head back against the pillows, grimacing as she tries to get comfortable. He knows the feeling of trying to find a good position where there isn't one. Tossing and turning, adjusting and shifting and fiddling.

It's made worse by the fact that Njord doesn't sleep beside him at night, doesn't take up all the empty space in that big bed. Of everything, that might be what Cerrick misses most from the dreamworld that was Holbeck.

He tucks away those thoughts and tells Edlyn about the better things—the food Brandr has prepared in Solveig's own kitchen, stealing the cook's limelight. He describes everyone who's come to visit him. Though they've come to visit Edlyn too, he illustrates Ivan's wild grin, Edda's kind smile and the motherly kiss she pressed to his forehead, the hours he and Brandr have spent talking. Cerrick has learned more about him in the past few days than he ever knew.

Cerrick omits the more serious things they've discussed, not wanting to ruin Edlyn's fragile sense of peace just yet. Most recently, Brandr faced the sobering reality that the Order of the Ice will never help them stage a coup. He's still searching for an ally to use in their place.

The five of them alone cannot take on Andor and his loyalists, even with a gemsha. Solveig's forces will help, and with her Cerrick thinks they could perhaps scrape by. But *perhaps* scraping by is not good enough for him or Brandr. Not now, not for the future they intend to build.

And then there is the matter of the gemsha, left to an uncertain fate in the harbor. Saints willing, it survived the attack. They won't know for certain until they return to Rinnfell and see if all their hard work was for naught.

Brandr's soft voice, whether he's recounting something pleasant as cooking or unpleasant as the woes of their rebellion, has become the sound Cerrick falls asleep to. Brandr regales him with the funnier tales of his five years in the Ice, the good memories he has of Andor, the first time he met Edda.

Edda has become a frequent topic of discussion for them both. She visits Cerrick too, but Edlyn reveals how much time Edda's been spending here with her. Cerrick still wonders about the hidden dark depths beneath her sweet exterior, considering the glimpses he's had so far. Punching the wall in the Oslands, the quiet danger that hides behind her makeup and silk.

Passing Brandr in the hallway on the way back to his own chambers, Cerrick notes that he's swathed in a billowing gray cloak instead of his usual green one.

Cerrick jokes that this cloak looks like something stolen from Edlyn. It has none of the characteristic Kryc decorations hanging from the front, it's simply a replacement for his green one. Laundry day, Brandr explains. Solveig and Ivan collaborated to quickly build a drying room with heat provided by the dust of Ivan's red flowers. Solveig is already mindblown by Os ingenuity.

Of course Ivan brought jars of the red petals across the sea, hidden away in his sack of plants, both of which are thriving now. Ivan is disappointed that the misbehaving plant survived the voyage, and he's threatened to put it out in the cold to pressure it further. His favorite plant is doing well, which he's deadly pleased about, and keeps it on display in his guest room for all to see.

Cerrick thanks his questionable priorities if it means he gets to have his cloak dried and no longer smelling like fire smoke within one day.

IN CERRICK'S SPARE moments, he devotes ample amounts of time to pondering Bertie's death. He can't wrap his head around his feelings about it, let alone the feelings he's expected to have. What *is* the tightening in his chest when he considers the fact that Bertie has finally joined Saint Renalie in hell?

He never has to answer to Bertie or make his dreaded payments again. He never has to fear walking the streets of southwest Rinnfell again. Cerrick and Edlyn can return to their apartment in peace.

Despite all that, it's no lie that Cerrick spent a long time in this man's service. He hated him, loathed him, but he considered him a brother in many ways.

An icy blanket of shame lays across his shoulders as Cerrick cries for him, mourns him in the deepest pits of his soul. Yet the tears come no matter how much he berates himself, wondering *why do you cry for him?* He doesn't have an answer. All he has, for the first time in a long time, is emotion.

He still doesn't let anyone see him like that. Good thing Edlyn is bedbound.

BRANDR IS SITTING ON the edge of Cerrick's recovery bed, sharing a memory of Edda from his endless supply. This one is about the time she took him to her house in Burfell. He's smiling, fondness plain in his eyes and on his face, and Cerrick can't help himself any longer.

"Why do you turn her down?" Cerrick asks.

"What do you mean?" Brandr turns his head, but he can't hide the break in his voice.

"Brandr, please. We're both too smart for this. Don't act like I don't know. Like even the Saints could see how you feel for her."

"I would like to think I have a little bit of privacy."

Cerrick laughs. "Not since you decided to start a rebellion with us. Tell me, why do you not just accept what she offers? What you both want?"

"You and Njord both want each other," Brandr retorts, facing him again. "Why are you not together all the time, happy as could be?"

"Because we have things to work through. Because I lied in Holbeck. He deserves better than that, than me." For a moment, emotion consumes him, and tears threaten to rise. He and Njord have avoided that conversation since Cerrick woke here. They don't want to disrupt the peaceful, joyous reunion they've shared on Kryc soil, and Cerrick doesn't want to face his own crimes.

He looks up from toying with the blanket to find Brandr smiling. "You see why Edda and I cannot be together."

"What? What have you ever done to her that remotely resembles my situation with Njord?"

Brandr shakes his head. A strand of hair falls in his eyes, making him look boyish and sly. "It's not what I've done to her, it's what I've done to others. My monstrosity in the Ice cannot be forgiven."

Anger boils in Cerrick more forcefully than he expected. He recalls Edda's frown every time Brandr lets go of her hand, every time he gently lets her down with a smile that hurts more than comforts. With effort, he sits up to face Brandr fully. "Does that mean I'm irredeemable?" he snaps. "Edlyn? Evan? Kara?"

Brandr casts his eyes away.

"Bertie is the only one among us who we won't forgive," Cerrick says. "Fuck him and his father and everything they did to us, every command we carried out for them, every coin we paid. But we exist with everyone else. We forgive, we tolerate.

"We don't have morals, us Ice members. What we are there never leaves our blood. Death doesn't faze us. What happens in that townhouse stays with us forever, but what we do have a choice about is how we react after we leave. How we live our lives.

"We hate Bertie because of how he treated us. We want revenge. He hates us because we left him. We don't hate him because he derives pleasure from others' pain. We do too, on occasion."

Brandr hangs his head, sighing in quiet resignation.

"Who cares if you're a monster?" Cerrick asks. "Edda certainly doesn't. We can't change our past, but we can control our future."

"She's everything I'm not," Brandr says. "I don't deserve her. She deserves better than me."

Cerrick has had those same thoughts many times, during too many sleepless nights to count. "She loves you, Brandr. I don't know what you're waiting for, because nothing's going to change. Your feelings won't, and her acceptance won't. You're fighting only with yourself."

Brandr sighs. "Being so close to her is a struggle. This rebellion has only made me fall more deeply for her. When I only had to see her at council meetings, when our paths crossed in the palace, that was enough. More than enough. It was almost too much to handle, seeing her smile at me. I wondered how she could. What she saw when she looked at me that wasn't a hideous beast."

"Well, I can see that it kills her for you to turn her away over and over again, knowing you feel the same. You wear it on your face, and you don't exactly hide it when you grab her for support."

Brandr smiles wearily. "I need her, just like you need him. You must agree we're both handling the situation rather selfishly."

Cerrick sighs, remembering every moment of Njord's smile, his touch, every time he's eaten up the glow in his eyes. Cerrick doesn't deserve any of that, but he takes it anyway. "Yes."

A moment of mutual brooding silence goes by before Cerrick speaks again, clearing his thoughts of blue eyes and a rumbling voice and endless warmth. "There'll be no better time than now to tell her. We're not going to have this peace for a long while. I would take advantage of that if I were you. I don't know what you're waiting for. Edda waits for you."

Brandr laughs softly, standing. "No, no. I don't want to sully your pain and Edlyn's by creating my own joy in the midst of your suffering."

Cerrick scoffs. "That's your excuse now?"

Brandr's hand finds Cerrick's shoulder and squeezes lightly. "Be the braver one of us. Fix things with your husband and let me look on from afar. Let one of us have what he wants, at least. Let one of us be happy."

Cerrick doesn't know if it's an admission, a request, a prayer, or a plea. He just nods, squeezing Brandr's hand on his shoulder. "Could you fetch Njord for me?" he asks in a rush before Brandr is quite out the door.

Brandr smiles back. "I won't have to go far. He's always waiting nearby whenever someone's in here. I can't tell if it's protectiveness or an innocent desire to get back to you as quickly as possible."

That warms Cerrick's chest through, and he's powerless against smiling like a lovesick fool. He supposes he is.

Indeed, it takes only seconds for Njord to take Brandr's place. He sits on the right edge of Cerrick's bed, hand on the covers. "You wanted me?"

I always do. "I think it's time we talked," Cerrick says.

Njord sighs. "The words every lover loves to hear. No, no, don't make that face—I agree. I find it difficult to bear this false perfection just as much."

Cerrick nods, taking a ragged breath. "How about we start with this?" He pauses, but there's no longer any hint of hesitation in his body. "I will never lie to you again."

Njord's face falls. Cerrick wants to wipe away the look of exhaustion and distrust that's resided on his face ever since Cerrick left Holbeck. "That's a dangerous thing to promise me."

Cerrick resists the urge to curl his arms around Njord's neck like he used to. He doesn't have the right. "It's what you deserve. If it's what it will take to earn your trust back, it's what I will gladly do, no matter the effort it might take." He remembers all too well the way Njord shuddered and put his head in his hands in the Ice townhouse.

That horror is imprinted on the inside of Cerrick's eyelids every time he closes them, impossible to forget.

Cerrick says, "I have hurt you...Saints only know how much." He'll never know how Njord felt the night he left the fire on for Cerrick, only for him never to show up. Cerrick never had to wade through the confusion, fear, and anger of riding to Rinnfell to search for him only to find out that he left of his own will, that he's not who Njord ever thought he was. That Njord is probably still stuck in the reeds of it, knee deep in muddled water.

"I can only guess how much more I'm going to hurt you by asking you to trust me again," Cerrick adds. His voice is thick, his heart is heavy. He can't take his eyes off the covers. "I'm sorry. Fuck, Njord, I don't know how to show you how much. I'm sorry I'm brash and don't think about how what I do is going to hurt those I love."

Njord takes his hand. "Cerrick, look at me. The only way you could me further is if you refused to love me anymore. Do you know what I see in you?"

A monster, Cerrick thinks.

"I see nothing," Njord says. "Everything."

Cerrick closes his eyes. He's weak to Njord's voice. Njord's words are his strength, the vice Cerrick is addicted to. He doesn't care how much it hurts him, how many knives it takes—he needs to hear the sweet warmth of that voice one more time. Always one more time.

Njord continues, "To me, it does not matter who you were before we met, nor who you are now. All that matters to me is that you love me and are willing to try again. It is you who is the block between us, not me. I wanted to be angry at you after I learned what you had withheld, but I could not be. Your choice made too much sense."

"What?"

"You were a spy who was trained not to trust. You were betrayed by two of your former bosses, both men you looked up to. That teaches distrust. You have alluded to a parentage which fostered a further need for distrust. In no world would you and I have had a marriage free of trust problems."

Njord smiles sheepishly. "I am not without my own meddling issues, Cerrick, no matter what you believe. I found it impossible to blame you for repeating the choice you'd been taught. You'd never before faced a situation where you wanted to choose differently—how could you know to do otherwise?

"Nevertheless, I knew distance was necessary. When you asked me to accompany you to the Oslands, I could not bear to see the anguish on your face each time you looked at me. Refusing was a selfishness on my part."

Cerrick doesn't think Njord could be selfish if he tried. He turns his head, trying to find shelter from the storm. Njord must read this as reluctance and disbelief, for he says, "Do you not think I deserve what I want?"

"You do," Cerrick says immediately. "Everything you could ever want and more. You deserve it all, darling."

"Well, I want you. So I deserve you. Simple as that. I want to start again." He pushes back Cerrick's bangs from his forehead to brush his lips against it, feather soft. His hand lingers on Cerrick's cheek, unbearably warm like storm rain. Cerrick finds himself speechless. "I trust you with all that I am. I hope, with time, you can learn to trust me with all that you are as well. We will not be perfect, yet we must try."

A lump forms in Cerrick's throat. "I—"

"Shh," Njord murmurs, tapping Cerrick's temple. "Quiet that loud head of yours. The only words I want to hear out of your mouth are sweet ones."

He's so close. Their faces are inches apart, and it's so quiet. So warm. So peaceful. Cerrick hasn't known a calm, easy stillness like this since—Saints, he doesn't know how long. He's rapidly losing focus with how close Njord's beautiful eyes are. "Can I kiss you?" Cerrick murmurs.

Njord smiles, some of the light returning to his eyes. "My love, you never have to ask."

Cerrick smiles as giddy euphoria rises in his chest, leaning in to kiss him. As his eyelids shut and their lips touch, Cerrick thanks every Saint that he's able to do this again. That everything has not gone to shit—well, at least with Njord. Cerrick thought he lost Njord forever. Like hell he's ever going to do anything to mess it up again.

Njord makes a soft noise of contentment against his mouth and pushes closer. It's so sweet, so achingly tender that Cerrick doesn't know what to do with himself. He wraps a hand around the back of Njord's neck.

Though his arm twinged with pain with every movement when he first woke in this bed, that pain has now faded to a dull sort of discomfort. He's willing to bear every ache as long as needed if it keeps Njord this close.

He has a comfortable plush headboard against his back and head, and every time Njord kisses him a little harder, pushes him a little more, he gets pushed back into that softness. Njord pulls him forward into his arms, and Cerrick finds softness there, too, with just the right kind of firmness in his chest and shoulders. Cerrick is caught between two wonderful, painless worlds, one of which is rapidly dissolving his focus. The heat of Njord's mouth makes his head fog up, like being caught in a storm at sea.

Cerrick meant for this to be nothing more than an innocent kiss taking advantage of rare alone time and celebrating the sweet relief of sorting their problems out. But it quickly fades into the heavy touch of Njord's hands on his shoulders, warm and firm, the heated passion of their mouths together.

"Cerrick," Njord breathes. "My love. My sun. You are the most beautiful man I have ever met. The way the light casts into your eyes reminds me of a sunset covered in thick clouds. Your hair is like wheat, your freckles like stars, your skin like the sand of Aeton's beaches. I never got to show you those beaches. I would've liked to. I would kiss you on the sand."

Cerrick doesn't mean to laugh, but he can't help it. He knows the awkward compliments are born from Kryc being Njord's second language, but it does pull him out of the moment, even if Njord's passion isn't inhibited. He punctuates his words with kisses that burn.

Saints above, Cerrick has missed this.

"Tell me in Aeton," Cerrick says when he can find the breath. Aeton, where Njord can express his thoughts more naturally.

Njord looks at him strangely for a moment, but then speaks again. Cerrick doesn't understand a word except *my love* and *I love you;* he realizes he's never heard Njord speak Aeton for more than a few sentences at a time. The language is beautiful. It's deep—at least, Njord's voice is deep—and the words flow into each other so smoothly.

The only sound in the room is Njord speaking what Cerrick presumes are sweet nothings to him. Cerrick is warm right down to his toes, Njord's arms around his waist, Njord pressed close to him with his lips on his neck, trailing down slowly like he's learning a new path.

He's murmuring words that dissolve into nothing. Cerrick reaches for him, ever closer, and shivers. Warm. He's so warm. The light from the lamps is golden, Njord is golden, and he's *so fucking warm*. Cerrick dreads to think of the cold outside.

Cerrick doesn't need to understand him. He understands Njord's meaning; *you are the sun and the stars and all the elements of the world, because just as they are vital to my life, so are you.* The moon, the crops, the sea and the beaches, the warmth of a summer day and the chill of a winter's night.

Your love is an ember, Cerrick thinks as Njord lays their mouths together again, though he doesn't have the breath, mental capacity, or the desire to interrupt Njord's ministrations and say so aloud. If he could say it in a language that Njord didn't understand, he would. The freedom of saying something your lover won't understand, even if they already know the sentiment—it's a joy, an escape from vulnerability.

Cerrick thinks, *You are the beginnings of a fire, the first stirrings of a storm. Possibly explosive, but never to me. To those all around us, but never me. Do you have any idea how that feels? To watch you and know you have the power to destroy the world if you had the mind for it, but you won't? And even if you did, you would hold me close so that I would be safe from your destruction?*

Njord doesn't understand his own power, that's the beauty of it. Njord doesn't have hesitations holding him back except those which are totally unfounded. If he knew his own power, truly nothing would hold him back.

Cerrick finds the frame of mind to remind himself of what this means. "W-what about the Order of the Phantom? You're staying with us? What about the international implications? An Aeton prince aiding Kryc rebels? You could get your family in trouble."

"I do not care. Yours is a worthy cause. I care only that I remain by your side." Njord pushes Cerrick back against the bed, moving like he means to clamber over him.

Cerrick reluctantly breaks their kiss, leaning his forehead against Njord's. "Are you sure about this?"

"Are you not?" Njord's voice is low, heavy, all breath. His accent is thick, his words slightly slurred as he gets used to speaking Kryc again. "Are your injuries disagreeing with you?"

"I'm sure, and I'm fine." He might not be healed yet, but he's sure as hell not going to let that stop them. "I just—" Cerrick doesn't know how to say he's still not sure if everything is alright between them, and he doesn't want to jeopardize things any further. They've only done this a handful of times, and never before have they done it in Kryos. Cerrick doesn't want to tarnish a second of this.

Njord smiles. His eyes are glistening, his hair framed by the dim light. "I know," he says. "I had those same worries for a while, too. But everything is well. We are—we are alright, yes? We have talked. We are okay."

Cerrick smiles, wrapping both arms around his neck and clasping his hands there. Njord has such a simple way of looking at the world. Cerrick used to think of it as naivety, but now he sees the truth: positivity. A determination to look at the world as if the sun shines on all parts of it, on everyone. "Yes."

Njord kisses him again. His weight over Cerrick is staggering, and it doesn't take long to lose himself in it. Hot touches, panting breath, moaned gasps of Cerrick's name—he could never last. He flies over the edge quickly. Njord's handsome face above him is more than enough alone.

After, Njord falls easily into a deep sleep, thankfully one without snoring. That is the one and perhaps only part of him Cerrick could do without.

Cerrick's arms loop loosely around Njord's neck, his head laid to Njord's heart. The rising and falling of his chest is lulling like the rocking of a ship. Despite that, Cerrick has trouble falling asleep. Not because he's restless or uncomfortable, but because he's happy to watch the peace on Njord's face.

Cerrick could be content to lie in this bed forever. He's awash in a bone deep comfort. He's warm and heavy, tangled up with Njord and just drowsy enough to be comfortable. Njord's body is warmer than any red Os flower, and it's on top of his broad chest that Cerrick finally drifts asleep.

CHAPTER TWELVE

It's a whole two weeks before Edlyn is well enough to leave the house.

The first time she's strong enough to get out of bed—or rather, the soonest Solveig lets her—is a momentous occasion, one the whole household celebrates. Solveig's wife Tyra finally graces them with her presence.

Brandr cooks a whole spread to celebrate the four steps into the hallway Edlyn takes before Solveig sends her back to bed. They eat a salad so fresh Cerrick can hardly believe it, along with decadent steaks, crisp potatoes, and cold berry juice. They share it all over a long table in the downstairs dining room.

Solveig had to carry Edlyn down the stairs after receiving dire threats about what would happen if she was left out. Cerrick could hear her all the way down the hall. Her body may be in disrepair, but her mind is as fierce as ever.

Solveig's dining hall is huge and airy, the walls painted tan like the rest of the house and painted gold by lamp and chandelier light. The floors are marble, and the whole room has a homely feel to it.

A fire burns in a giant brick hearth, and Ivan's flowers do the rest of the job of heating the room up. They sit around a long rectangular table adorned with golden chairs, their silverware sparkling in front of them. Portions of the ceiling are windows that offer them a view of the gray sky above, the rainclouds pouring down while they're safe inside.

This is an oligarch's house. Cerrick marvels at the fact that there are three oligarchs from opposite ends of the country all sitting at one table. One doesn't see this sort of thing outside the palace.

Njord compliments Brandr's cooking with kind remarks, but he grumbles that the fruit juice isn't comparable to the *bura* of Aeton. Cerrick is inclined to agree.

Just the mention of it hits him with a wave of longing for the serenity of Aeton. The indescribable beauty of the Middle Forests, the smiles of the people, the refreshing warmth of the sun. The only sun Cerrick wants to be associated with ever again.

Thinking of Aeton delivers him a sharp ache, but Njord slips an arm around his waist under their cloaks while the others are distracted, and the ache eases. As long as he has this piece of Aeton with him, he'll be fine.

"What do your family think of this?" Cerrick whispers amidst loud laughter from the other end of the table. The color has returned to Edlyn's cheeks, and she's happy as can be listening to Ivan's terrible jokes while rain pounds outside. She's also making fast friends with Tyra, a shy but kind Trygg art graduate who finishes Solveig's sentences for her.

"I told them I'd be gone indefinitely when I left," Njord replies, pulling him closer. Cerrick buries his face in Njord's neck just because he can. "They know that I'm here to stay for the time being. I've written them. And if you dare start feeling guilty about not writing me to tell me where you were, we're going to have words."

Cerrick smiles, kissing the skin he can reach.

"The point is my family love me, and they love you. I'm not needed in Holbeck right now. We're in peacetime, and Rosalia can handle my duties. She loves having something to do. My family is probably eager to be without me for a bit. They encouraged me to go, told me that anything was better than watching me sit around moping."

Before he can find a reply, Cerrick realizes the conversation at the table has ceased. He drags his face out of Njord's neck to find the others staring at them, some bothering to hide their smirks more than others. Cerrick's gut reaction is to scoot away, but a moment's hesitation lets Njord adjust his arm around his waist to pull him even closer.

"What?" Njord murmurs in his ear, a surefire way to get Cerrick to agree to anything. "What do we have to hide? I, for one, am happy to be able to show you off."

He's right, but it still takes effort to keep still and resume the meal with nothing more than an embarrassed smile. Cerrick can feel the heat rise to his cheeks, and the way Edlyn's eyes and smirk drag over him doesn't help. He doesn't want to pretend he and Njord are alone. He's thrilled to be at a table of the only people he can trust, and he wouldn't banish Edlyn's presence for almost anything in the world. But imagining it's just the two of them does help him relax.

Their latest message from Evan instructs them all to be prepared, for Solveig is about to be ousted—unless Andor has been leading Evan on with hints and half hidden meanings. Cerrick's stomach drops. At least Evan's safety seems secured; Andor trusts him and likely underestimates him as a young kid.

That day in Solveig's house is a grim, silent one, where they can do nothing but wait. That very evening, Solveig gets an official summons to the palace for a meeting with the council of oligarchs. Cerrick has never been in the presence of an oligarch when they've received such a message. Watching Solveig unravel that long scroll tied with a fancy ribbon is chilling.

She rides out just as night falls, with a sheet of snow falling on top of her. She bids them wish her luck. Cerrick doesn't sleep a wink that night, and come morning, all the occupants of the house sit around the hearth under blankets, waiting for Solveig to return.

She does, soaked from the rain, dripping onto the wood floor. She spends an hour bathing and warming up in her rooms, alone with her servants to tend her and her wife to speak to her. It's an endless wait Cerrick only manages to get through thanks to the mindless swipes of Njord's thumb over his hand under their cloaks. When Solveig descends the steps with a defeated expression and a sad smile, all of their spirits fall.

Either Andor is growing stupid or stupidly confident, giving away his plans to the shiny new oligarch Evan. He was never so careless around Cerrick, who always had to fight for even a hint of personal information, a hint about what Andor was thinking, what the next job might entail.

Edda and Brandr hug Solveig tightly; three grim faces united in injustice of the highest degree. It's a strange sight, both melancholy and joyous, fuel for the fire that they'll stoke until it boils over and explodes.

Solveig says Andor didn't immediately bring in her successor, didn't parade around what he'd done like he did with Edda. Solveig's determination to best Andor is quiet but fierce, her hand curled around her Pointstaff like she dreams of driving it into his chest. Her back is straight as a rod, her eyes cast into the flames.

The first time Edlyn's able to leave the house, Cerrick gets a taste of just desserts. His worry is slowly being replaced by a desire to fuck with her, to restore some humor to a humorless situation. It's their way of coping. The alternative is shutting down completely in the face of horror.

So, he offers to race her from the door of Solveig's home to the carriage carrying them into town. "Fuck you, I'm not suicidal," she tells him, but the heat in her voice is replaced by a laugh.

Solveig lives at the top of a mountain. The only path is an icy winding road. In the winter it's treacherous to traverse no matter what, but Solveig says not to worry, she's lived here enough years to have bested it. The only hard part will be getting to the carriages without turning an ankle in the snow.

Edlyn took the cane Solveig offered to make walking more bearable, and has been practicing with it around the hallway. Now, when Cerrick hears clicking and clopping just outside his door, he doesn't know if it's Edlyn or Brandr. Those two walk side by side now, talking, taking their time getting to the carriages with the leisure of royalty. Solveig and Edda follow at a moderate pace. Ivan and Inge and Tyra opted to stay.

Cerrick gets his race with Njord instead, a fast paced chase reminiscent of the hunt in the forest outside Holbeck. This time, he allows himself to be caught just that little bit faster so he can get thoroughly kissed against a towering tree before the others arrive.

Cerrick is bundled up in layers of wool *beneath* his cloak, with gloves to add, but all that doesn't banish the bite of the mountainous cold. Only the clutch of Njord's arms around his waist, hot and thick like freshly cast steel from a forge, and his mouth like liquid fire can warm him.

Then Edlyn and Brandr arrive with the rhythmic clicks of their canes—no element of surprise for those two, not anymore—and Cerrick and Njord pull apart to try and hide what they were just doing. Edlyn rolls her eyes and jerks her thumb toward the carriage.

Snow begins to fall as soon as they settle in, so Cerrick gets to watch it rain down within the safety of the warm, dry, carriage interior. He shares this carriage with Edlyn, Njord, and Brandr, the other women in the other. Cerrick notices the way Edlyn winces with every bump, the way she digs her teeth into her lip and looks out the window to hide her pain from the others.

He takes her hand under the folds of their cloaks. She squeezes back, not just in companionship but in necessity, an outlet for her pain. He bears every bone crushing squeeze happily.

His focus is on discretion, as it often is when he and the Phantom go out in public. Solveig, who has pledged herself fully to their cause, promised they wouldn't have to worry. Slairr is famously willing to challenge the government and call out its corrupt ways, and they're as loyal to Solveig as the Burfellans are to Edda. Wherever she goes, they'll follow.

While it's true Cerrick never met more ordinary citizens who opposed the government than he did at Trygg, he's not willing to wager his safety on the assumption that everyone in Slairr is. The idea that he can be safe just by being in Solveig's presence is nice but unrealistic.

As they descend into Steinberg on a winding road, his guard goes back up and his smiles melt into something to be unveiled when they're safely back in Solveig's mansion.

They start small, arriving calmly at the Steinberg library. Cerrick looks fondly to the clocktower across town, standing proud and tall, and the distant Trygg campus hidden behind the carriage's steamed up windows.

"I would like to take Njord to see Trygg," he says as they climb out of the carriage. The Steinberg library catches his eye, a tall building of waving and curving roof panels and asymmetric windows. He cranes his neck looking up at it.

People wave amiably to Solveig as they recognize her. Cerrick tries to ignore the way that little bit of notability prickles at him, even if it's friendly.

Brandr shrugs. "I don't see why not." Edlyn exits the carriage with Solveig and Edda's help, getting her cane beneath her. "We'll be in the library a while anyway. A respite from the cold. Take your time, be careful, meet us back here when you're ready."

And so Cerrick takes Njord's hand, tugs their hoods up, and guides him across town toward the place where Cerrick spent his first two glorious years of freedom away from his gloomy Grenivik home.

He's all too aware of the time they might be wasting by taking such an errand—Cerrick is eager to get back to Rinnfell, dethrone Andor as soon as possible, but he knows what Solveig would say. It's been only two weeks since the battle in the sea, the explosion in Rinnfell. Edlyn is still recovering, and Andor sure as hell isn't going anywhere.

Now that they've repaired things, Cerrick can use Njord for support the way he's always wanted to. He no longer has to plaster a smile on to cover his pain. He can cry in Njord's arms if he wants to. He can use Njord as a column of strength, lean against him and know he can hold Cerrick's weight. That alone is enough to put air back into his lungs.

Cerrick never guessed he'd wind up here, showing his husband the college he waxed poetic about in their Holbeck rooms. Most of the buildings here are free for public access, such as the library and the coffeeshops.

Cerrick points up at his old dorm building, noting the window he'd look out from every night. His roommates were lovers, and he chose to leave them be more nights than not. Banishing himself to the peace of the library or the Trygg coffeehouse while his roommates made love wasn't the worst thing in the world.

Njord insists on kissing him against the outer wall of the library. At Cerrick's pleased but disgruntled outcry, Njord shrugs and says, "I find it productive and necessary to kiss you against the side of every library we come across. We're about to meet Brandr in another one, so I'll have another chance there. I'd like to make a tradition of it."

Cerrick can only stare. There's more of a fiend in his delightful husband than he realized.

He rambles about every Trygg memory that comes to mind as he and Njord stroll leisurely through the campus grounds, Njord's arm warm around his shoulder.

When Cerrick pauses for breath, pauses to look at the tall red buildings around him, the foggy windows and blue roofs he still sometimes sees in his dreams, Njord speaks. "It's so fascinating to be allowed a glimpse of this. Your past life, your life before me, before any Order took you over."

"There was a lot more to my life before the Orders than that," Cerrick says, leaning his head into the crook of Njord's neck. By the way Njord pulls him closer and kisses the top of his head, he doesn't mind this frequent arrangement one bit. "Saints hope I'll never have an occasion to take you to my childhood home. That is a dark and dismal place. I swore long ago never to return."

They walk for a bit longer, savoring the peace of anonymity in a crowd of strangers, savoring the thrill of being able to touch like normal lovers. Cerrick can almost forget they're merely breaking from their rebellion for a few minutes' quiet.

They walk back to the Steinberg library, and the kiss Njord gives him against the side of it drains every thought from his head.

In that moment, he's glad he doesn't have to go anywhere except Solveig's house to eat and rest. He remembers fondly that glorious day he spent at Brandr's home before the rebellion truly began. When it was being formed before their eyes. When they were nurturing it into something real.

For now, Cerrick can forget the world.

The Steinberg library is blessedly warm, thick with incense. Its high ceilings arc and dip in height, and the carpet is soft beneath his boots, stained with coffee and mud in some places.

Edlyn is sitting alone at a table by the window. Brandr and Edda are seated side by side, caught up in their own world. They have a plan for drumming up support in Kryos laid out before them. Kara is their agent on the foreign side of things, but international support will mean nothing without domestic success.

Discreetly asking around for others who are itching for a rebellion, a desire to see Andor removed from power...word spreads, and word goes a long way. A simple conversation in a tavern can mean the difference between success and failure.

"Secrecy is imperative right now," Edda is saying quietly, "but once we emerge into the light, we'll need to spread our propaganda and recruit more than ever before. That won't change even if...things don't go as planned at the palace."

When Njord and Cerrick sidle up beside Edlyn, she acknowledges them with a kind if exhausted smile. "Had a nice stroll, did you?"

"Stop making it sound like we have an assignation every time we're alone in public," Cerrick says as he and Njord seat themselves across from her. "What have you found?"

Edlyn slides the book she has open across the table to him. "This was Edda's idea. To..." She taps the book.

After reading only a few sentences, he understands.

They're here to build a new country.

Njord hums, reading along with him.

"They're over there working on making this a reality," Edlyn says, pointing at the oligarchs, "while I'm supposed to be examining the history of Kryos and defining Sigrid and Erika's vision. What of theirs we should keep, what needs to be changed. Can you help me sift through these books?"

She speaks as if they're discussing the details of a fine dinner instead of the new era of a country that's been through six rebellions before. Cerrick steels himself. "Yes. Of course."

And so, for the rest of the snowy afternoon, the six of them sit against the windows in the library and drink coffee, reading books on Kryc history and the sixth rebellion. Between the town, the books, the coffee, and the smell of a library, Cerrick swears he's back in college. He studied hard the last rebellion, the way Sigrid and Erika formed their laws. All that knowledge comes rushing back now.

Njord largely stays out of it, saying, "It's your country you're building, I don't want to influence you," though he does proudly proclaim this is the most he's ever learned about Kryc history. Not even being a foreign prince afforded him this much. Cerrick can't bring himself to stop talking about it; this law and that, the dates Erika and Sigrid made this declaration and that decree.

Soon both Njord and Edlyn are staring at him with equal expressions of fond awe, and the other table has quieted down to listen to him. That attention, that delight on others' faces just from hearing him talk, isn't something he's used to. It makes Cerrick flush to know that he's appreciated so.

Edlyn pillows her chin on her hand at a lull in his rambling, flipping mindlessly through her book. "Is this how it started, too? Sigrid and Erika sitting at a table here, heads together, crafting their new country?"

"I doubt it," Cerrick says. "But it's a nice thought." The more he thinks about it, the easier it is to imagine: two girls not much older than him, in as fierce and committed a love as he is, planning their rebellion so that it doesn't explode in their faces.

That unfortunate irony is that it's a bit too late for the Order of the Phantom. They have a limited amount of time before the whole country knows what they're trying to do, and they must scramble to salvage that which has already been ruined. Bertie and Carr's deaths were lucky.

Burn down, build up. Right now they're drawing up the plans for their creation, and Edda's eyes shine at the mere discussion of it.

After minutes, days, hours, so many weeks of mulling this rebellion over in his mind, Cerrick finds the proper words to say.

"The people need a governing body they know will not betray them the first chance they get. Or at least, a government they can trust not to do so." He interlocks his fingers and rests his chin atop them. "Transparency is the key. No more secret Orders to spy on other countries, on the people within ours. No secret investigations into crime and rebellion. If the people have a complaint, or if we have a complaint, we'll say so. But when both sides allow feelings to fester, unchecked and unaddressed, that's when rebellions stir. That's when organizations like the Order of the Ice are founded."

"No private organizations?" Edlyn asks skeptically. "What if we have international problems? Other countries may not be so keen on our transparent pacifist policy. Other powers might simply take advantage of it and attack."

"I didn't say we couldn't keep defenses," Cerrick says. "Just that sneaking around and hiding things from our citizens has always blown up in our face. With a new approach, we'll keep our era alive for a little longer."

"That's what they all said, I'm sure," Edlyn says quietly. "I can imagine the Thorpes here, drafting the Thorpe Code, swearing that with seven people splitting the power and the land into equal portions, with the system to vote each other in and out, nothing could go wrong."

"You're not wrong. In fact, you're almost certainly right. But their system was not always bad, and nor will ours be. Just as they did, I have faith in this."

Edlyn smiles. "Who will rule in this supposed system?"

"We keep the system of separate dukedom rulers," Cerrick says immediately. Of this, he has been the surest. That part of Kryos is good at its heart, when managed correctly. "We'll use a different name than oligarch—something less intimidating. Dukes, maybe. Lords. Underlords.

"They'll rule with distinct supervision, and we'll implement balances to ensure they're not dealing in the darkness like Duchess Skad. We'll hold them accountable, and they'll rule beneath royalty. Two monarchs with ceremonial powers. Corruption lies within power, as it always has and always will, but there are ways to curb that. We will put greater power into the courts systems. We'll restore faith in prosecutions."

Edlyn raises an eyebrow. "This land hasn't had royalty for almost three hundred years. Crowns are out of style."

"There's much more to royalty than fashion and jewelry. Just take Aeton for an example." Cerrick glances at Njord, who's been sitting quietly through all of this. "With all of Aeton's royalty, all the land held beneath one person, they've never had a problem. Aeton is known as easy and reliable to negotiate with. Never even changed its name. You'll see them as a consistent ally of the land we call Kryos through all its rebellions and wars."

"By that logic, we'd always have to be an ally," Njord interrupts. "To the existing government or the rebellious side. And we've not always been a peaceful nation—you're not counting the civil war we had with the Ressegal territory that resulted in it separating from us."

"Even so, Aeton is so rarely engaged in conflict, and your wars are never as messy as ours." Cerrick lightly taps Njord's mouth to shut him up.

Edlyn asks, "And who, exactly, would serve as this royalty? Who would lord over the dukes? Who would hold the integrity of the country?"

Solveig, Edda, and Brandr began listening long ago, but they remained silent throughout Cerrick and Edlyn's discussion of the future. No doubt they'll have a detailed conversation about all the possibilities later. But now, a sort of quiet chill travels through the room, like the howl of wind drifting through a window on an otherwise silent night. Cerrick risks a glance at Edda. She's smiling with her fist clenched in victory.

Again, Cerrick wonders about Sigrid and Erika in their days of planning, what those first fragile days of rebellion must've looked like.

"What about you two?" Edda suggests. "Cerrick and Edlyn, king and queen of our new nation."

A pit opens in Cerrick's stomach. "I, uh."

"You don't want the job?" Edlyn asks. "None of you?"

Brandr and Solveig are smiling at them. "I sure as hell don't want to leave my home," Solveig says. "I'm happy to keep my position in the new era if the people will have me."

Brandr and Edda murmur assent. "The only question is how you feel about it," Brandr says. "A large responsibility, more eyes on you than ever before, but the opportunity to enact change. To hold power and use it for good. What do you think?"

Cerrick takes Edlyn's hand. Their eyes lock. They don't need words.

"We'd be honored," Cerrick says. "We won't let you down. We'll lead this nation."

Brandr rises half out of his chair to clap them both on the shoulder. Pride glows in his eyes.

"Does this mean I get to see you in formal clothes all the time?" Njord rumbles, startling a laugh out of Cerrick. "I fear my poor heart may never recover." He pillows his chin on his hand and smiles. "My lord. My king."

Ever since Andor's betrayal, Cerrick has been floating in a state of numbness, content to let the oligarchs take the lead. He's been struggling to find his footing with Njord, with his place within the rebellion, with his new role in the rapidly changing world…yet now, for the first time, that footing is becoming sturdier. The fog is clearing.

Cerrick will be a passive bystander no longer. He is finally ready.

CHAPTER THIRTEEN

They continue to find their respite from rebellion and worry. Walking the grounds of Solveig's estate between bursts of rain, feasting at her table, and doing nothing but rest and sleep and eat have all been wonderful. However, the respite morphed quickly into boredom, and Cerrick has been relying on Evan's letters and Brandr's stories as sources of entertainment.

In Evan's latest letter, he described unrest in Fura, demands throughout the dukedom for Brandr's reinstatement as oligarch. They have no problem with Evan, but Brandr was their lord for a long time, and his sudden departure came as a shock. Andor would never sanction his return, but Brandr doesn't want his old job back. He's of much more use to them here. Plus, Cerrick must consider what Edda said—that Brandr didn't intend to run for office again.

"We can use that," Brandr said when he'd finished the letter. Genius glittered in his eyes. "Stir up the nest. The people are angry about Andor getting rid of me with no notice, no warning, no justification. Evan's job is to encourage that notion." He writes a quick and zealous note on the matter.

"Only you could find a use for this situation," Edda said fondly, ruffling Brandr's hair. "Only you could find humor in it."

"What humor? We are feeling the turning of the tide, my dear. Rebellion is unfolding as we speak."

After two more restless weeks, midway into spring, they finally set out for Rinnfell for their first and hopefully only attempt at rebellion.

Mid spring in northern Kryos still spells winter in every sense. It's never truly warm enough in the north to go without a cloak, and this means Cerrick can doze under the warmth of soft blankets in the carriage, curled into Njord's side with Njord's arm wrapped around his back. Cerrick presses a nose into his chest, hiding from the rest of the world.

It's nowhere near the luxury of stretching out beside Njord in that big bed in Solveig's home—the most joyous occasion of the past few weeks is that Njord has gone back to sleeping beside him—but it's good enough. For a little longer, Cerrick can ignore the heaviness building in his chest at the very thought of facing all the problems they've amassed since the attacks.

To fill time, Njord quietly describes the ride from the chaotic Rinnfell explosion to the otherworldly calm of Solveig's house. Everyone was silent and grim, praying for Edlyn's survival while Solveig operated on her.

He strokes back and forth over Cerrick's bare back under the blankets now, his hand huge and warm. They can afford to do so since they have their own carriage. Solveig brought enough to bring an entire army. Her soldiers flank the carriages from their midnight horses.

Njord's voice lulls Cerrick to sleep. He'd never pass up the opportunity for a warm, comfortable sleep in his husband's arms, knowing he's about to become familiar with the feeling of aching exhaustion once again.

Cerrick's dreams are strange, and he wakes up only to be shushed back to sleep by Njord and the rocking of the carriage intermittently. He sees the heat of fire, feels the whine of arrows grazing his ear, smells the coppery tang of Edlyn's blood on his hands. He sees

Bertie's face and Andor's, thankfully silent this time. Their bright eyes are intimidating enough.

Through it all, running through his chest is an uncertain dread about what they'll find and who will be awaiting them in Rinnfell.

When they finally slow to a halt hours later and the carriage door opens, Cerrick is holding his breath. But—everything looks as they left it.

They've stopped on the northwestern side of Rinnfell, as close to the palace as they dare go. There's still no evidence that Andor knows they're alive, but like hell they're going to take that chance.

Edlyn exits the carriage with all the grace of a queen. Ever since that day in the library, she's carried herself differently, not only because she's healing more and more. She's still using the cane. Cerrick suspects she'll want to replace it with a staff that precedes her when walking into a room.

After years of secrecy and discretion, Cerrick was struggling to see the advantage of walking with something that makes so much noise, but now he understands. Edlyn wants something to announce her presence for her, classier than a herald or jingling knives.

Cerrick casts grim eyes toward the palace as they all duck behind a building. *We'll be seeing you soon, bastard. Stay out of our sight a little longer.* He says a prayer for Evan's continued safety while he's at it. Those reports of unrest in Fura are unfortunately the least of their worries. Cerrick wishes they were the worst.

Cerrick touches Njord's arm in what could be one of their last moments alone. "You are—here? With us? For good?"

Njord shrugs. "This is your thing. I am just here for you."

Cerrick nods as his cheeks burn. Another reminder that were it not for him, Njord would be safely back in Holbeck.

"No, no. I express myself wrong," Njord quickly adds. "I mean—this is your thing, I don't want to interfere and influence you and your rebellion. It is not for a lack of interest that I stay with you instead of going back to the sunshine. Do not mistake any of this as mere tolerance, my love. I could not leave you if I tried."

He gently caresses Cerrick's cheek, and Cerrick can't help leaning into it. He can't help anything when it comes to Njord.

Njord adds, "This is the most exciting thing I could've ever hoped to be a part of. Without this I would be sitting in Holbeck without anything interesting to do. My sisters and brother would tire of me quickly." Njord chuckles warmly. "There is nowhere I'd rather be than with you, whatever you're doing. I would willingly fall into the Gryting for you—with you, even."

"You're going to get yourself killed with an attitude like that," Cerrick whispers, on the verge of tears. He always scoffed at those who said they could face the whole world if only their lover stood at their side, but now he knows what they meant. He feels like he could defeat Andor in hand to hand combat if only Njord's hands were on his shoulders to steady him.

Njord winks. "I am good with Pointstaff. I shall be fine."

Cerrick touches Edlyn's shoulder just to check that she is indeed corporeal, as he has done every day for the last few weeks. She's gotten used to it by now and ignores him, staring down the long street of townhouses and apartments and seedy alleys that line the western side of Rinnfell, ending at the southern gate into the city. Cerrick shivers at the prospect of how close the Ice townhouse is. Here he is, squeezed between his two greatest enemies.

Bertie is dead. He has nothing more to fear there. The people left in the townhouse will have departed already, or the building may have been burnt down now that Bertie's not there to inspire fear and curb the chaos. Rival gangs will rejoice his death if they haven't already.

He glances at Edlyn and finds the same thoughts laid out on her face, a wide eyed sort of mystic curiosity. A pull, equally loathed and beloved, fills Cerrick's chest. He breathes out, stepping one foot closer to the Ice.

"We're going ahead to the docks," Brandr says, looking at them with a raised eyebrow. "We'll leave the carriages here, out of sight. You two take your time catching up. Be safe."

"You too," Edlyn says with a faint echo in her voice, as if she's not really hearing him. Like Cerrick, she's caught in a sort of trance, bound to the townhouse. Njord kisses his cheek before going off with Brandr.

As their carriage drivers—some of Solveig's most trusted soldiers—pull the carriages away into darkness, Cerrick grabs Edlyn's elbow and tugs her along after him. Thanks to Edlyn's cane, they walk instead of run to the sound of their friends' footsteps on the uneven cobble streets. They're heading in two equally unsavory directions.

They stop at the corner where their apartment lies, where Cerrick hasn't been in five months. He and Edlyn slip in through the black gate that's always remained unlocked. Evan would sneak through to visit them when they first refused to pay their debt to Bertie. He made a persuasive argument. The only one happy in that arrangement was Bertie, safe at home where he didn't have to face the consequences of his actions.

Edlyn's footsteps precede Cerrick's on the winding spiral staircase up to the second floor. Cerrick can't remember the number of nights he stumbled here into her arms after struggling not to go running back to the Ice, too tantalizingly close.

It was never that he *wanted* to go back. It was that he thought, hoped, *prayed* everything would go back to normal if he did, that somehow Bertie would magically heal all his hurts. Edlyn was there to hold him and pull him out of it, slap him into his senses when words weren't enough.

Cerrick doesn't have the words to thank her for that, especially knowing she was fighting the same pull. The personal connection she once had with Bertie herself. Fuck, he owes Edlyn so much.

She halts in front of their familiar beige door, the paint chipped and the wood dented from all the times they kicked it in rage. He never touched alcohol after the night that landed him in the Ice, but Edlyn did.

He had to rescue her from seedy bars many times, many times when she did not want to be rescued, only left alone. But when it came to the scarring impact the Ice left on them, they couldn't leave each other to destroy themselves. They intervened and thanked each other for it later.

Edlyn fishes under her clothes for the familiar little key to this door. Cerrick can't help but laugh. After all this time, after a dip in the Gryting and a brush with death, she's still managed to hold onto that key.

The click of it turning in the door is warm and familiar. Cerrick has mixed feelings about this apartment—for a long time, he dreamed of a real home with real comforts and walls that actually held heat. This was supposed to be temporary.

But at the same time, his hatred of it cools when he thinks about how it housed them in that tumultuous time. It was so teasingly close to their old home but just far enough to let them breathe.

It held Cerrick during his first bouts of nightmares, during Edlyn's drunken birthday, during the explosive fight between Edlyn and Carr that landed them all where they are right now.

Other than a bit of dust, the place hasn't changed a bit. To see it again hits Cerrick harder than he expected. Memories hit him hard—nights on that ugly, sunken in couch, the grating noise of Carr and Edlyn's fights, the crisp air that floated through the balcony door. They always kept it open. It faces a view Cerrick spent many mornings staring blankly out at, pondering.

He blocked out so much of those awful few months between the Ice and the Sun, yet it all comes flooding back now. After securing their jobs at the Sun, they were too busy to spend much time here.

Edlyn walks slowly through, sticking the key back under her clothes. "This place was so empty without you while you were in Aeton," she says. "So cold. So quiet."

Cerrick marches up to her and wraps his arms around her from behind, his hands taking hers and squeezing. He buries his face in the back of her neck. They're both quiet. Cerrick soaks in the sound of silence. This is what she had to live with day and night.

"I'm not your husband," she huffs, but her arms wrap over his and she leans back into him. Cerrick's heart swells.

"I'm sorry," Edlyn whispers.

"For what?"

"For ever taking up with that idiot Carr. If not for him—"

"We've had this discussion. If not for Carr, we wouldn't be here. And I'd much rather be here than living blindly in Andor's employ." Cerrick squeezes her waist.

They stand there in the melancholy peace for a few minutes before Cerrick comes to his senses and realizes they should probably be going.

Cerrick cracks open the door to his rooms, finding them just as he left them. His bed is in disarray, his possessions strewn about the cold wooden floor, his old cloak still hanging on its stand. His old cloak horns adorn it, and it's worn with holes that moths ate into the pale blue linen. It was the best he could afford while struggling under his debt to Bertie.

He runs his fingers over it now, noting the distinct absence of thick fur at the collar. He pulls his Njord cloak ever closer around his shoulders, savoring all that has come to pass these last five months.

Edlyn goes poking around her own room, strewn with various scented candles. After another minute's mourning, they lock up and leave, and Cerrick presses his hand to the cold wall to absorb every memory he's made here and freeze it into his bones.

Back out in the street, Cerrick faces the townhouse with a moment's apprehension. He and Edlyn exchange glances.

They should be getting back to Brandr and the Phantom. They should be kickstarting the rebellion.

They should.

It's not that Cerrick doesn't want to, it's that—

Edlyn grabs his hand again and races off.

The townhouse is everything that southwest Rinnfell represents. It's tall and black and miserable just to look at. Alluring and enticing until you're in too far to get back out. Remarkably, it's still standing.

Cerrick's blood is thrumming. He doesn't knock on the door, just busts it open and barrels in with Edlyn at his back. "Give me a knife," he breathes quietly. Edlyn presses one into his hand, cold and sharp.

The ground floor is dark as always, but people jump to their feet as a draught of cold air blows inside. No one here says a word as the door slams shut behind Cerrick and Edlyn. Cerrick doesn't recognize any faces, only the fear on them.

"Are we doing this?" Cerrick murmurs under his breath as one brave delegate steps forward.

Edlyn chuckles warmly. "You heard me the first time, didn't you? I want to see the Ice melt."

Cerrick shivers and nods.

"Now, to everyone here," Edlyn says, clapping her hands, "you know who we are, and you have everything to fear from us. No doubt Bertie told you to kill us on sight, but we're not going to hurt you unless you get in our way. We're going to burn this building to the ground, and you have two choices. Burn with it, with Bertie, and with your loyalties to this place, or walk out alive right now and join the order that's going to overthrow Andor Estensen today."

A few of the people look between each other. Cerrick is grinning wildly. To these kids, they must look manic. They are manic, but he feels so alive. *Embrace the monster,* Brandr told him all that eternity ago. Cerrick welcomes it with open arms and hands it a knife.

"Make your choice," Edlyn says. "Bertie isn't here to stop you. We'll be right back. I wouldn't dream of tattling if I were you. I don't think I need to tell you what will happen."

They won't have to worry about that, Cerrick knows as they head back out. Who would these people tell that wouldn't land them in a new set of trouble? It's what's stopped Bertie from reporting Cerrick and Edlyn to Andor all this time—he'd be incriminating himself too.

Edlyn and Cerrick make short work of gathering the oil and matches necessary to do their work. Bertie had them well acquainted with such dealers.

When they return, a timer is ticking down in Cerrick's head about the Phantom—if they're wondering where Cerrick and Edlyn have wandered off to, if they're waiting and wasting their precious time.

He hopes Brandr hasn't grown soft enough to let his useful Ice instincts dull. That he still knows how to take advantage of every moment. Hopefully he's embracing the monster as well, though it might be hard with Edda and Ivan's moral compasses on his back.

However, the rebellion is different.

No time to think about it. Only time to keep going, keep pouring the oil over every inch of the building. Cerrick doesn't need to go upstairs and say goodbye to his old room. He has nothing left to say, only a desire to know it's gone.

As they work, the Ice kids slowly shuffle outside. Those without cloaks cross their arms over their chests for warmth, and perhaps to make themselves appear smaller.

Cerrick tries not to stare at them. Where is the Saints given fear Bertie inspired in all of them? The fierceness? Are Cerrick and Edlyn that big a threat?

Cerrick wonders if he ever looked as green as these kids.

One of the Ice kids grows bold enough to approach Edlyn as she's pouring oil over Bertie's favorite rug. "Ma'am, Bertie is—"

"Stay or leave," Edlyn says, unforgiving. The young one flinches and retreats outside. Cerrick opens his mouth to scold her for needlessly scaring that child—that's what they are, children—but decides it's not worth the fight that would ensue.

Edlyn is living the revenge that she's been seeking ever since Carr betrayed her, ever since she left this place, ever since her two oldest foes attacked her and took glee in the fact that she'd die at sea.

The rebellion is one thing, but this—this means more to her, just as Andor's betrayal hurt Cerrick harder than it did Edlyn. Cerrick could let Bertie go easier than she could, just as she couldn't let him go enough to see Andor in his entirety.

Perhaps if she'd been the one toiling away in Holbeck, scraping together evidence only to come home and have all her hard work used to betray and condemn her. She has a family who still loves her, and has never sought replacements in any other parental figures. Cerrick has.

Cerrick, unlike the night they fought to escape, has no desire to see any innocents burn. All Ice members are Bertie's victims, even if they're not all innocent. He's sure they all have blood on their hands, but no one deserves to take the fall for Bertie's crimes.

The only one who has to pay for them is Bertie, dead thanks to Brandr. Cerrick prays to Saints Calith and Renalie that he's agonizing in hell right now, that he'll feel every bit of hurt when his townhouse kingdom comes tumbling down.

Cerrick makes sure all the people are out of the building—they left willingly to stand at his side—before allowing Edlyn to strike the match and throw it onto the building. She doesn't offer to share it with him, and he doesn't ask. He thinks of what Njord said. *This is your thing. I won't interfere, and I won't influence you.* He understands better now.

The building goes up easily. The heat of it is powerful and welcome—Cerrick takes every pleasure in warming his hands over it. He'll forever associate Bertie with these huge, destructive fires, between the ship and the townhouse. It's in a way beautiful.

Once the fire reaches the interior, the townhouse will blow up in an inferno.

Cerrick bathes in it for a moment, closing his eyes and inhaling the smoke. This is Bertie's death. He doesn't deserve to have his ashes scattered on the wind. He belongs to the sea now.

Edlyn is staring at the fire, the flaming colors reflected in the dark brown of her eyes. She's not smiling, not frowning, just watching with a transfixed expression. If Cerrick searches far and well, he'll find the sadistic glee that's always resided in her heart and in his. Monstrous.

Cerrick remembers what he first thought of Bertie, standing just a few feet away against the wall of this alley. Bertie's knife was on his neck, but Edlyn was close enough to ensure that he wouldn't get cut. She was screaming at Bertie to spare him, shrill, passionate.

Bertie wouldn't listen at first, and all Cerrick could see was the bright blue of his eyes, filled with a blazing passion. He didn't know someone could feel, let alone wear that much glee and hatred all at once.

Bertie screamed back at Edlyn, threatened her with death, making the naïve young Cerrick go wide eyed with fear. Edlyn didn't physically intervene, though Cerrick could see how badly she wanted to, how desperately she was straining to keep hold of herself. At last, Bertie let up.

Despite that, Cerrick was in awe of him. Bertie oozed leadership from every vein, expressing his power through subtlety. Cerrick wanted to impress him, get on his good side, but he also wanted to see what would happen if he pushed back. He spent the next year testing exactly that. How much could he get away with, how far Bertie would let him go. The answer? Much farther than Cerrick thought.

Cerrick gets the last jab now. This fire will remain in Cerrick's mind as another treasured painting. The rest will be held as a holy archive in his mind, an account he means to write. He breathes in and out with the smoke, which will serve as his ink. The paper is the burning townhouse, Bertie's crest.

He clenches his fists just to feel them, but he can't pretend forever that they're alone. The presence of the others behind them is glaring. Cerrick can feel their eyes on his back.

"Where will we go now?" one whispers, perhaps to their companion, perhaps to themself. Maybe to a Saint. Bertie always kept statues of Saint Renalie in the townhouse in mocking. He believed that individuals should relinquish any ties they might have to the Saints when they enter this order.

"I already told you," Edlyn says, her tone blank. Cerrick knows from experience on their bloodier jobs that it'll take a while to pull her back out of her own head. He knows when to let her float in purgatory alone, how long to give her the time she needs. "You'll accompany us on our rebellion against Andor."

Cerrick watches the indignation strike their faces, but he casts them a warning glance. "Better just to go along with it," he says lowly. "You'll be treated well there. Welcomed. I promise."

These kids don't believe in promises the same way as most people. They all nod their assent anyway, looking between Edlyn's dark form and each other.

Cerrick waits for Edlyn to get her fill of the fire. He would leave her to admire it as long as she wished, but he doesn't want her to get lost in it and lose time. He chances touching her wrist and squeezes it when she doesn't pull a knife on him. She nods, staring at the flame another long few seconds. Some of the life returns to her eyes, dark and ugly. Exactly what they need for what they're about to do.

They take off down the street hand in hand, smelling of smoke with ash in their hair and an army of Ice kids behind them. Edlyn's cane clicks to the beat of Cerrick's heart. They find the Phantom at the docks.

Cerrick looks around at the destruction wrought by Bertie's insurance explosion that drove them out of the city. The ground is scorched, and a crater pierces the ground. Inge's shack and all evidence it ever existed are gone. Much of the smoldering debris was cleaned away while they were in Slairr.

Cerrick ponders for a moment the details of Bertie's insurance attack on the harbor, but resigns himself to the reality that they'll never know what the details were. It matters little now. Bertie's last influences are burning down the street.

CHAPTER FOURTEEN

"We're back," Edlyn says, adjusting her cloak and fixing her hair. She and Cerrick both are covered in ash.

"Is that smoke?" Brandr asks, squinting into the skyline. "That looks like it's coming from the southwest. Is there something—"

"Don't worry about it," Edlyn cuts in. "What can we help with?"

Brandr looks at her, a slight smirk curling his lip. "We're waiting for Solveig's soldiers to return to shore," Brandr says beneath the glow of a streetlight. "They make up for the allies we lost in the Ice. They took a dingy to the gemsha ship to alert the captain of our needs. They fly my symbol. The captain will know allies approach instead of foes. Once we've cleared the palace, we'll rendezvous with Evan. He eagerly awaits us, according to his last letter."

Reality comes rushing down. They're truly about to use a gemsha to coerce Andor and his allies to hand over power and fight to convince them if necessary. Cerrick takes a deep breath. This could grow messy, fast.

Brandr must sense his distress, for he pats Cerrick firmly on the shoulder and pulls him into a hug. "Whatever happens," he grunts, "stay safe." With his other arm, he pulls Edlyn in. "Both of you. I won't lose you."

Cerrick curls his fist in Brandr's cloak, wooden carvings biting into his cheek, the smell of clean soap filling his nose. Stinging tears threaten to rise to the surface, but he pushes them back. No time for that now.

This, Cerrick thinks. *This is what it's supposed to be like.* Family. Not fear and frowns and endless arguments in a black house. This. Hugging, receiving words of affirmation. Confidence. Community. Cerrick might cry. *Family.*

They break apart at the sound of rushing water growing louder behind them. Solveig's soldiers dismount from their boat at the water's edge. The ship carrying the gemsha trails behind them, covered in a cloud of fog.

Cerrick's breath catches. He hasn't seen it in the daytime, yet it's just as beautiful as he remembers, gleaming proudly in silver. He recalls the brilliance of the cannonball firing into Bertie and Carr's ship, the painting Cerrick froze in his mind. He can't help wanting to see that again.

At the cost of the palace you love? he wonders.

It's Andor's home. It's what matters most to him. That's what matters. Palaces can be rebuilt, and they're planning to start rebuilding from the ground up, aren't they? Cerrick isn't sure he wants their new capital to remain in the dark and frigid north, though that's something to be considered later.

"Brilliant," Solveig breathes, taking in every detail of the gemsha she can glimpse from the shore. "Absolutely brilliant."

The ship lingers under the edge of the fog. Ivan boards the ship to tend his precious gemsha, escort it onto its new homeland.

"He treats that thing like his newborn child," Brandr murmurs. "As precious as his plants."

Solveig turns to them. "I exchanged letters with Oligarch Eir, discreetly asking if she would be willing to join us. She wrote back with a resounding yes—encoded, of course. She's on our side. She's only sorry she can't be here to help us; she simply couldn't reach

Rinnfell in time. In the future, however she may, she pledged her life and her aid to our cause."

Four oligarchs on their side, willing to go to war against the other three. What kind of strange dreamworld has Cerrick stumbled into?

If only Eir were here right now. Supposedly what grace she lacks in a fight she makes up for in enthusiasm. Any warm body they can add to their numbers will be of great help against the force Andor undoubtedly has built against them.

By now Brandr has noticed the group of Ice children hovering behind Cerrick and Edlyn, unsure what to do. "Do I want to know?" he asks, brow pinched.

"They're here to help us fight," Edlyn says. "That's all you need to know for now."

"Fair enough. Are we ready?"

Cerrick and Edlyn exchange glances. Everyone is waiting on them, looking to them for guidance. So much attention still makes Cerrick prickle, but he supposes he'll have to grow used to it if he's going to be king of this new country. He and Edlyn are the heart of this rebellion, the flame to the oil that was Brandr, just waiting to catch all these years.

"I don't see a reason to wait any longer," Edlyn says, considerably better at bearing the attention than he is. "Let's go finish what we were supposed to finish the last time we were here."

Brandr smiles, proud and pleased. "That's what I like to hear." He signals to Solveig's soldiers, not daring to use his voice in the busy seaside.

The Phantom is coming out of hiding for the first time. For the first time, they're striving to be seen instead of running from the light. Cerrick has always thrived on working in the shadows. The light has burned him over and over.

Cerrick goes over the route to the palace in his head. It's not far, but unfortunately, he's been told gemshas are slow even when they're being driven. Everyone in Rinnfell will have a chance to stare, and they won't be able to run away quickly. The gemsha's size dictates they take the main streets with the most visibility.

Brandr can pull the hood of his cloak over his face, they all can, but that won't save them from being pelted with fruit. Better fruit than knives.

Cerrick hopes it won't come to that with the civilians. He wishes they were in Steinberg where those who oppose the government reside in the biggest numbers. Rinnfell is in Andor's dukedom of Heynes, and it's filled with as many of his devotees as sworn enemies.

Njord, who has remained silent these past few minutes, takes hold of Cerrick's hand and raises it to his warm lips. Cerrick smiles up at him.

Emboldened and wishing for a bit of luck, Cerrick beckons Njord closer. He yearns for a precious memory to hold in his heart in case everything goes wrong from this point on.

Pulling him down by a hand on the back of his neck, Cerrick gives Njord a kiss with all his devotion and love and fear. Njord has always been able to handle his worst, and Cerrick entrusts him with it now.

Njord receives it like it's an honor to be the bearer of Cerrick's burdens. Unlike Bertie, Cerrick has no desire to see how far he can push Njord before he breaks. He hopes to push him the other way, straight into Saint Irena's heaven. By the testament of Njord's sweet words, he already has.

The gemsha slides down its ramp, descending slowly onto Kryc pavement. Cerrick holds his breath until Solveig's soldiers have pushed it securely onto solid ground. The gemsha is here, and Brandr is grinning like he's just waiting for a moment to resume control.

He climbs with childlike eagerness back up to the seat, to Ivan's disgruntlement. "Remember what you promised," he says.

"I'm not going to hurt anyone," Brandr says gently, handing his cane off to Edda for her safekeeping. Ivan nods, relinquishing the last of his control. Brandr flicks a few levers and pushes a few buttons. The gemsha roars to life.

He and Ivan have been reviewing the proper procedures on how to operate it during the downtime at Solveig's mansion. Brandr is measurably more confident than the last time he piloted the gemsha.

It's damn loud, louder than Cerrick remembers. Now, he doesn't have the roaring sea and storm to muffle the noise. He resists the urge to cover his ears, saving his voice for when he'll have to shout to be heard. The gemsha grates on his ears, rattling the ground, and he grimaces.

Unsurprisingly, the noise draws the crowds quickly. Cerrick pulls his hood up and the others follow suit. He exchanges glances with Edlyn just before her face disappears into that little window of darkness.

Brandr moves the gemsha as fast as it can go, which is even slower than Cerrick imagined. Himself, Njord, Edlyn, Edda, Ivan, Solveig, the Ice kids, and Solveig's soldiers flank the gemsha like an honor guard, keeping their heads down as the first hollers come from the crowd. Not yet jeers, just questions followed by exclamations when the gemsha enters the path of a waterfront merchant.

Cerrick keeps his mouth shut, determined not to explain himself to every person they pass. The curious yells turn to curses and jibes, just as Cerrick knew they would. He tries to block out both the noise of the gemsha and the people. *Someday they will understand,* he reminds himself. *Someday they'll realize we're doing this for them.* Every rebellion leader of the past must've had the same thought, and Cerrick isn't any different.

But we are. That's not a unique thought either. Njord holds his wrist to offer silent support, which helps, but Cerrick can't help remembering Sigrid and Erika Thorpe marching through the streets together. They held hands at the head of a much larger, much more organized, much fiercer army. While they did not make their demonstration in Rinnfell, as they were the ones to establish the capital, Cerrick imagines a similar scene.

The citizens of that time knew full well of their corrupt government, and fully supported a new era. Most of the country rallied harmoniously behind Erika and Sigrid, after decades of life under fraud.

Cerrick and the Phantom are suffering unique circumstances where no one knows the truth about their corrupt government—yet, that is.

Cerrick doesn't dare lift his gaze to check their progress, not with objects of various kinds hitting his cloak. The citizens are annoyed with a group of ragtags for disrupting the day's routine with their enormously loud machine, as many would be, but Cerrick hazards a guess that most of the mob are itching for a fight. The Phantom have merely provided an outlet for their angry energy.

"Crazy Krycs," Ivan mutters behind him, providing Cerrick a moment of choked laughter which he desperately needs. Njord's hand in his and the picture Cerrick imagines they must make are the only things keeping him tethered.

Will this scene become a painting? Is someone staring at this spectacle from their balcony right now, searing every moment of this into their mind? The strange sight of people in hooded cloaks moving in a slow procession through the streets, a tank at their side? Will the sight burrow so deeply into someone's mind that they won't be able to function until they put it to canvas?

Will the artist focus on the looming gray of the sky, or will they highlight the color of every cloak, every decoration? Will the gemsha be the focal point, or the hooded strangers? The crowd pelting fruit at them? Or will it be the palace, their ultimate destination?

Will people write their families to illustrate the strangeness of this moment, describing the hoods in an eerie or a reverent way? Will they mention first the noise or the unnatural silver gleam of the gemsha? Will they be truthful and say the crowd acted with scorn, or will they lie that the crowd revered them like Saints? Which of these many accounts will historians believe when Cerrick and the Phantom are all dead and gone?

Someone touches Cerrick's back in silent support—Edlyn, he guesses from the angle. So much silent support around him, so much from his two favorite people. He could die happily here, with them.

How much more must he endure until they reach the damned palace?

The Saints seem to be on their side today, something Cerrick hopes will be pointed out in the accounts and the people's minds. His own mind is already doing damage control, trying to predict the opposing argument.

Wherever the gemsha goes, the very ground seems to rumble beneath their feet. When the gemsha pulls to a halt, the rumbling stops with it, and Cerrick takes a full breath of relief.

He glances up for the first time, discovering that they're at the palace gate. The gemsha is too wide to ride up the path. If they wanted to cause unfettered destruction, it could simply tear its way through. as close to the palace as they can get.

Cerrick's hood should still cover his face, and though the urge to pull it down enough to see the entire street is irresistible, he keeps his hands rooted in his pockets. Some more wet fruit hits his head, and he ducks. He'll see the crowd in the paintings and drawings, it's not worth it to look now.

Cerrick glances south and finds the Ice townhouse still belching smoke into the sky.

Just a bit more anonymity.

Brandr swivels around the cannon of the gemsha to face the palace. He doesn't fire, doesn't even have his hand on the firing lever, but the people don't notice. They've never seen a gemsha before. They scream.

The first group of palace soldiers file through the same gates Cerrick passed through to work every morning. That first wave arrived quicker than they all expected. Cerrick's blood begins to run cold.

Njord lets go of his hand after one final squeeze, and Solveig shouts orders to her soldiers, who thunder past Brandr on horses to meet the palace soldiers. Cerrick's heart swells and then begins its familiar nervous pounding. His hand aches for the grip of a knife, though something more substantial would be better. At least Njord brought his Pointstaff. Cerrick looks at Edda, and to his shock, finds her wielding a Pointstaff herself.

He and Edlyn exchange glances. When did she—how—

"We are the Order of the Phantom!" Brandr screams, loud enough for all of Rinnfell to hear. He raises his hood, and the rest of them at last follow his lead and do the same. Cerrick shivers as the gray light of the day hits his face. "We lead the seventh rebellion of Kryos. We demand that corrupt traitor Andor Estensen resign his post immediately and hand over the reins to us, to the new era. Since we know he will not, we come to fight our way there instead."

The Phantom lets out a mighty cry, even the newfound Ice kids. They seem simply happy to have a purpose, some kind of explanation for the sudden upheaval in their lives. Njord doesn't roar with the rest of them, but everyone else who has a weapon raises it to the sky for the Saints to judge.

The crowd continues to yell, the gemsha roars on, and battle cries thunder in Cerrick's ears as more palace soldiers emerge to fight. More of Solveig's volunteer themselves. The hum of war buzzes all around him—noise and light to the beat of his racing heart. Edlyn shoves him in excitement.

Rebellion. This is what it looks like, no, feels like.

Brandr sits atop his great steed like a king, looking down at the Order he's created. If direct sunlight shone here, the silver gemsha would blind one and all.

Cerrick chances a glance up at the roof of the palace, the only safe place to rest his eyes. There are figures there. He squints and curses, grabbing Edlyn's arm.

Up on the roof, Saints know how, are Bertie and Carr, perfectly alive and intact. They look not to have a scratch on them. Cerrick wonders if they're a Saintly vision, but after blinking, they don't disappear.

"What the fuck?" Edlyn breathes. "What the *fuck*."

"Oh, yes," Cerrick says, unable to believe his own eyes. Among other questions, how—

That ship was on fire. The two splintered halves sailed toward their doom. They were to meet their fate at the bottom of the sea. Surely Cerrick is just looking at Saints come to haunt him, taunt him for his faults right before the biggest victory of his life. Bertie is inconsequential compared to this.

Bertie turns and locks eyes with him. A slow smile spreads across his face. He's attained a new bow and a new cloak, one that gleams.

A flash of anger flows through Cerrick's veins. He already mourned Bertie. He and Edlyn just laid Bertie's corpse to rest at the townhouse, lit his pyre. Cerrick can't do this again. How many times must he bury Bertie?

No time for a debate right now. The important thing is that the figures on the roof are not apparitions, they've noticed the Phantom, and they have the high ground. "We have to get up there," Edlyn says breathlessly. "Do you know the way?"

Cerrick's lips form the word *no,* but he hesitates to think. He explored much of the upper palace during his first few weeks of work, both to satisfy his curiosity and to prevent from getting lost. He opened more dark storage closets than he ever did in his own childhood home, and that led to discovering room after secret room.

Among all this exploring, he found a staircase to the rooftop. He closes his eyes and pictures the route, every turn, every point of danger. "I do. Follow me."

Cerrick glances at Brandr to see if he's noticed the two figures on the rooftop yet, but he and the Phantom are too busy contending with the crowd and the palace soldiers. Then, he ponders the top palace floor, wondering if Andor is watching from some unseen window.

Attempting to signal to Brandr in this chaos would be impossible, so Cerrick doesn't even try. Cerrick takes Edlyn's hand in his and makes a run for it—as quickly as they can with her cane, of course—weaving through the crowd filling the street. Brandr is the center of it all on the gemsha with Ivan standing beside him. Edda and Solveig fight side by side with Pointstaffs in their hands.

Cerrick wishes he had the time to stand and stare at the marvels they make. Three tall Krycs and a short Os man all of equally terrifying power. Cerrick grins wildly, drunk on the celebration in the air. Rebellion.

He lets out a whoop of joy and adrenaline, and then he spots Njord with his Pointstaff clutched in his fist. He's not partaking in the fight, a wise political move and a remarkable indication of self-control. Yet he matches Cerrick's smile with an intensity that's painfully bright.

Pride swells in Cerrick's chest. Without him, Njord wouldn't be here, and for once Cerrick surpasses that guilt. *Without him, Njord wouldn't be here,* at the dawn of the new rebellion. Witnessing history. Taking part in it.

Njord is the head of Aeton's military. The fight is where he belongs, even if he never lifts his weapon against another.

He waves to Cerrick, thrusting his Pointstaff high in an apparent toast. Cerrick blows him a kiss, dreaming of later, after all this is officially theirs. *I love you,* he mouths. His blood pounds to the beat of the gemsha's roar, warming him from head to toe.

He catches Brandr's eye for a split second. In that split second, Cerrick finds all the years shed from his face. Brandr's grin is wide and infectious. Their leader. The very center of them.

The Phantom slowly fights their way up the incline to the palace, driving the soldiers back inside. As they walk, Cerrick faces Edlyn, who's taking this all in with an open mouth. The sky might be gray, but she brings her own light. He squeezes her fingers. She looks at him, and he smiles at her.

Lord and Lady of Rinnfell. King and queen of the seventh era.

Cerrick leads Edlyn through the open gate, unlocked to let soldiers through unimpeded. It's a stroke of luck for them. "Please tell me we don't have to venture deep into the palace to reach the roof," Edlyn says between rhythmic clicks of her cane.

"Just hold tight," Cerrick says.

They push in through an unlocked side door and find the entire floor empty. All hands have been evacuated or called outside to fight. The empty office is eerie and dark and quiet save for a single golden light burning at the end of the hall.

Cerrick shivers with memories and pushes on, treading as lightly as he can on the carpet.

The closet leading to the staircase resides in the center of the top floor. As they walk through the halls, Cerrick finds every room deserted. They move quickly past, not wanting to take the slightest chance. They go from corner to corner with a pause to hide in the darkness before moving on.

Edlyn remains silent, though he can feel her tension and anxiety in every beat of her heart against his back. Cerrick is thankful, if surprised he still remembers the exact path.

Finally, the coveted dark door comes into view. Cerrick grins, allowing himself a moment's celebration before stepping out into the perils of an open hallway again.

Pulling on the knob, Cerrick groans and discovers his luck with unlocked doors has run out. The Saints send a challenge to humble him, as if he's not challenged enough. No matter. Nothing and no one can extinguish the fire from his veins with the sound of the rebellion in the street below, bleeding easily through the windows.

Edlyn gently brushes him aside and brandishes a large dagger. She bashes the butt of it against the lock, and the door swings open with a slight squeak. "Nothing to it," she says, ducking inside, unable to hide the breathlessness in her voice. Excitement and fear are mingling. He wonders if her heart is racing as fast as his.

Cerrick guides her up the dark spiral staircase. It ends at the ceiling, but he reaches for an easy to miss hook hanging from the ceiling tile panel. The hidden ladder nearly crashes into both their heads, but Edlyn helps him ease it to the ground. Cerrick gulps a mouthful of frigid air. He's never been so glad to see a gray sky.

They clamber up onto the roof one by one. Once Edlyn's gotten her cane under herself, drawing breath, Cerrick joins her. He pulls himself upright as quickly as possible, noting the burning eyes raking over him. Bertie and Carr stand there in the flesh, as real and unharmed as they looked from the ground. That doesn't make them any less of an ethereal, unsettling sight. A pit opens in Cerrick's stomach.

"You're alive," Cerrick breathes, far more reverential than he intended. He clears his throat as Edlyn stands at his shoulder. Her movements are slow and gradual like someone rising from the dead. Her gaze is hard. "How?" he demands.

"Luck of the Saints," Bertie says with an innocent shrug. He can make himself appear so very small with so much ease, yet his power is staggering. "I see you healed up, Edlyn. A shame."

"I am fucking sick of this," Edlyn says, marching up to Carr and grabbing the front of his shirt. "Carr, I have you to thank for opening our eyes to Andor's misdeeds and founding this rebellion, but that's the last compliment you'll get from me."

Carr gulps and shrinks back a bit from the pressure of Edlyn's fury. Few know what to do when confronted by such a force.

"What's she talking about, Carr?" Bertie asks. Cerrick delights in the panic in his voice.

"Noth—"

"Has he not told you who he works for?" Edlyn asks with glee. "What have you told him, Carr? Why are you two working together?"

Carr opens his mouth and spills the truth with less of a fight than Cerrick expected. When he notices the flash of a blade against the man's neck, things make more sense. "I told him I was Edlyn's—Edlyn's ex. I would help him take care of her and her partner Cerrick. Get them out of the way for good."

"Why?"

Carr casts his eyes at the ground like a scolded child. Cerrick hasn't missed hearing the perpetual whine in his voice. How Edlyn ever put up with this idiot amazes him. At first, she ignored his fervent advice to let this swine go. After she realized the depths of his treachery, she apologized to Cerrick for being so blind.

"I was sorry he got to have what I couldn't," Carr mumbles. "I wanted that with you. We deserved to have that. I wanted to see him dead for it, and I knew a man who would pay me well for my trouble. I decided to maximize my investment."

Edlyn laughs. "Carr, Cerrick and I aren't together. He holds no affections for women—not like that. For one, he's married, and for two, that is not the kind of bond we have ever desired to share. I have you to thank for helping me realize I have no interest in anyone at all. Oh, dear—seems I've given you another compliment after all."

"What haven't you been telling me?" Bertie asks, ignoring all this petty discourse and folding his arms. Just a hint of that cold disappointment, the darkness in his voice, is all he needs to get people to talk. Cerrick watches Carr fold like he folded to Bertie so many times. It's not just the threat of what might happen if you don't do what Bertie asks, it's the genuine desire to please him that compels an answer.

"He sold Cerrick and I out to Andor," Edlyn says before pathetic Carr can answer. Cerrick would've liked to watch him squirm and stew, struggle to force the words out, but this is faster. Cerrick wants to see this through, and he's keenly aware of the Phantom on the street below.

"After he discovered that we once worked for you, I threw him out of my life, much later than I should've. I was just waiting for him to strike and bring that knowledge to Andor, and he did. He works at the Sun."

Bertie's eyes flare. If there's one thing he hates more than Ice members who desert him, it's Sun members.

"I suspect Andor sent him on an undercover mission of his own, to investigate you," Edlyn says, exchanging glances with Cerrick. Her fist is still balled up in Carr's cloak, holding him on his toes like a ragdoll. "He was likely asked to pledge fake alliance to you in the name of your mutual goal; finding Cerrick and I. Infiltrate and disrupt the Ice once and for all. Bring all three of us right to Andor's feet. I'd wager it took Andor's help to get you out of the water alive, however he pulled off that miracle."

Bertie steps toward Carr, a sneer forming on his lips, but Cerrick has him before Edlyn can pull out another knife. Cerrick holds a blade to Bertie's throat, enjoying the way he squirms. "Easy," Cerrick purrs. "Betrayal isn't such a pretty thing, is it?"

"This is far from the first time," Bertie grits out. Cerrick looks into his eyes, really looks, and *sees*. It's not just that two Ice members dared to leave him, not just that they were useful to him, it's that he cared for them. Perhaps Edlyn wasn't alone in her struggle to sever her emotional connection.

Bertie's hand curls around his wrist, a warmer and gentler touch than Cerrick expected. He quickly rips Bertie's hand away, cursing colorfully at the way this man still fucks with his head. He shoves Bertie back with disgust, holding his knife out at arm's length. Bertie doesn't make another attempt to go for Carr.

As if nothing happened, Edlyn spits in Carr's face, "I'm going to show you that the fury—not just any fury, but I, *the fury*—cannot be killed so easily. A stray splinter of wood was not going to send me to Saint Renalie just yet."

Edlyn kicks out her right leg and pushes Carr off the edge of the roof.

He falls backwards like Cerrick and Edlyn did when Andor betrayed them, his mouth open in a silent, airless scream. His wide eyes pierce Edlyn's as he falls, flailing, betrayal sinking deep into his depths. She doesn't so much as flinch. Cerrick is frozen. He doesn't know where to look.

Is this what Andor saw when the two of them fell with their arms wrapped around each other, bathing in the scalding burn of his betrayal? Did he watch until they hit the sea, until he was satisfied they were dead? Cerrick never searched for his face in the shattered window. He was focused on other things at the time.

Cerrick watches Carr fall onto jagged rocks. Carr's body crumples like a ragdoll, lifeless and bloody, and is quickly swept away in the icy water. Cerrick watches to make sure he's dead, and finds not a sign of anything left. He feels nothing.

He wrenches his gaze back to Bertie, who's wide eyed like he's never seen a murder before. "Edlyn," he breathes, in a tone that suggests he might fall to his knees in worship. Cerrick would like to see that. "Edlyn."

She smiles. "How nice to hear you say my name like that, Bertie."

"Edlyn," he says again, like he can't think of anything else. Cerrick doesn't blame him. He wonders if this is how he looked the night he was initiated into the Ice, staring between a murderer and his equally brutal savior. Back then, he thought of her as a Saint. Now, he thinks much the same.

Edlyn's smile widens, her eyes crinkling as she walks to Bertie. She takes hold of the front of his coat, and for a bizarre moment, Cerrick thinks she's about to kiss him. That dopey expression of wonder and amazement rests on Bertie's face.

She says, "I'm not going to live in fear of you lurking in the shadows, trying to lure me back to your side. Your side, where you always said I was best. We could be unstoppable together, you said. A force that Kryos had never seen before. We could do anything together.

"Except I don't need you in order to be unstoppable. I can accomplish my dreams on my own. I need to see you buried, once and for all, for my dreams to become a reality. You've ruined enough dreams for a lifetime—I think it's time you started making some come true."

She lets him go and kicks him, quick as lightning. Bertie didn't realize he was standing so close to the edge, nor did he think to stand back after watching what happened to Carr.

The only difference is that he doesn't flail when he falls. His scream isn't contained, it's guttural, loud enough for all of Kryos to hear. It strikes at the very core of Cerrick's heart, rumbling like Bertie means to part the clouds and let the Saints have a look. Cerrick closes his eyes, torn between wanting to immortalize the image of Bertie falling onto the rocks and hiding himself from it.

This time, he hears the sound Bertie's body makes as it collides, and Cerrick opens his eyes again to make sure he's dead. Blood blooms out from the man's motionless head, his eyes unseeing on a rock so very far below.

The gasps of other people draw Cerrick's ear, and he turns, hand on his knife. Brandr and Edda are clambering onto the roof, winded and flushed but otherwise unharmed when Cerrick scans them. The gemsha is still humming far below. Solveig has taken over the helm, not giving an inch even without Brandr's guidance.

"What's going on up here?" Brandr pants. "We heard screaming."

Before Cerrick can answer, a metallic rattle comes from the other end of the roof. Cerrick whirls around, drawing breath at the sight of teal clad soldiers approaching the four of them. Those soldiers hold four sets of shining silver handcuffs. Behind them stands Andor, hand curled around his Pointstaff, eyes glaring with a vengeance and a fury Cerrick has never before seen from him.

And then Andor opens his mouth. All at once, like a boulder tumbling down, Cerrick realizes that Bertie's scream was *nothing*. Bertie's scream was weak, high, exactly the cowardly type of sound he would've complained about himself. Andor's voice carries the might of the Saints, a true rumble like thunder. Lightning that means to strike you down.

He could be an agent of the heavens, or of Saint Renalie's Hell. He strikes his Pointstaff against the ground, and that, *that* is the sound that could be heard in every corner of Kryos. Not Bertie.

A soldier clasps handcuffs around Cerrick's wrists. He doesn't complain or fight. He's too shocked to move.

There are three more clicks as the others are handcuffed. The soldier handling Cerrick grasps his chin and turns his head back towards Andor by force, taking sadistic glee in wrenching Cerrick's neck forward at an awkward angle.

Andor says, "Cerrick Montef, Edlyn Chao, Brandr Tofte, Edda Holman, and every last soul I find who assisted you—you are all under arrest."

Acknowledgements

As always, no novel would be possible to create alone. Thank you to my invaluable beta readers Etta and Jenny, who improved this book in ways I hadn't even thought possible. I appreciate all of the time and effort you poured into making this book the best version it could be. Your insights are appreciated more than you know. You're always a pleasure to work with.

Thank you as always to Pax, for your support, understanding, and unyielding positivity. How quickly time flies between bouncing around ideas for this trilogy to now, when it sits before us as a finished novel.

Thanks again to the Tumblr crew who gave life to this trilogy. Revisiting these books has brought back such wonderful memories of those fall months filled with community. I am eternally grateful for you.

Thank you to the *Hades* soundtrack, without which the battle scenes in this book would almost certainly not have been possible.

And lastly, thank you to my faithful readers, without whom I would not be able to continue creating these books. There is nothing that gives me greater joy than creating new worlds, romances, and characters, except perhaps your reactions. Reading comments and reviews is the only fuel a writer truly needs.

About the Author

Lila Mary has always craved fantasy romance books where queer characters existed just like everyone else—so, she writes them! When she isn't daydreaming in fantasy worlds, she can be found entertaining her cats. She was born and raised in California.

She can be found at:
lilamarybooks.com
lilamarybooks on Instagram